The Night of The Mothman

By R.E.Sohl

The Night of The Mothman by R. E. Sohl
© 2024, Curious Corvid Publishing
All rights reserved.
Published in the United States by Curious Corvid Publishing, LLC, Ohio.

No part of this publication may be reproduced, stored in a retrieval system, stored in a database and / or published in any form or by any means, electronic, mechanical, photocopying, recording or otherwise, without the prior written permission of the publisher, except as permitted by U.S. copyright law.

All works used with the express permission of each author.

ISBN: 978-1-959860-48-8
978-1-959860-49-5

Cover Design by: Mitch Green, Rad Press Studios
Formatted by Ravven White

Printed in the United States of America
Curious Corvid Publishing, LLC
PO Box 204
Geneva, OH 44041

This is a work of fiction. Unless otherwise indicated, all the names, characters, businesses, places, events and incidents in this book are either the product of the author's imagination or used in a fictitious manner. Any resemblance to actual persons, living or dead, or actual events is purely coincidental.

www.curiouscorvidpublishing.com

First Edition

A Suggestion from the Author:

Have you ever played a drinking game centered around watching a beloved, classic movie? Oftentimes, the rules of such games include a provision which states that whenever someone in the film says the title of the movie in dialogue that you must take a drink.

In writing this novel, I've discovered that I have used the phrase "The Night of The Mothman" several times in the actual text of this work. I now invite you to take a drink whenever you notice this. It doesn't happen nearly often enough to get you trashed, but perhaps it will give you a nice little buzz which will make the abomination you're about to embark upon reading slightly more palatable?

However, for legal reasons, I must urge you to please refrain from playing this game if you are under the age of twenty-one, are pregnant, have a history of alcohol abuse, or are driving or operating heavy machinery. Although if you're reading this book while driving or operating heavy machinery and this is not an audiobook edition, I have many questions as to how exactly you're managing to do that. And a mix of awe and horror regarding such actions.

Enough blathering! Now, go forth and try to enjoy reading this ridiculous attempt at art that I like to call *"The Night of The Mothman"* (take a drink!)

- Robert E. Sohl, Fairfax, VA June 26th 2023

Prelude: Hope In A Hopeless Place

Her life had become a revolving door of pain. An ever turning wheel of agony upon which she had nearly been broken.

She didn't know how long she'd been there. Weeks? Months? Years? Time no longer had any meaning. All that existed were the periods of intense torture, and the brief respites in between when she was left alone with the aching, throbbing wreckage of her body and these four walls.

She was in solitary confinement, but she knew there were others in here who shared her fate, she could hear their screams through the walls keeping her up when she was trying to recover from what they'd been doing to her. She studied her scars, scabs, and the purple/blue mosaic of bruises riddling her body. She wondered if she'd *ever* truly recover from this ordeal, psychologically if not physically. Before she'd been put in here, she'd seen shows on TV that talked about how solitary confinement was an inhumane practice that should be considered cruel and unusual punishment, something which caused deep mental trauma. She was definitely feeling all of that, but on top of it, her captors were inflicting literal physical torture upon on her as well, on a regular basis.

One of the most terrible things was that she had no idea why any of this was being done to her. They didn't need any information from her (not that she had anything of value to tell anyone), they never asked her any questions. She couldn't think of anyone she'd pissed off badly enough to warrant ending up here. Nothing about this whole thing felt personal. Were they getting off on it? It was hard to tell through those masks, but she didn't think so. Her tormentors were very cold, robotic and business-like. They seemed to take no obvious delight in the monstrous things they did to her, it all seemed so routine to them. Perhaps that was the most chilling thing of all? The idea that anyone could become so used to doing this to another human being that they seemed to be utterly bored with it. It was just another day at the office for them.

The only thing she was grateful for was that the torture didn't have any overtly sexual component to it; nobody had tried to rape her — yet. She lived in constant dread that it was coming, that it was an inevitable escalation of the helpless situation she found herself in. In a way, this dread was the worst aspect of it all. That, and the fact that they never turned off the fucking lights in her cell along with the endless screams from the other cells which made it impossible to sleep. How many other people did they have here? How many others were suffering like she was?

The room wasn't like the solitary confinement cells she'd seen on TV. Sure, there was the usual sink and a toilet, and the lack of any windows but that's where the similarities ended. For one, the room was unusually spacious, large enough to accommodate the steel table they strapped her down to, and the cart they wheeled in which held all the twisted instruments of their trade. For another, her feet were chained to the floor and her hands were shackled together, both by a cruelly short chain. It was extremely difficult to pick up her bland, tasteless food to eat it, or to pull down her pants to use the toilet when she could barely move her wrists apart, but she'd had plenty of time to master the art.

She had nothing *but* time. Time to think about how to get out of this place. She thought the answer might lie in another way in which her cell differed from the ones she'd seen on TV: they didn't slide her meals through a slot in the door, someone actually walked into the cell to drop off her trays, and collect the old ones. The masked guard who brought the food carried a holstered pistol, but she also knew he had the keys to her shackles dangling from his belt. He had to unchain her when they put her on the torture table, and presumably chained her back up when it was all over. She only had hazy memories of being chained back up. She always passed out from her ordeal, only to awaken later on the unyielding, frigid cement floor.

Her plan was a simple, desperate one. She would feign being asleep when the guard came in to exchange the trays. He had to bend down near her to do it. When he did, she'd jump up and try to get the chain shackling her hands together around his throat to choke the bastard until he was dead. She didn't have any regrets about planning to murder him. She figured anyone sick enough to participate in something this rotten had it coming to them. She also understood how risky this plan was. She was a tiny woman and had never been blessed with much physical strength. She was extremely sore and weak from everything she'd been enduring since arriving there. Her guard was a big man, and he had a gun. She was gambling that she'd be able to take him out before he could get it out of the holster. The truth was that she simply didn't care about the risks anymore. If he pulled his gun out and shot her, at least it would all be over. She was completely done with this, with *all* of it. This was going to end soon, one way or another. Either she'd escape or she'd die. Either option sounded equally appealing. She just wanted this to be over while she had some semblance of her sanity remaining, before this experience transformed her into something unrecognizable to herself.

If she did manage to kill or choke out her captor, she'd use his keys to remove her chains and grab his gun, then try to figure out how to get the hell out of the building she was in. She'd have to improvise that part. She didn't know where it was located or how it was laid out. They'd drugged her when she was brought here, she'd woken up in this place and had never seen the outside of it. She fantasized about freeing the other prisoners, of creating an army of them to slaughter the fuckers who'd done this to them, but she knew this had to remain a dream. She'd be lucky to get out herself, trying to liberate anyone else was too risky. No, the best way to help them was to escape and bring the authorities back here to shut this awful place down.

This plan, this hope was the small thread which her sanity hung upon.

Hope, she thought, bitter over the irony of that word. Her first name was Hope. She'd honestly never much liked her name, but now she had a renewed appreciation for it. She had decided that it was there to remind her not to lose hope - to never give up. She knew that if she ever completely lost hope, she would lose everything. She very nearly had. They'd pushed her so hard, but she refused to be pushed any further. It was time to push back — or die trying.

When Hope heard her guard come in, she slowly opened one eye, just slightly enough so that she could see the hazy outline of him through her lashes. With any luck, he wouldn't be able to tell she was awake studying him. She waited until he set down the latest tray of tasteless, gray muck that she'd been surviving on, and leaned forward to pick up the old tray. Summoning the tattered remnants of her strength, she jumped up, ignoring the protests of the thousand places where her body ached. She was full of adrenaline now, as she launched herself onto him.

"What the—" Cried the guard.

Hope clocked him on the temple with the side of her thick steel cuff, with animalistic fury. This dazed him long enough for her to get the short chain connecting the two cuffs over his head and under his chin. She pulled back repeatedly with as much force as she could muster, her back arching as his eyes rolled back up into his skull. He slumped over onto the floor, she tumbled off of him as he crashed down. Hope wasn't sure if he was dead or simply unconscious and she didn't care so long as he remained down.

Hope disentangled her chain from his neck and hunted frantically for the keys on his belt. With a snort of annoyance, she realized he was lying on them. She sat back and used the strength of her legs to push his limp, but heavy, body over so she could get to them. Within seconds, she'd scrambled to unclip them from the belt and fumbled to find the right one to unlock the cuffs around her wrists. It wasn't easy; she had to bite down on the key to maneuver it into the lock. Once her hands were free, she rubbed her sore wrists instinctively for a moment, then went to work on finding the key that would unchain her feet and using it.

With her body free, Hope wasted no time in removing the gun from the holster. She'd never used one before, never even held one, but how difficult could it be? You just aimed and squeezed the trigger, right? She trained it upon her captor and considered putting a round into the guard's head just to be safe. It would certainly feel good to shoot him. Then she quickly decided that the sound of the gunshot would bring others to the cell if the sound of their struggle hadn't already alerted them that something was wrong.

She dashed out the still open doorway and into the featureless hall, thankful it was vacant of any other guards. Hope held the gun out in front of her as she picked a direction and started moving quickly, yet cautiously down the corridor in a kind of half run. She passed other doors like her own and wondered how many of them were also occupied. Sometimes screams from within told her. For once she was grateful for those awful sounds, as she realized they had probably masked the sound of her fight with the guard. In the middle of the hall was an elevator. Hope thought about taking it, but decided instead on trying the stairs at the end of the corridor, if the door to it wasn't locked. Fortunately for her, it wasn't and she began sprinting up the staircase. Hope went upwards because judging from the number of stairs above her, and the fact that they started on the level she was on, it was obvious that this was a large building and her cell had likely been in a basement. She ran up a couple of flights of steps until she reached a sign with a large number "1" helpfully painted on it. *Perhaps this was the ground floor?* The door separating the stairwell from the rest of that level had a small window in it, she peered through it, making sure the coast was clear before pushing the door open with the barrel of her gun and stepping out.

Hope wandered down the hallway carefully, she caught sight of a long desk with a uniformed and unmasked guard sitting at one end of the hall. She quickly turned around and jogged in the opposite direction.

"Hey you, stop!" A voice from behind her shouted, soon the sound of running footsteps could be heard dogging her. She ran. An elevator opened up to her left and without thinking, she dove into it. A tall, thin man in a fancy business suit stood inside, gaping at her. She grabbed him roughly by the shoulders and shoved him out, right into the security guard, knocking them both to the ground. Hope was pleased to see that she still had an untapped reservoir of adrenaline fueling her strength. The doors to the elevator swooshed shut, just as she heard a bullet slam into the door and punch a bullet shaped outline into it. The elevator lurched upwards, obviously, someone had called for it on another floor. Hope cursed loudly. She was positive that she'd just been on the ground floor. She needed to get up, not down!

Thankfully, the elevator abruptly stopped on the next floor up. Maybe if she could find a window she could shoot it out and jump down without breaking any bones? The door opened and she was surprised to find nobody on the other side waiting for it. Hope wondered if they had somehow stopped it from going up any higher now that they were onto her? She stepped out into another empty hallway and ran for the nearest door and threw it open, hoping to find a window somewhere inside.

The man who now went by the faintly ridiculous name of Chesterfield Xavier (or Chester for short) was shocked to see the door suddenly flung open so forcefully that it slammed into the adjacent wall with a loud report. He was even more alarmed to see the wild looking young woman who rushed into the darkened room. She might've been quite pretty at one time, but now her blonde hair was a fantastically unkempt and frizzy mess that flared out around her head in all directions, giving her the appearance of a crazed lioness. Her face and arms were crisscrossed with countless dried, crusted scabs and bruises. One eye was almost swollen shut and haloed by a mean looking shiner. Her once sensuous lips were now cracked and peeling as surely as if she'd spent the afternoon crawling through the sun baked sands of the Sahara. The lady's clothes looked like filthy medical scrubs, smeared with dried blood stains and marks from who knew what other kinds of bodily fluids. Her untamed appearance was equalled only by the abominable stench emanating from her. She smelled like she hadn't bathed in weeks. Yet somehow, the woman seemed strangely familiar, he could've sworn he'd seen her somewhere before, but where? Then he saw the gun and very nearly pissed his pants. He managed to get control over his bladder, but he *did* drop the notepad and pen he'd been using.

He held up his hands, "It's okay, I won't hurt you—I swear!"

She just grunted and cast her eyes around the room.

"Is there a window in here? I need to get out of here!"

Chester shook his head, "There's no window in here, but I can help you get out. What's going on? Who are you?"

"You mean you don't know? You're not part of it?"

He shook his head again. For some reason, she seemed to believe him.

"My name is Hope Cooper, I've been kidnapped and tortured in the basement of this building and I need to get out of here! They're after me! You've gotta help me, mister!"

Chester's mouth dropped open. *Of course! The missing college student! He'd seen her on the news. What was she doing here? Why would someone at this place be keeping her locked up in the basement? He didn't even know that this building had a basement!*

"This doesn't make any sense. We do good work here, humanitarian work! We're helping the world, not kidnapping people," he stammered.

"I don't have time to debate this! Look at me! Do you really think I'm making all this up? Are you gonna help me escape or what?"

"Of course, of course!" He jumped off of the stool he'd been sitting on and started to cross the room towards her.

As he got up, something on the other side of the thick glass partition he'd been sitting in front of moved forward, pressing itself up against the glass. She was so surprised by it that she nearly dropped her gun.

"Oh my God! What is that *thing*? What are you people up to here?"

Chester glanced over his shoulder and chuckled. "Him? Don't be scared of him! He takes a little getting used to, but he's harmless."

Her one good eye was opened so wide it threatened to pop out. "Harmless? Are you fucking nuts? It's a monster! A real monster!" Hope raised her gun towards the glass wall and the *thing* on the other side. She squeezed the trigger, but nothing happened. She didn't understand that the safety was on. Neither did Chester.

"No! Don't! He's my friend!" He cried, positioning himself between him and the dark shadow of the beast.

Just then, the door flew open again. This time, an armed guard in a uniform appeared in the threshold and, without pause, emptied the clip of his pistol into the body of Hope Cooper. She did an almost comically grim little dance as the bullets tore through her slight, wispy frame, making her contort this way and that before her smoking corpse smacked into the floor, oozing blood from half a dozen different wounds. She looked up at Chester pitifully one last time, and stretched out a hand towards him, before the light went out of her, her hand falling into a pool of her own rapidly spreading life blood with a sickening squelch. Now Chester really *did* piss his pants.

The tall man in the fancy suit strode into the room, wearing an expression of rage on his normally bland face. "You idiot! You could've hit the asset!" He hissed at the guard. Then the newcomer noticed Chester.

"Chester! I didn't realize you were here yet! I'm so sorry you had to see all of that."

"What's going on here? What's this all about?" Chester demanded furiously. He couldn't believe that he'd just seen a young woman mercilessly gunned down right in front of him, someone who was looking to him for help.

"Believe me, the less you know about it, the better it is for everyone. Plausible deniability and all that. Don't trouble yourself with it."

"Don't trouble myself with it? Are you out of your mind? He just murdered that woman!"

"Yes, unfortunately, he was forced to use lethal force to protect you and our mutual friend from an armed and dangerous madwoman. Most regrettable, but unavoidable."

But Chester was no longer looking at him. To his astonishment, he saw clumps of a thick, dark liquid rising up off of the dying body of Hope Cooper and moving through the air, passing through the glass barrier where his strange friend seemed to be sucking it up through his bizarre, insect-like mouth.

Yes, this is how I feed.

Chester heard his strange friend's "voice" buzz through his head, and also realized that the others couldn't see what he was seeing either. They lacked his own unique sensitivity to such things. Or at least the guard did. The boss, Balthazar Hazleton, seemed to be somewhat aware of what was happening. He looked at Chester oddly.

"These things are unpleasant, but they are necessary, I assure you, if our work is to continue for the benefit of all mankind. Think of the bigger picture, the greater good! And we *are* doing good work here, *very* good work! You can't make an omelet without breaking a few eggs."

Chester stepped backwards to avoid the spreading tide of blood coming from his employer's most recent broken egg. No, fuck that! Hope Cooper wasn't an egg. She wasn't some abstraction. She was a real person who'd had a real life, and they'd just needlessly and casually murdered her, like it was nothing. Fuck this place and fuck these people! There was no way to justify this.

Balthazar sniffed at the air, then looked pointedly at Chester's soiled pants. "Why don't you take the rest of the day off? Hell, take the entire week off! I can see that this has got you quite upset, and understandably so." He threw an arm around Chester in a forced gesture of amity, but was careful to keep his own body at a distance from his urine stained pants.

"Go home and forget about all of this, and whatever you do, don't mention it to anyone else. You're quite talented and are an important part of our success as a company. I'd hate to see anything happen to you. I'll see you again a week from today and we'll put all of this nastiness behind us and get back to doing our important work, for all mankind."

But Chester was no dummy. He knew a veiled threat when he heard one. He always knew that there was something a little shady about working here, but he'd willfully ignored all the red flags because he believed in the mission, and he knew he'd never have another opportunity to work with someone as extraordinary as his "friend". But as he watched his friend continue to suck up the unearthly substance coming off of the dying woman before him, he was certain that he no longer wanted anything to do with any of this. But how could he get out of it with his own life intact? He was a prisoner of circumstances just as surely as if he was being held prisoner in the basement.

He didn't know how he'd put a stop to all of this, but he knew that he must. He owed it to himself, and to the woman who was still dying at his feet.

"Sure," he gulped. "See you next Tuesday".

Act One

ACT ONE

Chapter One: Hello From The Other Side

Athena Anderson Arden yawned. She was bored, there was no denying it. When the Jersey Shore Paranormal Society had been asked to investigate poltergeist activity by the owners of this home, it had sounded exciting. In all her twenty-four years of research into the more mysterious corners of the world, she'd never before encountered a poltergeist. The home owners had provided plenty of impressive videos they'd taken with their cellphones to whet her appetite. In the videos, doors slammed shut, chairs moved across rooms and books flew off of shelves. It could've all been easily faked by someone tugging on these things from off camera with a fishing line, but Athena's husband and fellow ghost hunter, Dennis had analyzed the footage looking for just such telltale signs of a hoax and concluded it was genuine. Dennis definitely knew his shit. If he said it was real, she trusted that it was. Much of the activity centered around Clair, the thirteen year old girl who lived in the old colonial house. It definitely seemed like a classic example of a poltergeist, a German term meaning "noisy ghost". The running theory was that such manifestations were not actually caused by a ghost at all, but stemmed somehow from psychic energy given off by children entering the tumultuous years of puberty.

It was a nice theory, one that had always intrigued Athena, but so far it just wasn't panning out. Athena was a gifted psychic herself. She could actually *see* psychic energy, and she hadn't seen anything unusual coming off of Clair. Since the group had been there, none of them had experienced or recorded anything out of the ordinary whatsoever. The closest thing to an indication that something was amiss was a feeling

Athena would sometimes get. It was like she was sensing a fleeting presence, someone or something that was watching her, then it would flee before she could be sure that it had been anything other than a figment of her own imagination. Things were so uneventful that despite her conviction that Clair wasn't causing the activity, they'd called her back into her bedroom and asked her to do some of the things she'd been doing in the past when the ghostly activity had occurred hoping to stir something up.

So it was that Athena was now sitting on the edge of Clair's bed, engulfed in darkness, while her best friend, Miranda Robbins, filmed them with a night vision camera from a chair in front of a desk across the room. Clair was just lying in the bed, streaming music from her phone to a Bluetooth speaker on the bedside table. The last few catchy notes of a K-pop song that Athena didn't recognize were fading out, only to be replaced by something she knew all too well. Not that she particularly wanted to know it, but it was unavoidable these days and had been for the past few years.

"Hello" by Adele now blared out of the speaker.

That's when it happened. Athena heard the pitter (yet oddly not the patter) of tiny feet upon the floorboards. In the darkness, she spied a blur of motion out of the corner of her eye and a second later, something was flung through the air, nearly hitting Miranda. Whatever it was that was thrown, it bounced off the wall behind her. Clair screamed, competing with one of Adele's more powerful notes which she was currently belting out through the speaker.

Miranda leapt to her feet, "What the hell was that? It landed right behind me!"

Athena heard a childish giggle and more pitters. Still no patters. That's how she knew she was definitely dealing with something unearthly. Then she actually *saw* it, the transparent form of a boy, no more than eight or nine years old, running past her and out the door.

"Hey!" She called after it. Who did this little shit think he was, throwing stuff at her bestie? Within moments, she was up and chasing the diminutive spirit down the hallway.

"Come back! I just want to talk!" She was almost out of breath, at forty-six she wasn't as fast as she used to be. She led a pretty sedentary lifestyle, usually without any regrets except for at times like this.

The spectral boy turned to the left and disappeared. In the darkness, Athena had assumed there was an open door there and started to follow him, only too late did she see that there was no door, he'd vanished right through the wall. Unable to halt her forward momentum, she banged her face up against it, nearly breaking her glasses. "Why you little—!" She exclaimed, then laughed as she realized that she'd just spontaneously done a perfect impression of Homer Simpson. Before she knew it, her husband Dennis was running down the hall towards her, Lars Ericson, another member of her team hot on his heels.

Dennis took her in his arms, "Are you okay? We heard screams and running and crashing—"

She rubbed her nose. Nothing felt like it was broken. "I'll be fine, only my pride is wounded."

Another scream pierced the dark, accompanied by a persistent banging sound. It sounded like it was coming from Clair's room. The three of them looked at each other, then all set off racing towards the source of the sound. As Athena came skidding into the room first, she saw that the kid now had the long, black cylindrical Bluetooth speaker in his hands and was banging it up against the wall, trying to smash it. Poor Clair was sitting up on her bed screaming herself hoarse. Athena realized that the others probably couldn't see the boy, so from their perspective this looked like the speaker was floating in mid air and launching itself into the wall repeatedly. The unflappable Miranda was dutifully recording the whole thing with her camera, while simultaneously trying to soothe Clair with her words. She couldn't help it, it was the mother in her.

"It's okay, honey it's just a speaker, you're okay. It's going to be okay," assured Miranda.

"It sure will be! I won't let him hurt you!" Athena added as she strode into the room towards the troublesome ghost. She could see him much better now, through the weak light streaming in from through the window from the streetlights. He was a little older than she had first assumed, perhaps the same age as Clair herself. He had unruly sandy blonde hair that was a little on the long side, coming down to just above his shoulders and a round, freckled face. Judging from the way he was dressed in bell bottom jeans, he'd likely died in the late 1960s or 70s. Or maybe even the nineties. That look had come back into style then, for reasons Athena had never fathomed. Fashion was depressingly cyclical.

The ghost wasn't happy to see her. "Oh shit!" He cried, then looked as if he was about to run off again, before he could, Athena pointed at him

and chanted something which sounded oddly like baby talk. The boy tried to drop the speaker, found that he couldn't and a perplexed look crossed his face. He tried to disappear through the wall again, but it didn't work. Now he looked angrily in Athena's direction.

"The others said you were a witch! What have you done to me?"

Athena smiled and took a step towards him, "I prefer the term sorceress. Witch, unfortunately has too many negative connotations to it, it makes me sound mean. Also I'm not a Wiccan, so it's not particularly accurate."

The ghost looked visibly confused by her comments. She'd have to keep it simple for him, he was just a kid. "Anyhow, I've temporarily bound you to a physical object, namely that speaker in your hand. I won't hurt you, I just want to talk."

"No you don't! I've heard of you! You're the witch who makes us cross over! You want to get rid of me! It's not fair! I was here first!"

Athena was taken aback by his words. She didn't know if she was more surprised by the fact that she was garnering a reputation amongst the ghosts, or the fact that they seemed to have some kind of a community in which they could get together to gossip about her. It was news to her, but she didn't have time to worry about that now.

"Calm down kid. I can't make anyone cross over who isn't ready to, and I wouldn't even if I could, it's unethical. If you wanna stay, that's fine. But if you are gonna stick around, I *do* wish you'd behave yourself a little better. What's with all the banging and throwing stuff around? What's got you so upset lately?"

"*This* is what it's all about!" He frantically waved the speaker around that he was now unable to put down. Surreally, Adele had still been singing throughout this entire episode.

Athena was confused, "The speaker?"

"No, the song! She plays it all the time! I'm so sick of it!"

Athena smiled wryly. She was sick of it too. Was that really what this was all about? "It's actually a really good song, but I agree it's been so overplayed that it's worn out its welcome. Why don't you just turn off the speaker?"

"How?"

"It's usually the little button next to the light."

"Oh." He pressed it with his other hand. Adele's voice disappeared from the room like a phantom.

"See, isn't that easier than tearing up the place?"

"It's not just that! She might be kinda hot, but this chick has terrible tastes in music! Why doesn't she ever play anything cool, y'know like KISS or something?"

KISS? Okay, so this ghost was *definitely* from the Seventies, Athena decided. Personally, while she appreciated the theatricality of KISS, she wasn't sure she actually liked their music very much. There were so many other bands that rocked harder.

"Is that really all that's bothering you? Oh! I never did catch your name, did I?"

"It's Jay. And yeah, that's my only problem, otherwise I'm okay."

"You're sure? You don't want to move on at all? To see what lies beyond this world?"

"Nah, being a ghost is pretty groovy. I'm much happier than I was when I was alive, really."

Athena thought that Jay's life must've been pretty shitty if he preferred being a ghost to being alive, but what did she really know about the secret lives of ghosts? Perhaps it was in fact far more "groovy" than she could imagine. She did believe him though, the activity had only started recently and he'd obviously been here for years. She wondered how long Clair had owned that Bluetooth speaker?

"I'll tell you what Jay, I promise to talk to Clair here and see if she can listen to her music with earbuds instead."

The ghost wrinkled his nose, "Earbuds?"

"They're like headphones."

Jay nodded in understanding, "And they have to play KISS. I want them to blast that stuff!"

Athena chuckled, "Okay, I'll work on that with them too. And in return do you promise to go back to being so quiet that they won't even know you're here, like before?"

"Sure, if you'll let me go." He pointed to the speaker that was stuck to his open palm as if it had been superglued to it.

"It's a deal. Have a nice afterlife, Jay." Athena chanted something and Jay set the speaker back on the side table he'd snatched it from. He gave her a sly smile and a salute, then disappeared through the wall.

Athena clapped her hands together in satisfaction and whirled around to face the others. Dennis and Lars were lingering in the doorframe. Miranda was sitting on the bed next to Clair, who was sobbing in a far more subdued way by now. Miranda was rubbing her back to calm her down while she continued to film.

"It's all settled now—I hope! I think we can turn the lights back on and call this investigation a wrap!"

Lars flicked a switch on the wall and light flooded back into the room. "What happened?" He asked. Lars was blessed with a very smooth voice, or rather, he'd cultivated one. His ambition had once been to be a TV news anchor, but that hadn't worked out for him. He couldn't prove it, but he suspected that he'd been just a little bit too ginger for prime time. He still worked as a journalist, albeit for the Asbury Park Press, one of the bigger local newspapers that hadn't yet been wiped out by the internet. Lars sometimes reported on the doings of the Jersey Shore Paranormal Society, before he decided to become a proper member of the team after participating in one of their more harrowing cases nearly two years earlier.

"Our poltergeist was actually a kid from the Seventies named Jay. He's been here all along, but the activity was stirred up by his disapproval of Clair's choice of music."

Dennis laughed, "Really? That's what caused all this trouble?"

"Apparently," Athena looked at Clair. The teen was wiping the tears from her eyes with her sweater sleeve. "He promised not to cause any more trouble so long as you listen to your music with your earbuds in. Do you think you can do that?"

The girl nodded. "Are you really a...sorceress?"

"Yes, but don't worry, I'm one of the good ones! We'll have to ask you to keep that as our little secret." She turned to Dennis, "And you're gonna have to edit my spell casting out before you upload any of this to our website."

"Well, yeah of course, duh." He hardly needed to be reminded of this.

Athena had been trained in how to harness her natural psychic aptitude to work magic by a wizard named Clark Kismet. He'd also been training her similarly gifted younger half brother, Mark. Both Clark and Mark were part of an ancient secret society of magic users called the Temple of the Old Gods. Athena had declined to join this group, she had no use for all their silly, secret handshake nonsense. She just wanted to be able to use her abilities to protect her friends and help restless spirits move on. Technically, Clark wasn't supposed to be training her unless she became a card carrying member, but he'd made a special exception in her case. In return, Athena had agreed to help maintain the group's secrecy, as well as the fact that magic was a real thing.

Mark would've normally joined them on this investigation, but both he and Clark were currently away at the Temple of the Old God's' headquarters on the hidden Greek island of Elysium. In a few days, Mark was going to be participating in a ceremony to honor his graduation from apprentice to full fledged wizard. For Athena, there would be no such solemn celebrations of her newfound mastery of the mystic arts in far off, exotic locations. She was magnificently jealous of this fact and everyone knew it, although she refused to acknowledge this to anyone, least of all herself.

Athena smacked herself on the forehead. "Oh! I nearly forgot! Apparently, our newfound spectral friend has a special request that you play him some KISS songs from time to time."

"What's KISS?" Clair asked.

"KISS! You know, Knights in Satan's Service?"

"That's not what it stands for!" Dennis corrected her.

She waved a dismissive hand at him, "Whatever! You know, Gene Simmons? The dude with the long tongue and the platform shoes who breathes fire? There's the cat guy, and the dude with the star on his face and some other guy and they all wear crazy kabuki makeup?"

The girl just gave her a befuddled look.

Athena's mouth gaped open in astonishment. KISS had been such a big deal during her early childhood, it was hard for her to comprehend that she was now living in a world where most young people probably didn't know who they were. *Oh, well,* she mused, *if you live long enough I suppose you start to see lots of things that used to be a big deal start to fade into obscurity. I'll bet she doesn't even know who the Fonz is either. What are they teaching the kids these days?*

"It's okay, I've got a greatest hits CD in the van I can let you have. I don't really listen to it anymore, it gets on a certain *somebody's* nerves whenever I pop it in," Dennis told the girl. The certain someone he mentioned was of course, Athena, who maintained the opinion that KISS put on such an elaborate show to distract from the fact that their music was fairly lackluster.

"What's a CD?" Clair asked innocently.

Now Athena had heard everything! Surely, it hadn't been *that* long ago when CDs were the dominant method of listening to music, was it? They still sold them in stores, didn't they? Was this girl determined to make her feel like she was one of the ancients?

Miranda came to the rescue, as she often did. She patted Clair on the shoulder and said "Don't worry about it. Just search for KISS on Spotify or whatever you use to stream your music."

"Blast a few of those songs on your little speaker a few times a week, and that should keep Jay happy and out of your hair. If he ever reneges on our deal, give us another call and I'll give him another good talking to."

Clair agreed to the unusual request, and the team invited the rest of her family (who had been hanging out in a neighbor's house while they did their investigation) back in. They packed up all their gear and congratulated themselves on another successful investigation, but as they pulled out of the driveway, Athena felt little satisfaction. A dark feeling of foreboding washed over her. Although he was no psychic, after over twenty years of marriage, Dennis was magnificently attuned to his spouse's moods, and he picked up on her distress.

"What's wrong?"

"I dunno. I feel like we're headed for some sort of a really big challenge or something. It's probably nothing." As she said it, she could practically hear her mentor, Clark Kismet chiding her for ignoring her instincts.

"Hmm. You know what I think? I think you're just bummed out that you're not getting a big celebration like Mark is. I told you we could throw you a party too if you want."

"And I told you I don't need a party. Anyhow, Clark hasn't said that my training period is officially over. I haven't earned it yet, even if I wanted everyone to make a big deal over it, which I *don't*."

"Uh huh, sure."

"I mean it! I don't need to have a fancy ceremony on some stupid island. I made my bed when I refused to join the Temple of the Old Gods and I'm perfectly fine sleeping in it. My bed is very cozy."

Dennis knew better than to press the issue. He hadn't survived in this marriage for this long without knowing when to drop a subject. If she changed her mind, she'd certainly let him know. He just wished she wouldn't be so hard on herself and allow herself to celebrate her accomplishments every once in a while. She deserved a party! She'd come so far in the past two years, and put her newfound powers to good use, sending lots of spirits who'd become too attached to the material plane to move on to whatever the heck it is which awaits us all in the great beyond.

Athena just continued to glare gloomily out of the window all the rest of the way home, unable to shake her palpable sense of dark foreboding...

Chapter Two: When Worlds Collide

Ugh, look at this sad turn out, Athena thought in disappointment for the forty-ninth time. She eyed the group bitterly, there were only seven of them, mostly consisting of blue haired little old ladies and a few folks who looked as if they might be in their early twenties. She'd organized this event at the library where she served as head librarian for her old schoolmate, Matt Spike, to discuss his latest detective novel *The Streets Will Run Red,* but was mortified by the small size of the audience. She'd been advertising it and talking it up to everyone for nearly two months now, and yet it had failed to attract many people. Matt and his wife Naomi had driven down to their old hometown of Barnegat all the way from North Brunswick to be here. She hoped he thought it was worth the trip.

She'd known Matt since middle school, and was delighted when he started making something of a name for himself as a writer in the early 2000's, she was always sure to stock all his books and display them prominently whenever a new one came out.

She stole a glance at Naomi. Or Dr. Naomi Waters-Spike as she styled herself these days. Apparently she was now a high flutin' history professor up at Rutgers University. *How did she keep herself looking so young?* She wondered with a twinge of jealousy. Naomi was a short, curvy woman with long jet black hair (Athena had concluded that it must be dyed, or surely there'd be some gray in it by now?) and an olive complexion.

She'd known Naomi for almost as long as she'd known Matt, but she'd never really considered her to be a friend. Unlike Matt, she'd never been a part of the Dungeons and Dragons group Dennis used to run. Not only that, but Athena was pretty sure Naomi had stolen her boyfriend in the seventh grade. That guy was kind of a jerk anyways, and she knew it was stupid to hold grudges over things that happened a lifetime ago, but it was hard to let go. She and Matt did look cute together, though. She wasn't too surprised to find out that they'd eventually become a couple. Even though they'd never dated back when they were all in school together, Athena always thought they looked as if they *should've* been, and often suspected that there was something going on between the two of them. Naomi was an author too, she had a few books published on various historical topics. Athena had at least one of them on these library shelves. She didn't stock them with the same devotion she did with Matt's books. Naomi's books were quite dry and technical, little better than textbooks, in her opinion.

The sound of polite clapping broke her out of her reverie. Matt had just finished up reading an excerpt from his novel, and was now fielding questions from the audience, such as it was.

Mrs. Clayton raised her hand. Athena smiled, she was one of her most regular of regulars. A retired teacher, Athena had watched her grow old over the years, she must've been in her early forties when Athena first started working here in the nineties and she used to bring her children to the library. Now the woman was in her sixties and as far as Athena could tell, her retirement seemed to consist mainly of sitting at home and reading, which sounded like the ideal life to Athena. Mrs. Clayton would read anything Athena recommended to her, and was a sucker for mysteries. Athena had turned her on to Matt's books long ago and she always eagerly gobbled them up.

"Hello, Matt. I'm a longtime reader—" she started off nervously.

"I appreciate that! Thank you," Matt interrupted. The older woman blushed slightly and Athena wondered if she had a little crush on Matt. He was certainly good looking enough, tall and a little on the slender side; although not nearly as skinny as Athena remembered him he had rugged features and a permanent five o'clock shadow. His short cropped once dark blond hair had mostly turned brown by now, and was even graying at the temples.

Mrs. Clayton had stopped swooning long enough to resume her line of questioning. "I've always wondered to what extent your cases as a private eye informed the plots of your stories?" That's right, Matt was also a private investigator.

Matt didn't take very long to ponder the question, it was one he got often.

"Being a PI in real life definitely helps with the realism of the stories when it comes to depicting the process of doing an investigation, but that's typically where it ends. My cases are mostly pretty dull and wouldn't make for very entertaining stories—"

"You do have a handful of ones that are pretty exciting," Naomi contradicted him with a wink.

"Yeah, but I can't write about those, or else I'd have to kill my readers, which generally isn't good for sales." The audience laughed at this exchange, but it piqued Athena's interest.

What are they talking about? She sensed that there was something deeper behind this exchange than a wish to protect the privacy of his clients.

"I do work in a few funny anecdotes from my years of working as a detective whenever I can, but the plots are from my imagination. I have lots of time to daydream and come up with them when sitting around in my car doing surveillance on people."

Matt called on another person who had their hand up. This was a pensive looking young man with short dark hair. Athena didn't know his name, but she'd seen him around from time to time.

"Did you decide to become a private investigator as a way of doing research for your books?" he asked in a somewhat nasally voice.

"Ah, the old chicken or the egg question? Do I write detective fiction because I am a detective, or did I become a detective to better write these kinds of stories? Well, it was my love of mystery stories which inspired me to become an investigator in the first place. I was a little disappointed to find out that it's not much like how it's depicted in those old noir movies, but what the hell? The money is good and I can't picture myself doing a normal job, so I stick with it. I think that no matter what, I would've ended up writing these kinds of stories. I've been making them up since I was a kid, it's like second nature to me."

From the way he answered that one, Athena was sure he got that question a lot too.

"No more questions? Anyone?" Matt looked searchingly at the group, "okay then, if anyone bought a book for me to sign, I'll be happy to sign it, so long as it's your own copy of one of my books. I don't think the library would take kindly to me defacing their property!"

"I wouldn't consider signing one of our copies to be defacing!" Athena chimed in.

This exchange elicited more smiles and laughter from the small party.

Athena saw Mrs. Clayton scoop up a small stack of paperbacks and practically sprint towards Matt to be the first in line. She shook her head and grinned. *She's definitely got a crush on him!* She didn't need to be psychic to see that.

Matt spent the next ten minutes or so signing books and chatting with the attendees. As the last one got their book signed and they began to disperse, Athena walked over to Matt and Naomi.

"Sorry about the size of the group. I was really hoping for a better turn out."

"Don't be silly! A small group is better, it's more intimate and less intimidating."

Athena could tell he was sincere, and it removed a huge burden from her mind. "I hope you guys are ready for dinner. Dennis texted me that it was ready a few minutes ago."

"I'm pretty famished. What are we having?" Naomi asked.

"Beef wellington. After watching Gordon Ramsay screaming at people for undercooking it for years, Dennis was inspired to take a shot at making it himself. 'IT'S RAAAW!'" She playfully said as loudly as she dared in a terrible attempt at a British accent.

They laughed along at her awful impression, the way that good friends will.

Athena led them back to her red brick, ranch style house in the Settler's Landing section of town. She was suddenly a little embarrassed by her house, she imagined it must seem pretty humble compared to what Matt and Naomi were probably living in. It had been Dennis' idea to cook dinner for them when he heard that Matt had accepted Athena's invitation to give a presentation at the library. He and Matt had been pretty good friends in middle school, but had drifted apart in the last few years of high school for no particular reason, it's just one of those things that happens sometimes. Dennis was eager to reconnect with him outside of Facebook, but after a long day at work, Athena just wanted to relax, not play host to company. She sighed, what's done is done, she had no choice. At least there was the beef wellington to look forward to, Dennis was an excellent cook and she thought that his rendition of the dish might even pass Chef Ramsay's notoriously tough standards.

She got out of her little blue Kia Rio and waited for Matt and Naomi to exit the SUV they'd driven down here. She didn't know which one of them it belonged to, but Naomi was the one driving it. They had to park on the street because Dennis' van took up most of the driveway. They had a garage, but it was so stuffed with his tools from his HVAC job and his ghost hunting equipment that it could no longer house a vehicle, to Athena's eternal chagrin.

Matt looked around as he walked from the car. "It's so strange to be back on these streets. I spent so many years dreaming about the world beyond this place, scheming to get out of here, eager to shake the dust of this place off of me. Then you come back as an adult, and it suddenly doesn't seem so bad anymore, and you wonder why you were so driven to leave in the first place."

"You don't get back here very often, do you?" Athena asked as Matt and Naomi caught up with her.

"No reason to. My dad passed away about five or six years ago and my mom lives with us now in one of those tiny houses we had made for her in our backyard. I haven't been here since I helped her clear out our old house and sell it."

"And those times we were all about business, no time to visit with any old friends," Naomi added.

"I'm sorry to hear about your father." Athena only had vague memories of the man.

"Don't be! He was a real piece of work, wasn't he?"

"He sure was! The only man I've ever met who was cheaper than you are, which I frankly thought was impossible," Naomi observed.

"Hardy har, har har!" Matt mock laughed. Athena shook her head and thought, *The more things change the more they stay the same. These two still carry on with each other just like they did in high school!*

As they all approached her front door they were greeted by the sounds of a barking dog within.

"That's our latest pooch, Bealzebarker," Athena explained, "don't worry he won't bite."

"What a cool name! Back when we had a dog, Mr. Creativity here just named him Mike," Naomi remarked.

"Hey, can I help it if he looked like a Mike to me? I must reserve all my creativity, like the precious commodity that it is, for my writing," Matt replied facetiously, then a melancholy look came over him. "He was a good boy, our Mike. When he passed away, I didn't have the heart to get another dog, besides there was no replacing him."

"So you guys don't have any pets?" Athena inquired, as an enthusiastic pet lover she wasn't thrown at all by the fact that Matt sounded more saddened when discussing the loss of his dog than he was over his father.

"Just a cat," Matt answered.

"Technically, he's our daughter's cat, but she's not allowed to have a pet in her apartment, so we got stuck with him, which is fine by me," Naomi clarified.

Athena fiddled with her door key as the sounds of barking grew more intense and were joined by an insistent scratching on the other side of the door. "We've got cats too! What's his name?"

"Zarathustra," Naomi revealed with a smile.

"Ah, named after the Persian prophet that founded Zoroastrianism? That's a pretty good one. You must've come up with that name." Athena couldn't help but show off her familiarity with the unusual moniker.

"I did, I'm impressed that you got the reference."

I might not be a history professor, but I'm no dummy, sister! Athena thought. She smiled at Naomi as she shoved the door open, "I'm a collector of interesting and obscure yet practically useless knowledge."

Athena was immediately set upon by Beazlebark, an enthusiastic beagle who promptly placed his front paws on her legs, his tail wagging in ecstasy.

"Down!" She commanded in that tone of voice which most people reserve for talking to animals and small children. The dog didn't obey until she acknowledged him by rubbing him on the top of his head, now satisfied, he went off to sniff curiously at the newcomers. Matt couldn't resist petting him, but he quickly lost interest and waddled off towards the more enticing aromas of dinner wafting in from the dining room.

"MATTY!" Dennis bellowed as he strode into the living room from the adjacent dining area, a wide grin on his face.

"Jesus! It's been years since anyone called me that!"

"Hey, Dennis! Lookin' good, man!" He meant it too. Dennis had been a bit on the husky side throughout their childhood, but it looked as if he'd lost much of that baby fat over the years, he was still big, but in a much healthier looking way. His sandy blonde hair was thinning, but he retained a mischievous twinkle in his remarkably blue eyes which made it apparent just how very much he was enjoying life.

Dennis gave his old friend a big hug, then stepped back to take another look at him. "Still rocking the fedora, huh?"

"I've always been a little fashion forward."

Naomi chuckled at that remark, "More like fashion backwards!"

"Hey Naomi." Dennis seemed to notice Naomi for the first time, in his defense, she was an extraordinarily petite woman and Matt was almost completely obscuring her with his long brown trench coat. Even though it was a warm day in late May, Matt still wore his coat and trademark fedora when outside. He really was a slave to his peculiar idea of fashion.

"Hey right back at you, Dennis," Naomi said politely, the two of them barely knew each other, having had few interactions in their school days. It was more like they knew *of* each other than actually *knew* each other very well.

"I have to hand it to you, Matt. We always thought you were just dressing up like a private eye for the fun of it, but you actually went out and really became one! And an author too!"

"You know what they say, dress for the job you want!" Matt said as he took off his hat and trench coat, which Athena took and put into a nearby closet. Matt took stock of the interior of the home. They were standing in a living room connected to a dining room, which was connected to a kitchen. The living room was furnished in a very standard way: there was a couch, a love seat, and a recliner, with a coffee table in the center. A large flatscreen TV was attached to the far wall, and the room was well lit by a large bay window. Matt smiled. His hosts had no idea that the reason behind his grin was that he had spent many of the happiest moments of his childhood in the houses of this neighborhood. Many of them shared an identical layout, and he found the familiarity of it oddly comforting. What made the room stand apart from those others was the array of framed movie posters on the walls, as well as the bookshelves crammed with an astonishingly diverse array of volumes, as well as a few glass display cases filled with action figures. Most of the movie posters and toys were related to Star Wars. Being a big fan of that galaxy, far, far away, Matt was immediately drawn to them like a moth to a flame.

"Oh! Nice collection!" He said as he tapped on the glass of one of the cases and leaned in for a closer look. "I used to collect these with my son Joe back when he was still a kid, but he kinda lost interest in it all pretty soon. I'm afraid we failed to pass on our Star Wars love to the kiddos."

"Thanks, man," Dennis said with a touch of pride. "How are your kids doing?"

"Joe is actually working with me at the detective agency now! I'm thinking of changing the business name to "Spike and Son".

"I thought he was a fine artist? I saw some of his paintings you posted on Facebook, amazing stuff."

"He was doing really well for himself in the fine arts world for a while, but it's a really tough kind of career and it doesn't help that the art scene in NYC is as corrupt as hell. One minute you're the hot new toast of the town and the next you're yesterday's news," Naomi interjected, "So Matt convinced him to come work with him at the family business to supplement his income. He hasn't given up on his art, he still creates things and sells them, he just needs a bit more financial stability now."

"Yeah, he's planning on marrying a girl, Mary Sherwood. She's a good kid, the sister of one of the girls who works in my office."

"Geez, Matt, it sounds like this private investigator thing has really taken off! How many people do you have working for you?" Athena said as she waved her arms to shoo Bealzebarker away from the dining room table, which was already completely laid out. It looked like Dennis had definitively been busy while they'd been at the library.

Matt's face contorted as he considered the question. It was something he didn't really think about often. "Hmm, five full timers and one part timer if you don't count me."

"And what about your daughter? You said something about her having an apartment? How old is she now?" Athena inquired as she motioned for them to take their seats at the table.

"Autumn is nineteen now, they're going to my school, Rutgers, for computer science stuff. They're renting a cute place off campus with their best friend, Celine," Naomi informed her as she took her seat. "It all smells really good, Dennis!" Her comment made him blush slightly. Dennis' face was an open book to the whole world. He was a man who completely lacked guile, and was honest almost to a fault.

"Thanks! No need to stand on ceremony, we don't say grace or anything, we're not religious, just dig right in!"

"Kids are a real trip, they grow up so fast!" Matt added as he picked up his knife and fork and proceeded to dissect the food before him.

"They do, don't they?" Athena responded, "We never had any of our own, which was a deliberate choice that I don't regret, but we've seen our nieces and nephews grow up way too quickly. It's hard not to feel like you're getting too old when you see all these kids suddenly turning into adults around you."

"I'll bet all that ghost hunting keeps you young, though. That's a really cool side hustle you guys have going," commented Naomi. Athena was surprised by her words. She didn't expect the distinguished professor to be so open minded about the paranormal.

"I thought you only dealt in scientifically verifiable facts."

"I try to, as much as possible, but you might be shocked to know how much of history is open to interpretation. Besides, we've seen a few things in our time that've opened us up to many possibilities."

"Careful," Matt warned "we can't talk about any of that or we might have to kill them, which is really bad table manners, not to mention just downright rude when you're a guest."

Athena's eyes narrowed slightly, *There they go again! What is that all about? Some kind of stupid running joke between the two of them, or something more?*

"Damn! This is really good, Dennis!" Matt said between bites "I don't know what it's *supposed* to taste like, because I've never had it before, but it sure tastes great and that's all that matters."

"It sure isn't RAAW!" Naomi laughed, imitating Athena's sad Gordon Ramsay impression from earlier.

"My man is, and always has been, an amazing cook," said Athena affectionately. Dennis blushed again like it was going out of style.

"Naomi is the master chef in our house. I can boil water, that's about the extent of my culinary skill," Matt confessed.

She shrugged, "The cooking is nothing, it's an Italian thing. You should've seen this guy when our paths crossed again after high school. He was skinny as a rail and living off of ramen noodles and hot dogs! But I fattened him up good!"

"So what's on the agenda for your next ghost hunt?" Matt inquired as he took a swig of the wine.

"Oh, it's no ghost hunt. We're the Jersey Shore Paranormal Society. We investigate all kinds of weird shit, not just ghosts, although to be sure, ghosts *are* our specialty," Athena said with a glint in her eye.

Matt was intrigued, "If it isn't a ghost, what is it then?"

"Go ahead and tell them, it's so cool!" Dennis gushed.

"We're going after Mothman, himself!" Athena grinned.

Matt was confused, "Mothman? I thought that was only in West Virginia?"

"The original sightings were in West Virginia back in the sixties, but there have been others all over the world. Most modern sightings actually happen in Chicago," Athena hastily explained.

"What the heck is a Mothman?" Naomi asked, looking a little left out.

"It's a cryptid. A legendary animal whose existence hasn't been proven by science yet, like Bigfoot. Mothman is like a big dark flying man with glowing red eyes and huge wings. We saw a movie about it once, remember? The one with Richard Gere, *The Mothman Prophecies*?" Matt reminded her.

Naomi bobbed her head in understanding. "Oh yeah, that movie was creepy!"

"Creepy, but also terribly inaccurate to the book it was based off of," Dennis said, a note of irritation creeping into his voice over that detail.

"But the book wasn't particularly accurate to the facts either," Athena replied. "The author exaggerated and made up all kinds of things to make the book more interesting."

"I still don't understand what Mothman is supposed to be. In the movie, didn't they imply that it showed up in West Virginia to warn people of a bridge that collapsed?" Matt was shocked that his wife remembered so much about the movie, they'd seen it so long ago.

"That's one theory, that it's some kind of a harbinger of impending doom, but there really isn't much to connect the creature to the collapse of the Silver Bridge in my opinion. Honestly, I've never been particularly impressed by the so-called evidence for the existence of Mothman. It's mostly anecdotal, plus a few unconvincing photos. People have tried to link his appearance to all kinds of bad things: the Chernobyl nuclear disaster, the 9/11 attacks—"

"Ladies and gentlemen, I present to you my wife, Athena Arden: the world's most infuriatingly skeptical paranormal investigator!" Dennis said grandly.

"Well, someone around here has to keep us grounded in reality."

"So," Matt asked between gulps, "when will you be going out to Chicago to look for Mothman?"

"Oh, we're not traveling that far," Dennis smiled slyly. "There have been sightings right here in New Jersey recently. They haven't made the local news yet, they've only been reported to us by someone who follows us on our website. So this weekend we're gonna go follow up on it."

"It could all be a bunch of hooey, it probably is, but look at Dennis! He's so excited by the possibility of Mothman being in New Jersey! How could I let him down by refusing to check into it?" Athena teased.

"You're excited too, you're just too cool to admit it."

"Mothman *is* a very cool idea, and I do wish it was real, I'm just not very convinced that it is. He's just so darned...improbable."

"Those people we met at the Mothman Festival a few years ago seemed sincere to me, they definitely saw something," Dennis shot back. Athena sighed, this was a debate they had often.

"Mothman Festival?" asked Naomi.

"It's a big annual event they have in Point Pleasant, West Virginia, the town where Mothman was first sighted," Dennis explained. "We went down there once and talked to some of the original eye witnesses. They have a really cool statue of the creature there too! We took a picture in front of it! I'll show you!"

He dug his phone out of his pocket and swiped on the screen a few times, then held it up for his guest to see. There was a picture of him and Athena standing before an immense chrome effigy of the Mothman. Dennis was smiling broadly in the photo, while Athena was flipping the creature "the bird" with her middle finger. He swiped the screen again and there was a picture of Athena sensually caressing one of the monster's legs, while sticking her tongue out as if she was about to lick the other one.

Naomi laughed at that last picture and nearly choked on her wine in the process.

"Those people were sincere. I'm a psychic, so I know they weren't lying to us. The trouble is that you can believe that you saw something, be completely honest about it, but it still doesn't mean that what you saw was really a flying man beast."

Dennis leaned back in his chair and crossed his arms, "My charming wife thinks that those nice folks somehow mixed up an owl with a seven foot bat winged creature with huge glowing red eyes."

"Hey, some of those owls can get really big, and their eyes can appear to glow when struck by light. It's less crazy than a flying man-shaped creature, and don't get me started on the impossible aerodynamics of such a monster."

Athena had conveniently forgotten that the flight mechanics of the wyvern she kept as a familiar were equally impossible seeming, yet he flew. "Well, we'll just have to see what we find this weekend, won't we? The person who had the sightings is very credible in my opinion."

"So how did you guys get started with investigating all this paranormal stuff?" asked Matt. Athena suspected he was trying to change the subject before this argument escalated.

"I've always been curious about the unknown, remember?" Dennis replied.

"I definitely remember you being really obsessed with the Jersey Devil. You even worked him into our D&D campaign, damn that thing was hard to kill!" Matt had nearly lost his favorite character during that battle.

"He sure was!" Athena agreed and smiled at Dennis knowingly. They'd had a run in with a creature which had been mistaken for the Jersey Devil about two years earlier, but she couldn't tell that particular story around the dinner table.

"I forgot all about that!" Dennis exclaimed. Athena reflected on what a strange thing memory was, how something like this expression of her husband's childhood Jersey Devil obsession could be so routine to him that he'd discarded all recollection of it, yet that same thing could make such a lasting impression on someone else.

"And how did you get roped into all of this?" Naomi asked Athena.

Athena leaned towards her, "I've always been able to see spirits, ever since I was a little girl. One day I saw one in that old house on West Bay Ave that's up the street from my library, you know the one? I swear it was empty the whole time we were in high school."

"Isn't that the one where those people were killed years ago?" asked Naomi.

"Yeah, it was a murder/suicide," Dennis informed her in a very matter of fact way.

Naomi made a face. Unbeknownst to her hosts, her own father had once been a cop in this town and he'd responded to that call. He hadn't shown up soon enough to prevent the tragedy, which had haunted him for the rest of his life and far beyond it too.

Athena took up the rest of the story, "So when I told Dennis what I'd seen, he bought all kinds of ghost hunting gear and we got permission to investigate. After that first case, we've been going at it ever since. I wrote a whole account of it once. I dabble in writing from time to time myself. I'd be honored to share it with you if you wanna read it. I'd love to know what a real author thinks of it."

Dennis interrupted her, "Uh, you might want to do some editing before you let Matt read it. It's a little *too* accurate." Her story also included their first meeting with the wizard Clark Kismet, which she'd since promised to keep secret.

Athena immediately caught onto his meaning, "Oh yeah. I suppose it is kinda rough around the edges in some places."

Matt's brows furrowed in apparent confusion over this peculiar exchange between his hosts. Athena hoped she hadn't aroused the detective's suspicions.

"I'd be happy to give you my professional opinion on it, whenever you feel like it's ready to be shared."

Athena was visibly thrilled by this idea, "Really? That would be so cool! I'll email it to you when I've polished it up some."

The rest of the evening passed pleasantly enough, but it was getting late and Matt and Naomi had to leave right after dinner, as they were both working the next day.

"That was a nice visit, wasn't it?" Athena remarked as she helped Dennis clear the plates off of the table.

"Yeah, it's weird seeing them again after all this time. Good, but awkward too. After so many years it's like you know each other, but you *don't* know each other anymore," he said, sounding a bit melancholy.

Athena placed a gentle hand on his arm, "Disappointed?"

"In a way, yes. Sometimes it's hard to recapture that..." he paused as he struggled to find the right words, "that *spark* that connected you as friends to begin with."

She felt bad for Dennis. Personally, she felt that the evening had been a success, even Naomi hadn't gotten under her skin, but it was obvious that Dennis had been expecting something more from it. He'd been so looking forward to reconnecting with Matt in person, but the experience had clearly left him feeling underwhelmed for whatever reason.

"Well, maybe we'll find you a nice Mothman to hang out with this weekend."

He chuckled at her words and started up the dishwasher.

A concerned Athena watched her husband shuffle past her, the usual spring in his step was gone, he suddenly seemed so tired and sad. For once, she sincerely hoped that she was wrong about the Mothman.

Again, she was seized by the same uncanny feeling she'd experienced after leaving their last ghost hunt. She hadn't been able to give it a name before, but now she was afraid that the meaning behind the feeling was all too clear: it was a feeling of impending doom.

Chapter Three: The Odd Couple

"The people from Humanaid are here," The voice on the intercom announced.

Matt Spike stabbed the response button with his finger, "Go ahead and send them in, Penny." He leaned back in his chair and swiveled to face his partner, Earl Rogers. Earl was a tall, heavy set African American man whose short hair was starting to go gray. He was reclining on a small couch to the right of Matt's desk.

"Well, we'll soon see what this is all about," said Earl expectantly.

"They're a pretty big company, this could be a great opportunity," Matt said cheerfully. It wasn't every day that a corporation like Humanaid wanted to hire his firm.

The door to the office swung open and two men in business suits pushed their way past Matt's office manager, Penny, a pixie-like woman with short, multi-colored spiked hair. From the expression on her face, it was evident to Matt that she didn't think much of them. He trusted her instincts implicitly, so her reaction put him on edge a bit. He straightened up in his chair and studied the newcomers. Earl sat up too.

One of the men was extraordinarily tall and lanky. He wore a rather flashy teal suit with a bright yellow tie and he carried a black briefcase. His skin was oily and his dark hair was slicked back. His companion was the opposite. He was dressed in a brown and threadbare suit that looked like it was about thirty years out of fashion. He was a squat, ruddy man with an unusually high forehead and short, dirty blonde hair.

What an odd couple! Matt thought.

The tall fellow held out his hand. "Hello, Mr. Spike, thank you for meeting with us. You may call me Mr. Swan, and my companion here is Mr. Keith, we're here today to represent Humanaid, I trust you've heard of our company?"

Matt took his clammy hand and as he shook it, he noticed something strange protruding from underneath the cuff of Mr.Swan's dress shirt. It looked like some kind of a metallic bracelet, but rather than wrapping completely around his wrist, it seemed as if it had teeth that were sunk directly into the flesh of his forearm. Matt blinked and it was gone, covered up by his shirt and jacket cuffs.

"I have to confess that I hadn't until you contacted us. I googled it, your organization's humanitarian work is quite impressive."

Humanaid was a company that supplied organizations like the Red Cross and FEMA with things like bottled water and a variety of other vital items when disasters struck. They seemed to enjoy a good reputation, although Matt supposed that if you wanted to be cynical, you could also say that they were profiting off of tragedy.

"Thank you," Mr. Swan said as he and Mr. Keith sat down in unison in the pair of chairs before Matt's desk. "I'm sure you're wondering why we're here, so I'll get right down to it." He opened up his briefcase on his lap and dropped a thin file onto Matt's desk.

"That file contains all of our information on one of our employees, a man by the name of Chesterfield Xavier," Mr. Swan said in his oddly deep voice.

"What a strange name." Earl remarked.

"I'm sorry, I forgot to introduce you to my partner, Earl Rogers," said Matt.

Both men waved at Earl in unison.

Mr. Keith spoke up for the first time, "It's something of a stage name, he had it legally changed a few years earlier."

"A stage name?" Matt echoed in confusion.

"Yes, Mr. Xavier fancies himself to be something of a psychic. He adopted that name when he began offering his so-called psychic gifts for sale," Mr. Swan's sonorous voice dripped with contempt.

"He's a pet psychic, to be precise. Claims to be able to mentally communicate with animals," Mr. Keith added.

"Yes, a regular Dr. Dolittle," Mr. Swan said distastefully.

"He certainly did *do little* for what he was paid!" Mr. Keith quipped.

Mr. Swan laughed, "Oh that's a good one, Mr. Keith! Well played!"

Matt and Earl exchanged worried glances from across the room over this strange double act.

Matt felt the need to take control of the conversation. "Excuse me, but why are you giving me a file on a...pet psychic?"

"He was employed by our CEO, who is a great lover of his animals. We would like very much for you to find him. He went missing a week ago and our company's internal security is unable to locate him. It's imperative that he be found. We have reason to believe that he stole sensitive company property before disappearing," explained Mr. Swan.

"If he stole something from you, why not go to the police with this?" Earl inquired reasonably.

Mr. Kieth piped up again "Because we are trying to avoid a scandal! While it is true that we are a privately owned business, we still have a number of investors. If they discovered that our CEO had a psychic on the company payroll, let alone a *pet* psychic, they'd lose confidence in him—and the company."

To Matt, this was the most logical thing the pair had said since walking into the room. "Makes sense. If I knew that my investment was going towards paying some crank who thought he could tell the CEO what his pooch was thinking, I might want to reconsider where I park my money," He opined.

"Quite!" Mr.Swan eagerly agreed, "Xavier was unusually well paid for his duties, yet for some reason he still felt compelled to take advantage of his access to our CEO's private residence to help himself to some rather important company property."

"Exactly what did he take?" Earl inquired.

"I'm afraid we're not at liberty to disclose that. It's a corporate secret," Mr. Keith told him hurriedly.

"We're not even completely sure that Xavier is responsible. It just seems a terribly convenient coincidence that the two things should go missing at the same time, and that Xavier had access to the, er, missing item," Swan said, trying to downplay the importance of this aspect of things although it was obviously the main reason why they wanted to find the man in the first place.

"I wouldn't concern yourself with what was taken or if he took it. Our own internal security team will get to the bottom of that once he's back in our custody. All that we ask is that you locate him, discreetly, and inform our people once you have," Mr. Keith told them.

"Yes, discretion!" Mr. Swan thundered with relish. "Discretion! That's the key word! That's what we're depending on from you gentlemen! Nobody must know that Humanaid is behind your search for him. In the interest of maintaining discretion there are a few other conditions."

"Such as?" Matt hoped his voice didn't sound as sour as he felt about this new wrinkle. He always kept his client's information discreet anyway as a matter of professional ethics, and didn't like being dictated to like this.

"You are not allowed to contact or interview our CEO or any other employees of Humanaid in the course of your inquiry.

Indeed, the identity of our CEO is confidential. He prizes his privacy a great deal," Swan said severely.

Earl blinked in surprise. "I didn't know you could even run a legitimate business and remain anonymous!"

Mr. Keith appeared to be insulted by the implication. "You can! It's called an anonymous LLC. It's done all the time! It's perfectly legal, we wouldn't have a big government contract if we weren't a legitimate business!"

Matt was certain that the big government contract they had with FEMA, the Federal Emergency Management Agency, was precisely why they were so worried about keeping all of this a secret. If word of how eccentric the CEO truly was got out, of how he might even be mishandling government funds by spending them on unusual things like pet psychics, the government would be under pressure to drop their contract with Humanaid.

"This is a bit unusual. Limiting who we can talk to like that will also limit our chances of actually finding him. It's not a good idea to tie our hands like that before we even get started," cautioned Matt.

"We disagree," Mr. Kieth said hotly, "there's no point in talking to our other employees. He had no contact with them. He worked exclusively with our CEO, at his private residence. Very few people within our organization even knew that he existed, let alone was an employee of the company."

Matt rubbed his stubbly chin in agitation. Earl shifted uncomfortably in his seat on the couch.

"Gentlemen, it's apparent that this troubles you, but your agency comes highly recommended and we have the utmost confidence in your abilities. We are willing to pay up to triple your usual rate for a job like this, whether you are successful or not," Mr.Swan assured them smoothly.

Mr. Keith opened his mouth to add more honey to the pot, "As well as a substantial bonus when you do find him."

"Well, when you put it like that, I don't see what we have to lose," Matt admitted.

"Would you mind if I spoke to my partner in private for a moment? Perhaps you two could wait out in the hallway for a couple of minutes?" Earl asked.

Mr. Swan inclined his head, "But of course. We understand, don't we Mr. Keith?"

Mr. Keith nodded enthusiastically. "Take whatever time you need to discuss it amongst yourselves." The two men stood up at the same time and walked out of the room, closing the door gently behind them.

Earl practically jumped off the sofa and launched himself over to where Matt sat. "Have you gone crazy?" He whispered, "This whole thing sounds fishy!"

"I admit it's a little weird, and they're a little weird, but that's a whole lot of money to turn down! Think of how epic our next office Christmas party will be! I could give Penny another raise—"

Earl cut off Matt's list of justifications. "You don't need the money that badly, we've got enough and you know it. You wanna know what we have to lose here? Our reputation, that's what! What if this guy is really some sort of a corporate whistleblower who stole evidence of their wrongdoing and they want to silence him? Are we just gonna turn him over to their corporate goons to do with him as they please if we find him? That's not who we are!"

"Of course not! That's why despite what those two say, we're gonna try to find out *what* he took before we decide to turn him over. You're right, while the money would definitely be nice, we don't necessarily *need* it. It's not about the money, that's just the icing on the cake. I want to take this case because there's a real mystery here and I want to know what it is. It's just too juicy to resist."

Earl sighed in resignation. Matt might call him his partner, but ultimately it was Matt's detective agency. He founded the business and he still called the shots, Earl was really more of a second in command when Matt wasn't around. And he knew how stubborn Matt could be once he made up his mind about something, and how much he loved a mystery.

"I'm sorry pal, you know how much I respect your opinion and I have similar reservations about this too, it's obvious that there's a lot more that they're not telling us, but I just *have* to know what's really going on here. I'd be happy if you'd help me figure it out, but if you wanna sit this one out, I can understand."

Earl gritted his teeth. It was at times like this that he questioned his unreasonable loyalty to this man. Unfortunately, he owed Matt much. Not only had he literally saved his life, but he'd also dramatically improved it by giving him this job, which was so much more fulfilling than his last one. Most importantly, he'd also given him his friendship and you couldn't put a price on that could you?

There was also the small matter that Earl also loved a good mystery and was dying to know what was really going on too, even though all of the alarm bells were going off in his head, warning of impending disaster.

"Okay, okay. I'll go get those two weirdos back in here and let them know the good news, that Spike and Rogers are on the case." And he couldn't help but smile a little as he said it.

Chapter Four: The Day of The Mothman

The gnarled, claw-like hand of the thing shattered the ground itself, fumbled blindly for purchase, and having found it, began hauling itself from the dark pit into which it had once been banished.

"No! You're never coming back! Never!" Athena screamed into the unnatural wind that now howled through the forest, stirring the trees, whipping at her hair and nearly knocking her over as the creature locked its terrible, bloodshot gaze upon her.

Despite its roughly humanoid shape, it bounded towards her like some sort of an ape, its skin crawling and bubbling up over it in a sickening way, its twisted maw slavering in anticipation of the meal it planned to make of Athena. Before it could reach her, a red blur arced down from the sky, carrying it up into heavens. Athena whooped in triumph as her wyvern, Daniel flew the monster away.

Her joy proved to be short lived, to her horror, the monster somehow grew in size so quickly that it was too large for Daniel to carry in his feet, forcing him to drop it. The creature landed on its feet with a ground shaking thump, mere feet away from Athena!

She turned and started running, the monster gave chase, making the earth shake with each giant footstep, pushing thick pine trees aside as if they were blades of grass. The terrible snapping of the trees as they broke rang in Athena's ears, and she had to dodge several of the shattered boughs as they came crashing down around her. The beast extended its misshapen mockery of a human hand towards her, he almost had her in his grasp!

Once more, Daniel swooped down and let loose a bright plume of flame at the outstretched hand, cooking it. The stench of scorched flesh turned Athena's stomach as the creature bellowed in pain. The burnt skin healed itself with astonishing speed, and the creature grew even larger than before, so large that he was taller than the level at which Daniel was flying. She looked on helplessly as the humongous monster snatched Daniel out of the air with one hand, grabbed the other end of him, and ripped him into two pieces.

"Noooo!" Athena screamed as Daniel's blood rained down upon her. She buried her head in her hands and began sobbing uncontrollably. As she did so, she felt as if something was being drained out of her very being. She looked up to see a thick, black oily substance coming out of the pores of her skin and floating up into the air. She looked over and saw the monster which had been chasing her turn black and dissolve into amorphous clumps of this same substance, only to drift high up above the pines.

All of this dark stuff coalesced in the sky, almost blotting it out completely, then it took on a definite shape. The shape of a giant moth, unfurling its monstrous wings over the whole forest. A pair of immense red eyes appeared within the form, burning like twin suns.

Athena squinted up at it, and she felt a powerful urge to find him, but who was *he*? Suddenly, bizarre alien vistas flooded into her mind. There was a burnt orange sky stretching endlessly over a veridian sea. Strange winged creatures screeched and hollered over this sea, and even stranger ones occasionally burst out of its depths. Titanic waves crashed against jagged, rocky cliffs on the shoreline, which pierced the sky like daggers, their surface dotted with craggy caves, and within those caves, dozens of red eyes stared back at her, staring into her very soul. She felt as if her head would burst, she wanted to scream, but she had no voice, and could only croak hoarsely....

The sound of her barking dogs dispelled the unearthly visions, bringing her crashing back to reality. There was a loud thumping and scraping noise which sounded as if it was right above her bedroom. Both Bealzebarker and even her most senior dog, the normally impossibly lethargic Mr. President, were looking towards the ceiling and barking with an uncharacteristic fury. Dennis was already on his feet, grabbing the set of new nunchucks he kept on the bedside table to deal with possible intruders (as if he knew how to use them).

"It sounds like something's on the roof!" He shouted when he noticed her stirring on the bed. "I'm gonna see what it is!" He was already out of the room before she could tell him to be careful, the dogs following closely on his heels. She heard beating wings, as if a whole flock of birds had just taken off, then the sound of the sliding glass door opening and closing.

I'd better get out there before he gets himself killed, she thought groggily. She hauled herself from the bed with a groan, and was soon rushing to follow the others.

When she caught up with Dennis, he was standing out in the backyard staring up at the roof. The dogs danced around his feet excitedly.

"Well?" she asked.

"There's nothing there. Whatever it was, it was gone by the time I got out here. Pretty weird, huh? You heard it, didn't you?"

"I did," she looked him in the eye. "I had the nightmare again. Only this time it ended differently."

A look of concern took hold of his face, "Different how?"

"This time, Mothman was in it, only the energy of it felt distinctly feminine, so maybe it was more of a Moth*woman*?

When I got to the part where Daniel gets killed there was all of this negative ambrosia leaking out of me—"

"Negative what?"

"Negative ambrosia. It's what Clark's name for negative psychic energy. Grief, suffering, pain, self loathing—that kind of thing. Well, it came out of me and it turned into this giant Mothman, er, Mothwoman in the sky. Then I saw all these weird alien scenes, I think maybe it's wherever they come from."

"Wait! Are you trying to say that you mentally connected with Mothman in your dreams?"

She looked down. "I dunno. Maybe. Or maybe I'm just scared of going on this investigation today? You know, things didn't work out so well the last time we hunted a cryptid."

This was a massive understatement. Their last cryptid hunt, nearly two years ago, had ended in the death of Tyler Lambert, one of the members of the JSPS. On that occasion they'd been searching for the Jersey Devil, and instead found something far more sinister in the woods. It was the creature which had plagued Athena's nightmares ever since. Unable to kill it, they'd sealed it in a pit deep beneath the earth. The whole incident is what had made Athena decide to properly develop her psychic abilities and learn magic, so that she'd never have to suffer the loss of another teammate. Yet here they were, about to go chasing after another dangerous cryptid, despite all her feelings of impending doom.

He wrapped his big arms around her. "We don't have to do this if you're not comfortable with it. We can still call the entire thing off."

She thought of how deflated he'd looked after their dinner with Matt and Naomi. She couldn't stand to see him disappointed like that again, and she knew how much this investigation meant to him. Then there was the matter of her own curiosity. The rational part of her brain told her that Mothman was a bunch of bullshit, but the other part of her brain was telling her that she had indeed made a mental connection with Mothman or Mothwoman or whatever the fuck it was. Maybe it had even just been up on her roof? And she knew that her mentor, Clark Kismet, whom she'd come to love like a second father, wouldn't want her to ignore this intuitive knowledge. And a part of her, that eternally youthful part of her which still longed for adventure, was hungering for answers as to what all of this meant.

"No way! 'Goonies never say die', remember? The investigation will go ahead as scheduled for today." And that was that. There was no arguing with Athena at this point, and after nearly a lifetime together, Dennis knew it.

Several hours later on that balmy Saturday afternoon, the entire team was assembled in the driveway of Athena and Dennis' home. The "entire team" in this case being only Miranda and Lars. Normally, Athena's brother Mark would've been there too, but he was off on the island of Elysium for his graduation ceremony. Athena didn't like going on investigations without her brother by her side. Especially one like this that was potentially dangerous and which she had such grave misgivings about. Unfortunately, for the past year, as Mark became increasingly consumed by his newfound devotion to sorcery, his absence from the team was the new normal. It broke her heart that he wasn't there.

The team had just finished loading up Dennis' van with equipment from the garage. They weren't bringing nearly as much of it with them as they normally would for a ghost hunt. They were just bringing some of his specialized video cameras along, like the FLIR thermal imaging and night vision ones, as well as motion activated trail cameras which could be mounted on trees.

Athena regarded Lars as he shut the van's back door. Perhaps her brother couldn't be there, but she was happy to finally have Lars with them as a proper member of the team. He'd been hanging around their periphery for years, occasionally going along with them on ghost hunts in order to cover their activities for the Asbury Park Press. He'd always used journalistic impartiality as an excuse to resist officially joining the group, despite his clear interest in all things weird. All that had changed after his involvement in the Jersey Devil case, he'd dropped his pretense of impartiality and much of his air of enigmatic aloofness after that incident had bonded him with the team.

"Where exactly does this guy live?" The ginger reporter asked.

"Somewhere in Eagleswood Township, along the bay," Dennis replied.

"Oh! That's not far away at all!" Miranda remarked cheerfully. She was right, it was only a few towns away and a couple of minutes south of them.

"I'll text you the address in case we get separated on the way," Athena promised as they split up into their separate vehicles. Athena would ride with her husband, while Miranda would accompany Lars in his white SUV.

As they drove down Route 9, Athena glowered out the window. "Uh, oh! I know that look! What's bothering you now?" Dennis asked.

What was really bothering her was the absence of her brother, and the fact that she couldn't attend his ceremony. Of course, she wasn't about to admit that, so she instead picked something which had been bothering her a few days earlier.

"How credible is this guy we're going to see—really?"

"Well, he *is* a doctor."

"A doctor? But doesn't he post stuff on our website under the screen name 'JohnBigbootay69'?" She asked skeptically.

Dennis laughed, "He does! It's a reference to a character from that old 80's movie *Buckaroo Banzai* I like. Also, he's a proctologist, so you see, the joke works on many levels—"

"Clever. Okay, so what's the 69 part about then?"

"I'm pretty sure he was born in 1969. He's a good guy, I swear! He's been posting stuff in the chats for years now. He's one of our most loyal followers. He even gives to our Patreon, *generously*, so be nice! It's gonna be cool to finally meet him in person."

"Uh huh, sure. So why is such a distinguished doctor of the anus always posting and chatting on a paranormal website?"

"If I remember correctly, he saw a UFO while he was taking out the garbage as a kid. It made quite an impression on him and he's been into this stuff ever since."

Athena blew out a long breath, "Oh boy! A UFO nut! Just what we need!"

Dennis shook his head in bemused exasperation. "My love, if it wasn't for the fact that you've been able to see ghosts for most of your life, I don't think you'd believe in them either!"

"You're right about that. For me, seeing is believing, it's the only logical way to approach it all."

"I would've thought that learning how to do sorcery would've made you a bit more open minded."

"Quite the reverse. Knowing that so many seemingly impossible things are, in fact, very possible means I have to work even harder to maintain my grounding in reality. Otherwise I'll end up believing in Lord Xenu and giving all my money to the Scientologists or some other nonsense."

Athena happily noted that Dennis appeared to be unable to refute her logic. Rather than fighting that fruitless battle, he seemed to be concentrating on finding a parking spot as they approached the home of Dr. John Kozloski, otherwise known as 'JohnBigbootay69'.

Dr. Kozloski greeted the team graciously, and Athena felt a little guilty about all the doubts she'd been casting on him. He lived in a sprawling split level home with a backyard facing the Barnegat Bay. He took them through the tastefully furnished house and out into the backyard, the ground of which was covered with countless smooth, white stones rather than grass, which was quite normal for many homes this close to the shore. There was a small dock in the backyard and a fishing boat was anchored there. A family of ducks swam peacefully by. The ever-present seagulls wheeled in the sky overhead. It was a nice view. Being an expert on the ass apparently had its benefits.

Lars and Dennis set up a camera on a tripod in a shady spot on his patio. Miranda held a smaller, hand held camera so they could get shots from different angles to edit together later when they posted this interview on the JSPS website. Mrs. Kozloski, a good looking lady who was obviously a few years younger than the good doctor, brought them all Cokes (and a water for the health conscious Miranda). Everyone made themselves comfortable on the patio furniture and they finally started recording.

"Do you want me to blur your face or distort your voice when we edit this?" Dennis inquired politely.

Dr. Kozloski waved a hand in dismissal. "Well, unless someone finds a cure for colon cancer soon, I don't think reporting a Mothman sighting will significantly impact my business, so don't trouble yourself."

"His patients already know he's a little crazy!" His wife teased.

Athena nodded. She supposed you had to be a little nuts to want to make a living off of sticking your fingers up people's asses. She wondered if the doctor was abducted and anally probed when he had his UFO sighting? The thought made her giggle, but that was okay because everyone assumed she was laughing at Mrs. Kozloski's joke.

"Okay, go ahead and tell us about your sighting," requested Lars. He usually conducted the interviews these days, as a journalist, he knew the right kinds of questions to ask. Also, his smooth as silk announcer's voice just sounded better on video than Dennis' which lent an extra patina of legitimacy to their endeavors.

"It happened two weekends ago. We were out on our neighbor, Tim's boat. It was me and my wife Bonnie, and Tim's wife Maddie. Tim's mother had recently passed away. She'd spent the past year living with Tim and Maddie and she'd wanted her ashes spread in the bay. It was starting to get dark, so we started heading back. As we were moving down the river on the way to Tim's dock, a whole bunch of birds suddenly came flying out of the woods off to our right like something had scared them. We had to duck to avoid getting hit by some of them. Then we heard the sound of more beating wings, *big* wings." He paused to take a drink from his Coke can.

"That's when we saw *it*. It came flying out of those same woods. It was brown—"

"I thought it looked more like a really dark gray," Bonnie Kozloski interrupted.

He smiled indulgently at his wife, "Or possibly dark gray. The light was starting to fade, so it was difficult to be sure. The wings were white though and like those of a giant bat; they were maybe ten feet wide. It rarely beat its wings, it just seemed to mostly glide on them. It had a humanoid shape, except for the head, which seemed to be built right into the body. I didn't see any neck. The hands were like three or four long claws, the feet almost seemed like hooves. You couldn't really make out many details of the face except for the eyes. That's the thing that stood out the most, those terrible eyes! Round as saucers and were a deep red. I'd say it was maybe six feet tall and very muscular, especially in the legs. The thing started circling in the air over us, right above the boat! Tim throttled it, despite all the signs that say not to leave a wake, and we tried to get away from it. It chased us for a while, we were still kind of far away from Tim's dock. It had no trouble keeping up with us. After some time, it seemed to lose interest and just flew off back in the same direction it had come from. Before it flew away, it let out a horrible screech that wasn't like anything I've ever heard."

Mrs. Kozloski spoke up, "I don't know that I've ever been that scared in my entire life! You could feel it looking at you, and when it did, it made all the hairs on the back of your neck stand up!"

"Do you have anything to add, regarding its physical description?" Lars asked her.

"No, aside from disagreeing about the color of it."

"Did you perhaps get a better look at the face?"

"Not really. It had a face, but the eyes were so distracting that it was like you couldn't concentrate on it long enough to make out any details."

Dr. Kozloski leaned forward, "He says he's seen it two other times since then, our friend Tim. Both times it flew away before he could remember to take a picture."

Athena pursed her lips in annoyance. *Of course they didn't get a picture, even though all these people probably had their phones on them!* Yet, she sensed no duplicity from the couple.

"It sounds like we should be talking to Tim and his wife," she commented dryly.

"They should be home today. I can call them for you, I'm sure they'd be open to helping you. I already told them I was planning on reporting it and they said you could talk to them too if you wanted to," the doctor said.

"That would be great! Maybe he could show us that spot in the woods too?"

"Like I said, I don't see why they wouldn't help," the doctor grinned and pulled out his cellphone.

A breeze blew in from off the bay, stirring Athena's long brown hair. She was hit with another wave of that awful feeling of foreboding which had been plaguing her so much lately.

Dr. Kozloski put his phone away, "They said you can come over right away. I'll show you how to get to their house, it's just down the street."

"Great! Let's go bag a Mothman!" She said with a false cheerfulness she didn't really feel, trying to mask her anxieties from all the others.

Chapter Five: The Case of Chesterfield Xavier's Strange Disappearance

Matt Spike sat in his office that same Saturday morning waiting for Earl to arrive so they could get started on the case of Chesterfield (AKA "Chester") Xavier's strange disappearance. You shouldn't be surprised that a private investigator was working on a Saturday, they typically keep very unusual hours. Matt only met with new clients during the week, but he did investigative legwork on the weekends when necessary. He usually liked to farm out jobs that would spill over into the weekend to his more junior investigators (ah, the perks of being the boss!), but with the kind of money Humanaid was paying him, he didn't trust this particular assignment to anyone other than Earl and himself.

Earl wasn't late to work that day so much as Matt was extraordinarily early. He lived closer to the office and he wanted to get an early start. While he waited he reviewed some information Penny had managed to snag for him before leaving for the day the night before. It was the official missing persons police report for Chester Xavier's case. It turns out that Chester had once been married and had a child. His ex-wife was the first one to notice that he wasn't around anymore when it was his weekend to pick up the kid and he failed to show up or even call. Apparently, this was very unlike him. Chester was no deadbeat dad. She drove by his house and saw no sign of him or his car, after calling and continuing to stop by his house all weekend she finally contacted the police the following Monday. It wouldn't be until the next day that Humanaid also noticed that he'd failed to return from work after taking a week off and began their own efforts to locate him immediately, they must've been very eager to recover whatever it is that they think he stole from them.

The police report wasn't helpful at all. The cops hadn't really put any effort into looking for him yet, which didn't surprise Matt in the slightest. He'd seen this a thousand times before. Unless it was a particularly young missing child, or the family constantly pressured the department for results or got the press involved, the police often didn't do much more than take note of the fact that the person in question was presently unaccounted for and put out an APB for someone matching their description. Missing people was a large part of what kept him in business, that and folks who suspected that their partner was cheating on them.

Matt was stirred from his review of the useless police report by the sound of Earl's keys in the lock. "I'm back here!" he called as he heard the door slam behind his partner. A moment later Earl entered the room and threw himself onto the couch as he often did.

"So what's the plan of attack for today?"

"This guy doesn't have many known relatives or friends that we know about yet. According to Humanaid's HR files he's got an ex-wife and kid that he has down as the beneficiaries on his life insurance. He's also got a mother who's still living listed as an emergency contact. Their own security guys already interviewed them, but I think it's worth our time to talk to them again, their people aren't pros at this like we are. Who knows what kinds of stupid questions they asked, or important ones they failed to ask?"

Earl nodded, chewing over the information. "Agreed. I take it you want to split it up? I talk to one while you talk to the other?"

"You know me too well! I'll take the mother, she lives in South Toms River. I'm familiar with the area, I used to have some family down there. You can deal with the ex. She lives in Neptune, I'll forward you the address. She's the one who first reported him missing, by the way. He was supposed to take their daughter for the weekend and failed to show. It sounds like the divorce was amicable, well about as amicable as these things ever are!"

"It must've been. If he still has her listed as the beneficiary on his life insurance. Which of course, is also a possible motivation for making sure he goes missing. We've seen it all before, haven't we?" Earl said wearily. He didn't like to assume the worst about people, but bitter experience had told him that it was foolish not to.

"Unfortunately we have. That's another reason why we need to re-interview these people. I trust your gut instincts about a person a hell of a lot more than I do some 9 to 5 clown from Humanaid that I've never even met before. While you're there, ask about anyone else she might know about in his life. Old buddies, former co-workers, stuff like that. This guy *has* to have more people in his circle than just his mom and his ex."

"Roger that," Earl said listlessly.

Matt raised an eyebrow. "What's wrong? It seems like something's eating you this morning. You aren't still pissed at me for taking this case are ya?"

"No, it's not that. I've been thinking about those strange men that Humanaid sent over yesterday, Mr. Swan and Mr. Keith. I can't shake the feeling that I've seen them somewhere before."

"Deja vu?" Matt suggested.

"Nothing like that. I don't think I've actually met them. I wouldn't forget meeting such a weird pair! It's more like maybe I've heard of them before or seen pictures of them somewhere. For the life of me, I just can't remember where! I wonder if it might've been from my old job?"

"You mean back when you were a cop?"

"No, I mean my *other* old job."

"Oh," Matt leaned back in his chair, a slightly troubled expression on his face. The job Earl was referring to was as an agent of the ABC, the secret organization which inspired the legends of the Men in Black. In fact, that's who he was working for when their paths first crossed about thirteen years earlier. "Do you suspect that maybe you did meet them back then and they wiped your memory of it?" he asked his partner cautiously.

"I sure hope not. Shit like that is one of the reasons I wanted out of that life. Messing with the brains of civilians is bad enough, but doing it to your own teammates is unforgivable. As far as I know, they never did that to me, but then again, I wouldn't know, would I? The entire time I worked for the ABC, I lived in constant fear that they'd screw around with my head like that."

Matt couldn't imagine what that must've been like, living with the idea that the very organization you worked for could alter something as private and fundamental to your being as your memories. "I'm sorry, pal. That must be a tough thing to deal with."

Earl stood up. "It is, but you get used to it. You have to. It's amazing the things you can train yourself to get used to. Anyway, if I really did meet them before, they didn't show any signs that they remembered me either, so maybe it's not all that important. I don't wanna talk about it anymore, I just want to get started on this case."

Matt stood too, retrieved his fedora from where it had been sitting on the desk and placed it on his head. "I can't argue with that! Let's go find this guy, not for the corporate creeps that hired us, but for the little girl who needs her dad, and the old lady worried about her son.

About an hour later Matt found himself standing in front of a modest faded green ranch style home in South Toms River. It was only a few blocks from his own grandmother's home. They'd been unusually close because she frequently watched him when his parents couldn't or didn't want to. He'd lost her when he was in his junior year of high school, but the pain of losing her had never completely faded. Matt had thought about driving past his grandmother's old house on the way here, but had decided against it. He hadn't been back there since he'd helped his father clear it out after her passing; he recalled half expecting to see her peeking at him from around every corner. It was a decidedly spooky feeling. He wasn't sure he could bear to look upon that yard where he'd played as a child and see what's become of it since.

In fact, he was now wishing he'd let Earl handle this one, even being this close to grandma's house was stirring up all kinds of long dormant feelings that he'd rather not try to deal with at the moment.

Focus on the job, he told himself as he walked up the concrete path to the door.

It swung open before he got there. The attractive blonde woman who stood in the doorway looked far too young in Matt's eyes to be anyone's grandmother, she was probably only about a decade older than he was. Then he recalled that he was uncomfortably close to being fifty and realized that her age was about right.

Well, either way, grandmas sure don't look like they used to! he mused. He wasn't just thinking about the beauty of the woman standing in the doorway, but about how he'd noticed that most people in general didn't quite look as rough around the edges as they aged as they'd seemed only a generation ago. Seventy was the new fifty.

"You must be Matt Spike," the woman said.

Matt had called ahead to make sure she'd be home before leaving the office.

"One and the same! Thanks for agreeing to see me on such short notice," he replied as he mounted the trio of worn looking concrete steps.

"I don't mind if it'll help find my Ronnie." Ronald Hofnagel had been Chesterfield Xavier's original name according to the file given to him by Humanaid. The woman who was holding the door open for him was Joan Hognagel.

"I'll do my best." Matt promised as he stepped into her home. He was standing in a tidy living room. He could see into the kitchen, which was dominated by a large, bright red refrigerator almost completely covered with magnets from Joan's many travels over the years. Matt was also struck by the number of cats lounging around on various surfaces or milling around. They were cats of every size, shape and color. He counted about eight between the kitchen and living room. He detected none of the foul aromas or hints of ammonia from a litter box that one sometimes encountered when visiting a home with this many cats. Joan kept a tidy home indeed.

She noticed the direction of his gaze. "I hope you're not allergic to them, I should've asked when you called."

"No, it's fine. I have one myself."

"What? Only one?" she laughed. She led him into the kitchen and offered Matt a seat at the table. He sat down and set his hat down in front of himself. "We've always had a bunch of them. I guess that's where Ronnie got his love of animals from, from me. He sure didn't get it from his father, Ronnie Sr, God rest his soul!" She pointed to a blue and white porcelain urn sitting atop the sideboard which apparently held the earthly remains of her late husband. "Ronnie Sr. barely tolerated it. He used to always say that sharing the house with a bunch of fuzz balls was the price he had to pay for having such a beautiful wife. He was a flatterer, my husband." She sighed, "now I'm just a lonely old crazy cat lady. Oh! Where are my manners? Would you like anything to drink? I just made some coffee."

Matt never could refuse a cup of coffee. After telling her how he took it, she poured him a mug (shaped like a cat, with the tail forming the handle) and set it down in front of him. He thanked her and started to raise it to his lips.

"You might want to wait a minute and let it cool down," she warned, and he set it back down with a smile. He decided now was a good time to get down to business.

"So when was the last time you saw your son?"

She scrunched up her face in concentration. "What's today? Saturday?" Matt nodded in the affirmative. "It's so hard to keep the days straight once you're retired! Let's see, if today is Saturday...it was about two weeks ago, a Wednesday I think. He was taking a week off from work and decided to come visit me. I remember that he looked sort of upset that day, like he wanted to tell me something but couldn't figure out how. When I asked him about it, he just said he was bothered by something he'd seen at work, but it wasn't important."

That got Matt's attention. What could he have possibly seen at work that had been bothering him so intensely?

"Did he talk about his job very often?"

She shook her head. "No. He always told me wasn't allowed to, which I thought was a little strange. Why, I didn't even know that the company he worked for was Humanaid until their people showed up to ask me questions last weekend! He was just happy to finally be making steady money as a pet psychic. His decision to fully devote himself to using his powers to help others was a big part of what broke up his marriage."

Matt's eyes narrowed. She'd just unleashed a lot of information all at once there for him to try to digest, but one thing she'd said in particular caught his attention. "Did I hear you right? Did you say that Humanaid's investigators were here last weekend?"

"Yes, I'm sure of it because it was the same day when my ex-daughter-in-law, Britney first called, worried that he hadn't shown up to get his daughter Vicki from her house. It was only maybe an hour later when the men from his job stopped by, which I thought was unusually quick! They said he was supposed to return to work the day before and they really needed him back there so he could do something important for them. I also thought that was weird, because I could've sworn he told me he didn't have to go back to work until Tuesday. "

Matt decided to chance taking a sip of the coffee. To his delight, it was not only no longer hot enough to burn his tongue, but it was delicious. "I was told that Humanaid began their search for him this past Tuesday," he confided.

"No, it was definitely before that. I couldn't understand what could be so important that they needed a pet psychic so urgently for, but I have a few ideas."

Matt was floored. If Joan had her dates straight, Humanaid had been looking for Chester days before the police report would be filed on the following Monday. What could have motivated them to falsify their own records of the investigation to make it look like they'd only been seeking him since Tuesday?

"So why do you think they were trying to find him? What do you think he actually did for them?"

"Well, from what I understand the company has something to do with assisting in disaster relief. You've seen those search and rescue dogs haven't you? The ones they send into collapsed buildings and tunnels after an earthquake or something? I figured they needed him to talk to those dogs, so he can tell the rescue workers what they've seen."

Matt was impressed. It was a good theory. He didn't have the heart to tell her that Humanaid only sold supplies used in disaster relief, and that his son was employed so the eccentric CEO knew what his pets were thinking. He certainly wasn't about to tell her that the reason why they were so desperate to find him was because they thought he'd stolen something from them. No, it was much kinder to let her go on believing that her boy was involved in heroically saving lives.

"That could be. But why all the secrecy then?" He already knew the official answer, but he was interested to see what she thought. He was fascinated by how other people's minds worked.

"They're a big company. They're probably embarrassed to be associated with a pet psychic. Very few people are open minded about his gifts."

Yup, she sure nailed it, Matt thought, *or at least that's what they're happy having us believe.* "But you don't have any doubts?"

"I've seen it firsthand, for his entire life. He's always had a special way with animals. They love him, and he loves them, all animals, even the nasty ones like snakes and bugs! That's why he became a veterinary assistant. There's all kinds of people on TV who claim they know what animals are thinking, *The Dog Whisperer*, that guy on that show, *My Cat From Hell*, but my son is the real deal! He was hoping that someday he'd get a show of his own too, once word got out about his powers, but it never happened."

Matt was skeptical himself. The people on those TV shows she'd just mentioned never claimed to have psychic abilities.

They were highly educated about the behaviors of the animals they specialized in, and knew how to correctly read their body language to interpret what they were feeling. Matt suspected that her son had a similar skill set, but was marketing it as something supernatural. Not that he didn't believe in psychics or the supernatural-he knew all too well from experience that such things existed, but he also knew that the genuine articles were exceedingly rare. Most people who claimed to possess such powers were charlatans intent on fooling others, or even themselves.

"And that was the main source of the tension in his marriage? Deciding to become a full time pet psychic?" Matt asked, recalling one of her earlier remarks.

"I wouldn't say it was the *main* reason, but it sure was *a* reason. It's always more complicated than just one thing. Deciding to pursue being a pet psychic full time was a bold decision, and not one that his wife fully supported. She's a good girl, I can't really blame her. Money was tight, and Britney ended up supporting the family on her income alone more often than not after he stopped working as a veterinary assistant. It was tough on them all, but it was especially on him because he felt like she didn't really understand him or his dreams, or believe in him. I guess they'd already started to grow apart from each other before all of that. People change. They weren't the same people they'd married anymore. It happens sometimes ya know?"

Matt counted himself fortunate that he *didn't* know, at least not firsthand. He wasn't the same person he was when he'd married Naomi, and she'd changed somewhat too over the years, but he felt that they'd grown closer together rather than apart.

"It's a pity. They're still very good friends. And the pet psychic thing really did pay off for him eventually, if only she'd toughed it out with him for a little longer! He had to move back in with me for a few months after the divorce, but since he landed that job at Humanaid he's never had to worry about money again. I keep praying that they'll get back together again soon, especially for the sake of little Vicki." Joan Hofnagel looked visibly upset. She raised the trembling hand that had been cradling her own cup of coffee to her face and took a sip to conceal her pain.

Matt decided it was best to change the subject somewhat. "How did he ever come up with that new name for himself: Chesterfield Xavier?"

She chuckled. "Oh that's not a new name, it's a very old one! Ronnie had a crush on a girl down the road when he was a boy. He used to write her love letters and stuff them in her mailbox. It was cute. He would sign them 'Chesterfield Xavier' to remain anonymous. Nothing ever came of it though. He got the name Chesterfield from his father's favorite brand of cigarettes. The Xavier part came from some character in his superhero funny books."

"I know the one." Matt smiled. It made sense that if Ronald Hofnagel Jr. believed he was a psychic, he'd identify with Professor Charles Xavier from *the X-Men* comics, a character that was one of the most powerful psychics who'd ever lived in that fictional world. Matt looked at the clock hanging on the kitchen wall and realized that he'd allowed himself to go off on too many tangents, indulging his own curiosity about these people's lives too deeply. It was time to focus more on questions which might help him bring Chester back home.

"Does Chester, er I mean Ronnie have any relatives he's close to aside from yourself, Britney and Vicki?"

"No. There's not much family to speak of. Me and Ronnie Sr. ran away from home together and never looked back. We cut all ties with our own families long ago. We traveled all over the country for a few years until we put roots down here." She gestured towards her fridge full of magnets from dozens of states and their associated tourist traps. Now that he was in the same room with them, Matt could see how old most of them were, yellowed and faded with age. He could also see where Chester got his romantic streak from.

"It sounds like quite an adventure."

"It was," she replied wistfully.

"So he doesn't have any brothers or sisters?"

"It wasn't for lack of trying! Ronnie Sr. Had a really low sperm count. It's probably a miracle I ever even got pregnant even one time! He used to blame it all on working at that nuclear power plant for thirty years. You know that one down in Forked River? Oyster Creek?"

"I sure do! I used to live in Forked River for a few years when I was a little kid." That nuclear power plant, with its single tall, thin smokestack loomed large in Matt's early memories.

"What about friends? Anyone he's close to?"

"I'm not sure anymore. There's nobody that I remember him talking about recently. My son was always a painfully shy person, he never had many friends aside from our pets. And I think the few he did make as a kid he lost track of when he grew up. He never dated much either, Ron Sr. and I were always afraid he'd never give us any grandchildren. We were as surprised as anyone when he told us he met a girl when he was in college and they were getting married. At least his father lived long enough to meet his granddaughter."

Matt pulled a small notebook and a pen from the inner pocket of his trench coat. "Do you think you could write down a few names of the few friends you do remember him making for me. Give me their addresses and phone numbers if you have them too."

She took the offered writing implements. "Of course, if you think it'll help."

"There's no harm in being thorough," Matt replied. Not long after handing it to her, she returned the notebook and pen. He was disappointed to see that there were only four names neatly printed on it. "Thank you, I'll follow up on these." He planned to check Chester's social media accounts and see if any of these names were still on his friends lists, and how often he interacted with them. You could figure out a great deal about someone by snooping around on their online profiles. If any of them seemed to be in regular contact with him, he'd pay them a visit too.

Matt stood up and put his hat back on his head, on his way out, he noticed several photos hanging on the living room wall. In one of them, Chester, a short, ruddy guy with long black hair was standing next to an Asian woman and a small child that was an obvious blending of the two of them. They all stood in front of a white cottage, the ocean was just visible behind them. Joan noticed him staring at it.

"That's him with Brit and Vicki, on vacation a few years ago, in happier times." She told him, although he'd already deduced as much. Seeing the man in the picture with his little girl beside him renewed Matt's determination to find him.

"Thanks for your help, you've given me a lot to think about." Matt said as he walked out onto the steps.

"I hope so. Please bring my Ronnie back, he's a good man and a good father."

"I will."

Matt hated making promises he wasn't sure he could keep, so he'd just have to find a way to make this particular promise come true. Too bad that he still felt every bit as clueless about how to do that as he did when he'd first arrived there.

Chapter Six: Forgive Those Who Trespass

Tim Maitland pointed out through the kitchen window to the dock in the backyard. "That's where I saw it for the second time. I was standing right here washing out a cup to pour my coffee into one morning and it was perched on top of that post with all the rope wrapped around it. It was just sitting on it, crouched like a gargoyle, staring right back at me. It felt like it was going on for a really long time. We were both kind of locked together in this staring contest, then it stood up, spread its wings out and just kind of floated up into the sky." His voice trembled as he recounted the story. Tim was a middle aged man of average height with dark hair that was balding in the back.

"But you didn't think to take a picture?" Dennis asked, hoping that the disappointment he was feeling wasn't evident in his voice.

"No, it was almost like I was hypnotized by it. I felt like it was looking right into my soul, like it could read my mind. It was the weirdest feeling!" He chuckled in a self deprecating way. "Yeah, I know how crazy that sounds. This whole thing sounds crazy, but it really happened! Anyway, I couldn't have taken a picture because my pajamas don't have any pockets, so I left my phone on the charger."

"I didn't see it myself that time. I was still asleep in bed, but he woke me up right afterwards. He was all shaken up, it was obvious he'd just seen something very upsetting." His wife Maddie, a wispy brunette in her fifties, added.

The JSPS had already gotten the couple to confirm the account of their neighbors' sighting on video. The details all matched up consistently. Now they were eager to learn about their subsequent encounters with the Mothman.

"I might've forgotten to take a picture, but there is some physical evidence." Tim announced with a grin.

That got Athena's attention, one of the frustrating things about Mothman was a general lack of physical evidence. At least Bigfoot had the decency to leave behind some tracks, but Mothman wasn't so kind. "What kind of physical evidence?"

Tim crossed the kitchen and pulled open his backdoor. "Follow me."

They all followed him out into a backyard that wasn't very different from the one they'd just been in at Dr. Kozloski's house. There was another patio with some furniture, a rather nice grill, and a dock which had a boat anchored at it. This boat was larger than the one owned by Dr. Kozloski, which seemed humble in comparison. It was no yacht, but it was impressive nonetheless. Athena didn't know what Tim did for a living, but clearly he was doing something right. Her sneakers crunched on the stones in the backyard as Tim led them onto the dock, and paused before the post he'd just been pointing to.

"It left these scratches on the post it was sitting on." They could all see three deep gouges in the top of the post and running down one side. A series of smaller scratches surrounded them. Athena was not at all impressed with this "evidence". Anything could've made them as far as she was concerned. Miranda, holding her camcorder, zoomed in on them. Dennis took a few photos with his phone.

"You're sure those weren't there before?" Inquired Athena.

"One hundred percent certain." Tim said firmly.

Impulsively, Athena stretched out a finger to brush the surface of the post. Immediately her mind flooded with strange, alien vistas like the ones she'd seen earlier that morning. She swooned, and dark spots appeared in her vision. Dennis was there in an instant, catching her as always, in his big, strong arms.

80

"Are you alright?" He asked as he held her.

"Thanks, I will be." She said straightening herself up and attempting to regain her dignity.

Miranda knew the distant look in her best friend's eyes all too well by now. "You saw something, didn't you?"

"Cliffs beside a strange sea, all beneath an alien sky. Same thing as this morning." Of course, she'd already told the whole team about her unusual morning. "I wish I knew what it meant!"

"It means that she was here," Tim said a little smugly.

Athena's ears pricked up. It wasn't his strange pride in owning something that Mothman had recently used as a scratching post, it was something else.

"Did you just say *she* was here?"

The man shrugged. "Did I? I hadn't noticed. Must've been a slip of the tongue."

Athena wondered about that. When her mind had brushed up against something strange this morning, she'd felt a distinctly female energy emanating from it. She'd just felt a similar sensation when touching the post.

"Can you tell us about the next time you saw it?" Lars inquired.

Tim laughed. "I can do you one better, I can take you out to the spot where it happened if you're up for a little boat ride this afternoon?"

Dennis looked as if he was going to squee. "That would be awesome!"

Athena wasn't so sure about that, she'd forgotten to bring any Dramamine with her.

The salty breeze tickled Athena's neck. Despite spending her entire life living near the shore, she didn't enjoy boat rides because she had a tendency to get sea sick. So far, her stomach was behaving itself, this was probably because Tim couldn't speed as he carefully maneuvered the boat along the lagoon which led out to the Barnegat Bay, which was actually the far end of the Mullins River. The river grew steadily wider as they drew ever closer to the bay. They passed a few homes on one side, the other side was all wetlands and woods.

"What *do* you think these latest visions of yours mean?" Miranda asked her as they slowly boated past Dr. Kozloski's backyard.

"Hard to say. I got the feeling that it was Mothman's home. It's pretty hard for me to swallow. I'm open to the existence of Mothman, but I also don't really think it's very likely to be real. Yet I can't deny how vivid these visions feel, how utterly alien it all is. Not just the things I'm seeing, but the mind behind them!" These visions, plus the general feeling of impending disaster that had been plaguing her lately were almost too much to bear. She didn't mention that other feeling though, she didn't want to worry her friend unnecessarily.

"Too bad Clark isn't around. He could probably just tell us what the Mothman really is. He's probably been to wherever it comes from and had tea with it!" Miranda mused.

Athena laughed. That did sound like something her mentor would've done. "Unfortunately, he hasn't. I actually did ask him about it one time. For once he had no idea what it really is or where it comes from. Which, I have to confess, only fueled my already skeptical feelings about it. I mean if Clark hasn't run across it in all the years he claims to have been alive, it's probably just bullshit. Or at least that's what I used to think. Today has been... eye opening. There's *something* out there that my mind keeps on connecting with and it sure seems like Mothman, er lady."

"Who knows if such earthly concepts as gender can even be applied to a creature that's so alien?" Lars chimed in cryptically, having overheard their conversation.

"Who indeed? Thanks for the deep thoughts, professor!" Dennis teased. The reporter ignored the good natured ribbing, he was used to it from Dennis.

"What do you think Mothman really is, Lars?" Miranda respected Lar's opinions, she knew that he was often remarkably well read up on the subjects and locations of their investigations.

"I'm trying to remain impartial, keep an open mind." He started. This was a common stance from Lars, who always kept his own biases close to his chest. He squinted in the afternoon sun. "But that said, I find the ideas of John Keel, the author of the *Mothman Prophecies* to be intriguing. He believed that Mothman and a whole range of other strange phenomena, like UFOs, the Men in Black, etc were "ultraterrestrials," beings from a dimension that intersects with our own. They've always been with us, throughout human history, taking on different forms to suit the era. A hundred years ago the UFOs were perceived as airships-basically big blimps. The aliens would've been seen as being demons or fairies by our ancestors."

"Yeah! Jacques Vallee had a similar idea. He wrote a whole book about it, *Passport to Magonia*. I've got it back at home!" Dennis broke in enthusiastically. Jacques Vallee was a famous UFO investigator.

"Well we know they're wrong about the Men in Black, or should I say the ABC? We've had our own encounters with them and they're all too human. I'm quite familiar with the ultraterrestrial hypothesis. It is a cool idea, but I don't see much evidence for it. It's a classic case of trying to explain one outlandish thing with something even more outrageous." Athena said dismissively.

Tim cut the motor, the boat continued to drift on its momentum. "Over there! It was perched on one of those tree branches about three days ago as I was driving by." They looked over to where he pointed. There was a stand of sturdy looking cedar trees near the water's edge. "This is basically the same spot where we saw it the first time. It came flying out of those trees."

Athena studied the skies over the trees. She could see a narrow band of glittering purple in the air arcing over the spot. It shifted, swaying back and forth as she watched. She knew that this was what Clark called "the Scar"-a tear in the fabric of reality left behind from a fantastic battle waged by rival armies of wizards thousands of years earlier. Every so often the Scar would open up and all manner of strange things could and sometimes did come pouring out of it. One of her own ancestors, Marlena Anderson, had once acted as the "Guardian of the Scar", tasked with dealing with the horrors that used it to enter our world. She also knew that the others couldn't see the Scar. Despite her psychic abilities, she'd had to undergo special training from Clark to be able to perceive it. From the state of the Scar in this area, she could tell that it had been open recently, perhaps in the past month, but it was definitely sealed now.

"The walls between worlds are especially thin around here," Was all she said, not wanting to burden the others with what she'd just noticed, or invite too many awkward questions from Tim and Maddie. Was the Mothman a visitor from one of the worlds on the other side of the Scar, like her familiar, Daniel was? Perhaps Keel and Vallee weren't so wrong after all.

"What's funny is that on all the occasions when I saw this thing, I was thinking about my late mother. The first time was right after we'd scattered her ashes in the bay. The other two times I was also reminiscing about her."

Mourning her is more like it. Athena could feel the palpable waves of grief coming off of him as he said this. She began to tear up a little herself, just from catching a whiff of some of the powerful feelings he was repressing. Sometimes being a psychic really sucked. She thought about her own dreams this morning, dreams in which she was crying over her wyvern, Daniel, who had perished in the nightmare. She thought about the Mothman's reputation as a harbinger of doom and had a sudden insight. *It's drawn to powerful feelings of loss! But why?*

"Man, I'd love to go exploring over there!" Dennis declared longingly.

"I could drop you guys off there and swing by later to pick you up if you want? I've had half a mind to check it out for myself, I'd be really interested to see what you turn up," Tim offered.

"Honey," Maddie chided, "that side of the river is part of a nature preserve! I don't think anyone is allowed over there, they might get in trouble for trespassing!"

"And now you see why I haven't explored it for myself! She's right though. That is the Edwin B.Forsythe National Wildlife Refuge over there. Visitors are only allowed in specific parts of it."

Athena was determined to get her answers. "It's alright, we promise not to step on any wild bird eggs." She did hate to inconvenience the couple by making them pick them up later on. She leaned in close to Dennis and whispered to him.

"Now that I know where this spot is, I could just do a teleportation spell to get us all back here so these two don't have to get stuck playing water taxi for us."

Dennis looked alarmed by the suggestion. "Er, with all due respect my love, I don't think that's a great idea. You haven't quite mastered the art of teleportation yet and I don't want you losing any more of my equipment. Those FLIR cameras are damned expensive!" Dennis was still upset about the camera that had failed to rematerialize when Athena had teleported the team beyond the locked gates of a graveyard several months ago.

"That was a long time ago! I'm much better at that kind of spell now, I've been practicing," she protested.

Dennis stood firm in the face of Athena's pouting. "I'm sorry, but I'm gonna have to put my foot down. We're doing it the old fashioned way today or bust."

"Fine. Whatever," Athena sulked.

And so, in short order, phone numbers were exchanged and the team agreed to spend the next three hours exploring the area before calling Tim for an extraction. He brought his boat as close to the marshy banks as he dared, and the team was able to hop onto the shore. Poor Miranda, despite being the most athletic member of the group, miscalculated her leap and almost ended up in the water. Dennis shot an arm out and caught her before she could tumble backwards. She smiled back at him gratefully.

"Happy hunting everyone! Good luck!" Tim shouted as he pulled the boat away from them. They all waved back.

Maddie shivered as she watched the members of the Jersey Shore Paranormal Society disappear into the tangle of cedar trees and reeds. "Those are either the bravest bunch of people I've ever met, or the stupidest! I'll be happy if I never see that *thing* again, the last thing I'd ever want to do is go chasing after it! Are you sure we didn't just drop those people off to their deaths? That thing is a real life monster!"

"That creature has had three chances to kill me and it hasn't lifted a finger against me yet, I think they'll be fine." He reminded her, trying to forget the way it had chased them that first time, and the awful feeling that engulfed him whenever he stared into those terrible red eyes.

Chapter Seven: It's Britney, Bitch!

Britney Hofnagel held the pair of barking German Shepherds back by their collars as she admitted Earl Rogers into the living room. The petite woman with short dark hair offered him an apologetic look before bellowing "VICKI! Take Max and Shrek outside!" A girl who looked to be around twelve years old appeared from around the corner and called to the dogs. They immediately lost all interest in Earl, coming to her with an eerie obedience. They followed her down the hall and out of sight. Earl breathed a sigh of relief. Big dogs scared him. He was bitten by one as a kid and had the scars on his calf to prove it. He noticed how quickly the animals had heeded the girl and wondered if the child had inherited any of her father's alleged gifts.

"So sorry about that! They're usually really friendly around strangers. They've been acting a little funny ever since Ron disappeared. Come in, sit down!"

Earl found himself a seat on the nearby sofa, Britney settled into a recliner diagonal from it.

"Those were his dogs?"

"They're *our* dogs. I let him have them in the divorce. He's so attached to them that trying to hold onto them seemed cruel. The poor babies were all out of food when I found them. I don't know how long they'd been like that, I couldn't leave them alone, so I brought them back home with me. That's how I knew something was really wrong. If Ron had known he was going to be away from home for awhile, he would've arranged for someone to pet sit them. He also wouldn't have ever given up a weekend with his daughter without at least calling first to cancel." She lowered her voice and leaned in closer, "This is all so weird. I'm really worried that something bad has happened to him."

Earl noticed how she refused to call him by his new name of 'Chesterfield'. "How's your daughter taking it?"

"It's difficult to say. She doesn't really talk to me anymore like she used to when she was younger. It seems like she's taking it well, but who knows what she's really going through on the inside? Do you have any kids?"

Earl smiled. He did indeed, and he'd much rather be spending the weekend with them instead of working, but such was the nature of the job. The only good thing about working on a Saturday is that most people are home and therefore easier to reach when he needs to interview them like this. Earl's wish to start a family was one of the biggest reasons why he'd left the ABC and taken Matt up on his offer to work for his firm. It wasn't that ABC agents couldn't have a family, many of them did, so much that it was that Earl didn't want to have to keep so many secrets from them about what he did for a living. A relationship based on a foundation of lies didn't strike him as being a particularly stable one.

"I've got two boys, twins. Only a few years older than her."

Britney arched an eyebrow. "Twins? Oh my! That must've been quite the challenge!"

"It was tough when they were little. 'Double the trouble' we used to say, but my wife and I got through it. Now it's like they barely need us anymore, it's strange to go from being at the center of someone's universe one day, and the next you feel like you're somewhere out by Pluto!" He didn't know why he was confiding all of this to her, wasn't he supposed to be asking all the questions? Yet there was something warm and inviting about her which immediately put him at ease and made him feel like he could trust her. She definitely wasn't giving him any "I made my ex-husband disappear for the insurance money" vibes.

She stood up. "Oh, so you know what it's like then! Hey, do you want something to drink? We've got water, Gatorade, milk—"

"No thanks, I just had something on the way up here. So what do you think happened to him?"

Britney wandered into the adjoining kitchen, pulled open the refrigerator, and produced a pitcher of iced tea, setting it on the counter. "I'm almost afraid to think about it. We had a lot of money problems. Fighting over money is the main thing that tore us apart. Working as a veterinary assistant became really depressing for him, having to help put so many animals down. It would depress anyone, but it was worse for him because he could *feel* them dying." She looked down at the counter for a moment, as if lost in the memory, then shook herself out of it. She opened a cabinet over her head and hunted for a glass before resuming her account.

"He couldn't take it anymore and decided he wanted to use his powers to give us a better life. He truly believes that once people understand what he can do, that he'll be rich. I wanted to believe too, and he *does* have an amazing power that I can't explain. I tried to understand, really I did, I tried to be supportive. He burned through all our savings trying to promote himself, flying out to LA to pitch ideas for a show to Animal Planet and other networks." She poured herself a glass of iced tea and returned the pitcher to the fridge, then sat back down diagonally across from Earl.

"For a minute it looked like there might be some interest, but then everything fizzled out. I think coming that tantalizingly close to scoring a major success screwed up his mind. Instead of getting discouraged, he became completely obsessed with making it big." She looked down into her glass.

Earl thought he spied the glimmer of a tear forming. She sighed and looked up at him.

"In the meantime, he wasn't bringing in enough money doing his pet psychic thing, and I begged him to go back to his nice, stable job at the veterinarian's office. I pleaded with him to do only work as a pet psychic as a side hustle, or if he couldn't bear to work as a veterinary assistant, to take any other kind of job just so we had more money coming in. But he was adamant about putting all of his time and energy into it until it paid off. We almost lost this house until I took a second job so we could hold onto it. That was it, I'd had enough at that point and kicked him out. I prayed that he'd come to his senses and get a more steady job so he could contribute something meaningful to the household, but he didn't." She paused to gulp down the rest of her iced tea, then slammed her glass down on a side table with such force that it was obvious to Earl that she'd startled herself.

"The way I saw it, his dreams of fame and wealth meant more to him than this family did. I never cared if I was married to a rich man, but I *do* care about ensuring that my daughter and I always have a roof over our heads and food on the table. It didn't seem like he did anymore. He said he was doing it all for us, but it felt like he was only doing it for himself. He wasn't the same man I'd married. So I had to divorce him, he left me no choice! I think he was given his powers for a reason too, but it was to help other people and their pets, not himself! God won't reward him with wealth until he learns how to put other people first." She frowned and looked up at the ceiling as if entreating the Almighty to chime in a word of agreement.

"Anyhow, then he got that mysterious new job working as a pet psychic and all of the sudden, the money started pouring in. He moved out of his mother's house and bought a new one even bigger than this one. He was doing really well for himself and I was happy for him, but I had a hard time believing that he was really getting paid so well just for reading the minds of animals. I've always wondered if he borrowed the money from someone. Maybe he was trying to make it look like he could really rake in the dollars by being a pet psychic so I'd take him back? Well, what if whoever he really got the money from suddenly wanted it back and he couldn't pay up?"

"Who are you thinking of? The mafia? Did he know anyone like that?"

"Not that I know of, but he had his secrets. I always thought that it was really strange how he wasn't allowed to say anything about his new job aside from the fact that he was working for them as a pet psychic. He wasn't even allowed to tell me the name of the company! And those guys who showed up looking for him, supposedly from the company he works for, were really weird! I think they're looking for him because he owes them money too. I looked up the name of the company they said they work for and it's some corporation that does disaster relief stuff. That doesn't make any sense to me. Why would a disaster relief company hire a pet psychic full time and pay him so much? I think they just made all that up. Hell, as far as I know *you* could've been hired by one of his creditors, since you can't tell me who really sent you."

"In my case, while I can't tell you who hired me, I can assure you that it's got nothing to do with his creditors. What were the men who came to talk to you from the company like? Was one of them tall with slicked back hair, and the other one short with a high forehead?"

"Yeah, those are the two, you know them?"

He nodded. It looked like Mr. Swan and Mr. Keith had been personally leading the company's investigation. "We've met. I can tell you that they really are with his employer." *Or at least that's what they'd have us believe,* he thought and not for the first time wondered what they'd really gotten themselves mixed up in.

What real proof did they have that those two worked for Humanaid? He hated to admit it, but Britney's theory made sense. It certainly made more sense than the strange story they'd been given by Swan and Keith. Perhaps Chester had taken out multiple loans from shady lenders and one of them had already made him pay the ultimate price for defaulting on it, while the others he owed money to were afraid he'd skipped town to avoid paying and hired Matt's detective agency once their own efforts to find him failed? But why all the subterfuge? Legitimate lenders hired detectives to find delinquent borrowers all the time. Earl couldn't deny that all signs pointed to those two weird characters being involved in something criminal. He recalled their claims that Chester had possibly stolen something of great value from the home of the CEO, something they refused to disclose. Maybe what they were really after was money he'd borrowed?

"Suppose, just for the sake of argument, that Chester, er *Ron* decided to go on the run, maybe to get away from people he owed money to like you suggested. Where do you think he would've gone?"

She thought for a moment, then shrugged. "I really can't think of any places he'd go to in particular. I don't think he's hiding anywhere. He wouldn't have ever abandoned his dogs. He wouldn't have disappointed his daughter without an explanation. I think someone really bad got to him first. You need to concentrate on figuring out who that is."

Earl could see how upset she was as she said it. "You still love him, don't you?"

"Do you ever really completely stop loving someone once you've totally given them your heart? Even after they've burned you a thousand times? I don't know how to do that. But life is tough and sometimes love just isn't enough. Unfortunately, you can't eat love! Love alone can't give you a roof over your head! I was really hoping that he'd changed. Yeah, I was suspicious about his newfound success, but I was also hoping that even though we were divorced, we could still work things out and learn how to be a family again someday. The divorce was only ever meant to be a wake up call, something to scare him into getting his act together. But he was too damned dense to see it that way, he started to move on, got himself a new girlfriend. It was hard enough to come to terms with the idea that he'd totally given up on me, but now I have to figure out how to deal with the fact that he's probably dead, and how to explain all of this to our Vicki..." her voice trailed off and it was obvious that she was holding back tears. Earl couldn't help but feel sympathy for her. If she was trying to throw suspicion off of herself, it was working. He cursed himself for his failure to maintain his professional detachment and fought down his own emotions. Then something she'd just said registered in his brain.

"He has a new girlfriend? I wasn't aware of that!" It was true, none of the files he'd been given mentioned a new love interest.

She laughed bitterly. "Not so much a new girlfriend as an old, unrequited love. Some girl he used to obsess over when he was a teenager. He used to write her love letters under that stupid stage name of his. They never hooked up back in the day. He was too shy to ever tell her who was really behind all those love notes. He never wrote me any love notes! She found him on the internet once he legally changed his name to the same alias he used when he wrote those letters. They started chatting, met in person, and one thing led to another. I want to hate him for it, but how can I? I'm the one who divorced him! And like I just said, do you ever really stop loving someone you've given your heart to? Obviously he never did, or he wouldn't have ever revived that old alias. I'll bet he never stopped loving her either. She was always there, somewhere in the back of his mind. It's not fair! She'd never noticed him like I did, never really saw him or appreciated him like I did until it was convenient for her, after she'd been burned by a bunch of bad relationships. I wanted to be a better person, to be happy that he'd finally gotten together with the kind of woman that he really wanted to be with all this time, but it's hard. It's hard to let go, you know? Even though I know he's no good for me, I still wanted him all for myself." She laughed again, in a very self conscious way . "I can't believe I'm telling all of this to you, a total stranger! I guess I don't have many people to talk to, and sometimes it's easier to talk to a stranger than someone you've got a relationship with. Shit! I need a therapist, don't I? Fuck! I can't afford a therapist! Please pardon my French!"

Earl couldn't help but chuckle at her little profane outburst either.

"It's fine, I've heard it all in my time."

"You used to be a cop, didn't you? You're giving me major cop vibes here. My uncle is a cop and you're just like he is."

"I was with the force for almost ten years, up in Connecticut," Earl revealed. He'd been a cop until the ABC recruited him after he'd had an encounter with a UFO.

"So how do you like it? Being a private eye?"

"One thing is for sure-the pay is a helluva lot better." It was an oversimplification. Yes, the money was good, but why he really stuck with it was because he loved his relationships with his coworkers. Matt's detective agency wasn't just a workplace, it was a second family.

She smiled. "I'll be sure to tell my uncle that! He's always threatening to quit. I've never met anyone who hates his job and loves it so much at the same time."

Earl nodded in understanding. "That's definitely the nature of that particular beast! Could you give me the name of Ron's new girlfriend, and any contact info you might have on her?"

"Of course. But I'm telling you, it's just another dead end. I've already talked to her. She has no idea where he's disappeared to either. I don't see why she'd lie about that. But feel free to look into it for yourself. I might not be a detective, but I'm no dummy, either. I've been racking my brains trying to figure out what happened to him. Trying to hold onto the hope that he's still alive out there somewhere. I've already called everyone I know that he knew well. Nobody seems to know anything useful."

"I could use that information too, if you don't mind? The names and numbers of all those people you've contacted or anyone else you think he might've been talking to recently." He opened up a briefcase he carried with him for holding his trusty laptop, and handed her a notepad and pen that he kept in there.

"Sure," she took it and opened up the contacts on her phone to begin transcribing names and numbers. It was probably more efficient if he just gave her his number and asked her to share the contacts, but then his phone would be clogged with all kinds of new contacts he didn't recognize. Unfortunately, this was the best way to keep them all straight. When she was done, she handed him back the notebook and pen. He was sad to see that the page was only about a third full. Chester didn't seem to have many friends. He felt like he hadn't gotten much to work with out of this interview, other than the sobering idea that Chester might've been murdered. He put his things back in the briefcase, took out a business card and gave it to her.

"Thanks for your time, if you think of anything else. Give me a call."

She told him that she would and he took his leave. He got back into his car and drove off. He started heading for a diner that was one of his and Matt's favorite restaurants. The two had agreed to meet up there to compare notes and plan their next moves after their interviews were done.

As he drove, a memory randomly popped into his mind, as they sometimes do. Suddenly, he recalled where he'd seen Mr. Swan and Mr. Keith before!

He couldn't wait to tell Matt what he'd just remembered, it put a new spin on everything!

Chapter Eight: On Ebon Wing

Miranda slapped the back of her neck, flattening a mosquito in the process, then shook the resulting nastiness off of her fingers, her face contorting into a grimace of disgust. "Why do these cryptid investigations inevitably lead us into mosquito infested places?" she complained.

"Chill out, I've got some Deep Woods Off! in my backpack that you can use." Dennis told her as he slung the bag off of his shoulder and searched for the insect repellent. He handed it to her in short order. As she sprayed her exposed arms and legs with it, Dennis assessed their surroundings. "Since we're stopped, we might as well set up a few trail cams on some of these trees." He held up a compact, rectangular camera that had also been in his backpack.

"Yeah, might as well, since we're just wandering around here with no idea where we're going," Lars said pointedly, looking at Athena.

"I'm sure she's gotta be somewhere nearby. I can *feel* her," Athena replied defensively.

Lars took a trail cam from Dennis and crossed over to a nearby cedar tree. "That's what you've been saying for the past hour," he remarked sourly as he tightened the camera's strap around the bough of the tree. "In the meantime, we're getting eaten alive by bugs and these shoes are probably ruined forever." He pointed down to a pair of once shiny black shoes that were now hopelessly encased in layers of mud.

"I'd say I'm sorry, but seriously Lars, who aside from you, doesn't wear sensible shoes on a monster hunt? You did it to yourself." It was true, even when they were in high school together Lars used to always dress way too formally, often wearing business suits to school. She was still a little shocked whenever he didn't show up in a button down shirt with a tie.

"I didn't realize that today's activities would involve traipsing around in a swamp for hours!"

"Hey, if you don't want to be the first person to clearly capture the Mothman, or Mothwoman or whatever it is on video, you can always head back to where we landed and wait for the boat!" she fired back.

"C'mon you guys! We're a team! Stop all this fighting! I know that we're all a little hot, sweaty, and our feet are completely soaked, but we're also hot on the trail of one of the coolest and most elusive cryptids of them all! This is what the JSPS is all about!" Dennis enthused as he finished setting up his camera. He dug around in his backpack and produced a few sticks of meat wrapped in plastic. He held them up triumphantly. "You know what'll cheer you guys up? Snapping into a Slim Jim!"

Miranda looked at them distastefully. "No thanks, you *do not* want to know what's in those things!"

"I already know what's in them-nothing but pure meaty deliciousness!" Dennis punctuated his point by biting into one.

Athena took one of the Slim Jims too. She didn't like the judgey way Lars looked at her as she did so. "What? Malnutrition is a thing! We're probably all so cranky because we haven't eaten in a while." *God help me, I'm surrounded by health nuts!* she thought as she took a bite.

"I'm cranky because I'm stuck in a swamp! Maybe I will head back." Lars was positively whining now.

"No way, never split up! That's horror movie rule number one!" Dennis protested.

"This is no horror movie, unless there's one called 'The Day of the Mosquitoes'." Lars answered sarcastically.

"Nah, but I do think there really is one simply entitled 'Mosquito'. As for this not being a horror movie, I will remind you again that right now we are literally out here looking for a monster." Athena parried back.

"Yes, and without much progress."

Athena pulled her phone out of her jeans pocket and checked the time before replacing it. "It may feel like we've been out here for a long time, but it's only been a little bit over an hour since we got off the boat. C'mon, give me a little more time. I'm telling you, I can feel it out there somewhere and we're getting closer all the time. By now you've gotta know that my psychic senses are for real."

Lars frowned, she had him there. "I *have* seen you do some pretty amazing things that I can't explain rationally."

"Great! So it's settled! Follow me!" She marched forward without waiting for a response. A moment later, her bravado was rewarded by the sound of squelching footfalls reluctantly following behind her.

Lars looked at Miranda wearily. "We're all going to die of West Nile Virus before we ever get to the Mothlady, aren't we?"

She just smiled and handed him the can of Deep Woods Off! she'd gotten from Dennis.

As Athena trudged through the wetlands, she was guided by a persistent buzzing sensation in the back of her head which she'd come to associate with her recent visions of the Mothman, Mothwoman, Moth*person*.

It feels like I really do have a bee in my bonnet! She mused. As it got slightly more intense, she assumed that also meant she was getting closer, but it was just a theory and there was no way to tell for sure. She'd just have to trust her gut, which told her that was exactly what it meant. As she walked, she tried to fight down her own fears. A part of her was screaming "what are you doing out here leading your husband and best friends straight to a monster? Didn't you learn your lesson? Didn't that end in disaster last time?" She had resolved not to listen to that particular voice inside her head. She told herself that she was a powerful sorceress now, and she could protect herself and her friends if the Mothperson was hostile. It was the entire reason why she'd learned how to do practical magic to begin with. Yes, she liked this latest inner voice much better than the previous one!

She decided to distract herself from this internal tug of war between her impulse to run away in terror and her need to prove herself by filling in the others with some of her recent observations. If nothing else, getting the more analytical part of Lar's mind engaged by her latest ideas might distract him from how miserable he was at the moment.

"I hate to say it, but I'm beginning to think that there's something to this ultraterrestrial thing after all." She announced loudly.

Dennis, walking behind her, was the first one to bite. "Really? What's changed your mind?"

"The condition of the Scar over us. It's all purple and slightly wiggly. That means it's been open sometime in the past few weeks." Her friends all knew what the Scar was already. They knew that her familiar, the wyvern Daniel, came from one of the many worlds on the other end of it.

"Are you thinking that your Mothlady comes from somewhere on the other side of the Scar, like Daniel does?" Lars asked.

"Exactly, although probably not the same world that Daniel migrates from, I've seen what that place looks like in his memories. The Mothplanet is much, much weirder. So yeah, we might really be dealing with something from another dimension. That part of the ultraterrestrial hypothesis seems to be correct."

"What if this creature flew through the Scar when it was open, then got stuck here? Could you open the Scar up again long enough to send it home?" Miranda wondered aloud.

"No, not yet. Only Clark knows how to open and close the Scar at will, he hasn't shown me how, he says it's too dangerous."

Lars knitted his brows in confusion. "How do you summon Daniel then?"

"It doesn't always work. He spends part of the year, during the summer, in our world, so he's usually somewhere nearby enough at that time of the year where he can receive my psychic summons. If it isn't summer, and the Scar isn't already open somewhere nearby, he can't come when I call." Athena frowned. All this talk about her familiar had her missing him, it had been awhile since she'd last spent any time with her extremely unusual pet. She thought this was perhaps one of the reasons why he kept on getting killed in her nightmares. She wanted to change the subject, so she decided to tell the team about one of her other new theories about the cryptid they were after. She wasn't sure how they'd take it, but they had a right to know what they might soon be facing.

"I have another idea about the nature of the thing we're after. I think it's attracted to negative psychic energy, the kind given off by feelings of despair or anger. Remember how Tim told us that he was thinking about his dead mother whenever he saw the creature? And this morning, I had a nightmare where Daniel gets killed and I think she landed right on my roof! We didn't get ourselves outside fast enough to see her, but we heard her, and I believe that my mind made contact with hers. In both cases, someone was experiencing grief."

"Why would it be attracted to that kind of thing?" Lars asked her.

"I was confused about that too at first, then I remembered that in my nightmare I could see the negative psychic energy coming out of me, then floating up to form into something that looked like a giant Mothman in the sky. I think it actually somehow eats the stuff! Some ghosts can make themselves more powerful by absorbing the fear they cause, and there are entities on the astral plane that can do the same thing. I think it's kind of like that. However, those are all spirits, it's unusual for a physical being to be able to derive sustenance that way- but maybe not impossible if it really does come from some other dimension."

"Interesting," Lars began, "for all we know, it might not even be a physical being at all, even though it can interact with our world strongly enough to leave claw marks on a post. It could just be some kind of an extremely powerful spirit."

Athena hadn't considered that. "That's possible I suppose. Either way, my theory fits in with the idea of Mothman being a harbinger of doom, an idea that I was skeptical about up until today. I mean, if Mothman is trying to warn people of impending disaster, he's doing a real shit job of it! Nobody ever understands the warnings until well after the fact, at which point one can easily dismiss it as a false correlation between unrelated events. So what's the point? But what if Mothman isn't really here to warn us, but to feast? Perhaps it can sense an event in the future that will cause lots of suffering, then it literally swoops in to suck it all up?"

"Or it causes the event." Dennis added ominously.

"Shit, Athena! This thing you're describing sounds more like some kind of demon than a cryptid!" Miranda said in alarm.

"The Angel of Death himself!" Dennis sounded more excited than frightened by the concept.

Athena sighed. As she feared, they definitely weren't taking the news well. Except for Dennis, nothing could blunt his passion for strange beats.

"Don't flake out on me guys. It's just an idea I had, I could be completely wrong. Besides, even if I am right, I don't get the feeling that it causes the tragedies it feeds off of. Lord knows there's probably enough misery and sorrow in this world at any given moment to feed a crapload of these creatures. I didn't sense that it was evil. It's more like a kind of giant scavenger, a sort of psychic vulture. It doesn't kill, but it'll pick at the corpse."

"Delightful all the same!" Lars said sardonically.

"Well I'm not worried," Dennis declared. "I'm married to an ass kicking witch who will protect me!"

Athena beamed at his vote of confidence, even if he did call her a witch rather than a sorceress.

"Dennis, being married to a witch doesn't make you invulnerable, it makes you Darrin from *Bewitched*." Lars replied sarcastically.

Miranda snorted in laughter.

"Hey!" Dennis exclaimed. "I'm not Darrin, I'm way cooler than Darrin."

Athena rolled her eyes. She was beginning to regret sharing her insights. She resolved to keep her mouth shut for the rest of the journey until she had something truly important to tell them. She produced a stick of gum from her small purse, popped it in her mouth and squelched onwards.

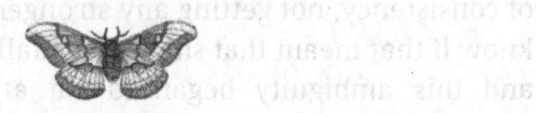

The group continued on in silence for some time. Dark clouds gathered overhead, offering some welcome relief from the harsh early May sun. The marshlands yielded to a more heavily wooded landscape, with bristly pine trees beginning to outnumber the cedars. Between the clouds overhead and the claustrophobically dense forest, it felt as if a great darkness was surrounding them and constantly pressing in on them.

Despite the oppressive atmosphere, Athena was quite determined to press on. She was far too intrigued by the idea that there was something real and tangible behind the legend of the Mothman. She'd always dismissed it all as being nothing more than an interesting bit of modern American folklore based on misidentifications of far more mundane animals. The idea that she'd be the first person to discover what the Mothman truly was, a secret that wasn't even known to her know-it-all mentor, the great wizard Clark Kismet, was impossible to ignore. She was so close to learning how accurate her theories about the creature might be and how much were mere flights of her own fancy. She couldn't give up. She loved a good mystery and she knew she was on the cusp of unraveling this one. She hungered for the truth, she had to know what it was! And it wasn't just for herself, there was Dennis to consider. He was a true believer, all this Mothman stuff meant so much to him. She couldn't disappoint him after his recent let down over how awkward and unfulfilling his reunion with Matt had been for him. He was her rock, he'd always been there for her, ever since they were kids. She hated to let him down, she never would, not on purpose at least.

The buzzing in Athena's head had assumed a curious level of consistency, not getting any stronger or weaker. She didn't know if that meant that she was actually getting closer or not, and this ambiguity began to eat at her. She had to do something. She had to ensure that she wasn't fruitlessly leading them all nowhere. Finally, she came to a halt so abruptly that Dennis bumped into her back and nearly knocked her over with a muttered apology. She swiftly regained her balance and turned to address the team.

"I'm going to sit down and meditate for a moment, see if I can make contact with it again and get a clearer idea of where we should be heading." She half expected Lars to say something snarky like "Aha! So you admit that you don't know where we're going!" but to her relief he didn't. The group looked too exhausted to offer much of a reaction. All of this hiking had numbed them. She found a dry spot to sit down. The others followed her lead, obviously grateful to give their feet a rest.

Athena closed her eyes and stretched out her awareness, putting herself into a kind of trance like state. It wasn't very long before the strange visions of that other world began to play out in her mind, stronger than ever before. And there was more, so much more. She was beginning to better comprehend the significance of some of the things she was seeing, as this new understanding dawned on her, she felt like information was also being pulled from her, her life began flashing before her eyes. It was too much for her to handle-simultaneously reliving her life at breakneck speed, while also learning about a new and alien world. She began to shake, and could feel a trickle of blood dripping down her upper lip. She struggled to break the connection, but she couldn't, she was frozen in place, powerless. A panic began to rise within her which she fought to get a handle on.

Fear is the mind killer, I must not fear. She remembered this mantra from one of her classic science fiction novels, but it was true, and it helped her regain control over her feelings. Fear would get her nowhere, she had to instead focus on somehow making the being on the other end of the mental connection understand that this was too intense for her to handle.

Please, slow down, this is hurting me! She sent the words to it, but it didn't seem to understand her. Instead, she refocused on sending it the feelings behind the words.

Dennis watched his wife wildly convulsing and spasming with great alarm. He shot to his feet, a cold fear running down his spine as he noticed the blood gushing out of her nose. He'd never seen anything like this happen to her before. He shook her by the shoulders.

"Athena! Snap out of it! Wake up!" She didn't register any reaction to his words.

"Omigod! What's happening to her? Dennis! *Do* something!" Miranda pleaded.

"What do you think I'm trying to do?" He shouted back as he continued to shake her out of the trance.

He took a deep breath, he couldn't believe that he was about to do what he was thinking of doing, but Miranda was right, he had to take drastic measures before it was too late. In all the many years they'd been married, he'd never even thought about raising a hand to Athena, she was as much of a goddess to him and her namesake had been to the ancient Greeks, but he had no choice. He'd seen this done in countless movies, he prayed that it would actually work in reality. He slapped her forcefully across the cheek, wincing at the red welt which immediately appeared.

To his tremendous relief, it seemed to do the trick! Athena stopped shaking and her eyes flew open.

"She's coming for me," she mumbled weakly. Her eyes had a glassy, dazed look to them, like she was still half asleep.

Then they all heard it, a great rustling of the trees and a rushing of the wind that blew their hair back. Flocks of birds burst out of the forest, honking and twittering in panic as they raced past them. Just beyond them, they could make out a large, dark blur rushing towards them through the trees at a fantastic speed. The thing didn't flap its huge, bat-like wings, but rather glided silently and swiftly onwards as if propelled by some unseen force. Its deep crimson eyes shone with a terrible intensity, paralyzing them all with an unspeakable, primal fear. It swooped down and grabbed onto Athena by her shoulders with its claw-feet, effortlessly snatching her off the ground and into the air. She didn't try to fight it, hanging limply in its grip as if accepting her fate.

The JSPS looked on in impotent horror as their leader was lifted high above the trees by the terrifying monster, and carried out of sight. Dennis was the first to shake himself out of his shocked stupor.

"Don't just stand there! That, that fucking *thing* took my wife! After it!" He was already crashing through the woods in the direction where it had disappeared as he screamed the words, heedless of the scratches from the countless branches tearing at him. Nothing could stop him now! He wasn't sure if the others were following and he didn't care. He'd rescue Athena from that monster-alone if he had to, or he'd die trying!

He just wished he'd brought his nunchucks with him.

Chapter Nine: Plan of Action

When Earl pulled up to the Broad Street Diner in Keyport, NJ, he spotted Matt's car in the parking lot and knew he'd already be waiting for him inside. Stepping into the place was almost like traveling back in time to the 1950s with its vintage chrome look. He supposed that's why Matt liked it so much, his friend often struck him as a man out of step with time, a holdover from a bygone era. The past didn't hold much nostalgia for Earl, and the era this diner evoked wasn't a particularly great one for his people, although thankfully he was born a few decades too late to have experienced it firsthand. At least the food was good. He found Matt tucked away into a corner booth looking at something on his phone and sipping what was probably his forty-ninth cup of coffee that day. Sometimes he wondered if his friend was secretly a test subject in a ghastly experiment to see how much caffeine a person could endure in one day before their heart exploded.

Matt looked up and noticed him. "Hey, Earl! Over here!" he called out loudly and unnecessarily, waving his hand frantically. A few customers turned to check out the disturbance, making Earl suddenly feel like an animal in a zoo.

Earl sighed. He loved the man, but sometimes he was such a dork! He slid into his seat opposite Matt. He didn't bother to look at the spare menu before him, he already knew what he was going to order. He got the same old thing every time. He was a creature of habit who found comfort in his routines.

"So how was the visit with the ex? Is she the femme fatale in this little mystery?"

Earl shook his head, everything was like a noir novel to Matt. "No, she's just a young single mother, mourning her divorce from a man she still has feelings for, who she now fears is dead."

Matt whistled in appreciation. "Wow, you got all of that off of her, huh? Still carrying a torch for good old Chester! You must've really turned on the charm for her to open up like that to you."

"Not really. I don't think she has many people to talk to, she readily volunteered most of the information. It's kind of sad, actually."

"I know what you mean, buddy. The mom was the same way. A real open book, she even told me about how her husband had a super low sperm count. Too much information, anyone?" he chuckled. Earl did too.

"So you said something about her thinking he's dead?" asked Matt.

"She seems very convinced of it, says he wouldn't leave his dogs uncared for and skipped out on his weekend with his kid otherwise. She thinks he owed money to the mafia or something and they made him 'disappear' when he couldn't pay."

Matt smirked. "The Mob, huh? Oh boy! If I was set to collect insurance money on someone, I'd want to deflect the blame onto the Mob too! Something like that is next to impossible to prove! Nobody connected to the Mob will talk to a pair of gumshoes like us!"

"She seemed sincere to me. The woman was practically in tears."

"Crocodile tears! Are you sure she didn't work her femme fatale magic on you?"

Earl was starting to get irritated with Matt's attitude. Blaming it on Britney Hofnagel would put a tidy bow on the whole case, but he knew it wasn't that simple.

"Look, you said earlier that you trusted my gut, so prove it! I'm convinced that she'd like nothing more than to see him walking through her door again. The problem is, she might be right, he might be dead."

"Shit, I did say that, didn't I? And I do trust your instincts, sorry, man. If you say she's not responsible, I'll drop it. But what makes you so sure he's taking a dirt nap too?"

Earl leaned forward and spoke in a low voice. "She doesn't believe that he ever had a great paying job working as a pet psychic. She thinks he borrowed all that money. Those two stiffs who hired us also paid her a visit. She believes he owed them money too and that's why they're so desperate to find him—"

"They lied about when they started looking for him!" Matt blurted out excitedly. "Chester's mom said they showed up the same day the ex noticed he was gone, but days before she reported it to the cops and long before Humanaid says they began their own investigation. Isn't that suspicious? Why falsify the records they gave us like that?"

"It's *very* suspicious. She doesn't think they work for Humanaid at all. I think she's right because on the way over here I remembered where I'd seen those two before." Earl revealed with a smile.

Before he could go into more detail, the waitress arrived and asked Earl for his order. They visited this place often enough that he could just say "the usual" and she understood his meaning. Matt had already finished his food before Earl showed up. She took his plate, and he ordered a pie for dessert.

"Well, don't keep me in suspense here," Matt said impatiently.

"Back when I was an ABC agent, they were involved in a high profile, scandalous crime. I never actually met them, but everyone in the agency knew all about it at the time. It was the subject of lots of gossip. Those two men, Swan and Keith, are members of one of the Lesser Houses of Magic known as the Order of the Feathered Serpent. They were caught selling the secrets of how to use real magic online back in the early 2000's."

"The Order of the Feathered Serpent, huh? Never heard of 'em, can't be too high profile," Matt commented.

"The Order isn't. It's very small, mostly based out of Mexico, but they have branches in Texas, which is where our friends hail from. The high profile part comes from the fact that a member of the Hazleton family was involved. One of them was working as an ABC agent and found out what Swan and Keith were up to. Instead of busting them like he was supposed to, he helped them cover their tracks-in exchange for a piece of the action!"

Matt nodded. He'd heard of the Hazeltons. Amongst the people within the Guilds, which was a loose union of the various secret societies of the world, they were extremely famous-almost like royalty. In the 19th century, a woman named Esmeralda Hazelton had been instrumental in reforming the most powerful of the Great Houses of Magic, the Temple of the Old Gods, into the more benevolent organization that it is today. Matt's own wife Naomi, who moonlights as the 'Supreme Archivist' for the Guilds, had literally written the book on it. Actually, it was several books. She authored a sprawling series of volumes entitled *The Magna Historia Mundi* (meaning 'The Great History of the World' in Latin) which explained the role of the Guilds in shaping human history. It was only circulated amongst the Guilds, but was quite popular with them.

"Hmm," Matt began, "I guess sometimes the apple *does* fall pretty far from the tree."

"Yeah, unfortunately not all of Esmeralda Hazelton's descendants are as distinguished as she was. This particular one had no great talent for magic, he wasn't accepted into the Temple of the Old Gods, despite his family name. So he joined the ABC instead. He'd grown up in luxury, but he wouldn't inherit a share of the family fortune until his father passed away. He got greedy. The salary of an ABC agent wasn't good enough for him, apparently. Eventually, another agent found out about what Swan and Keith were up to, and how Hazelton had covered for them for his share of their profits. Swan and Kieth were booted out of the Order of the Feathered Serpent, and went to jail. Hazleton's family connections shielded him from doing any hard time, but he was kicked out of the ABC. Even up at the branch in Hartford we heard about it."

The waitress delivered Earl's food, a Cajun shrimp penne, and he dug in. She gave Matt his pie and they thanked her. "So those two are really a pair of wizards! I saw one of them, the tall one, wearing something strange on his wrist. It was like a metal bracelet that looked like it was digging into the flesh of his wrist."

"That's a magical Inhibitor." Earl informed him. "They can't work any spells while wearing it. Only another magic user can take it off. After all these years, they're probably out on parole. The Inhibitors won't be removed until they've finished their sentences. That must be why they hired us. They can't use their magic to find him. You know, the ABC never did find all the money they'd made on their internet scheme. They'd done a good job of squirreling it away. What if Chester borrowed some of that money? Maybe that's what he 'stole' from them."

"It could be. Thanks, Earl."

Earl was puzzled. "For what?"

"For not saying 'I told you so' about not taking this case. You're right, those two probably don't even work for

Humanaid. I don't know why they picked that particular company or came up with such a weird cover story. I guess they just wanted to look like they were affiliated with a big, reputable company so we'd take them seriously." Matt said bitterly. He felt like a fool.

"So where do we go from here? We've already taken the job, and I *would* like to give that poor woman I met and her daughter some closure if possible."

"Yeah, and I practically promised his mom that I'd find her son. I think we should stick with it, and I'd still like to know more about what's really going on here. But if we do find Chester alive, I'm not so sure we should actually tell our clients! I think we should just let his immediate family know that he's okay, and tell those two clowns that we can't find him."

Earl knew that Matt wasn't taking this decision lightly. Doing what someone had hired you to do, then lying to them about your actual success was a serious breach of professional ethics, and Matt was justifiably proud of his reputation. Earl was proud of him too, for having the decency to set that aside in order to do what was truly right. And was it really so unethical to deceive their clients? They hadn't started it. They were less than twenty four hours into the job, and they'd already gotten wise to various things their current employers had lied to them about.

"Yeah, Chester doesn't sound like he's such a bad guy. Maybe he got a little carried away with the idea of getting famous from his psychic powers, but I don't think we should turn him over to a bunch of criminals to do God only knows what to him! If he borrowed lots of money, it was probably just so he could put his broken family back together. Britney thinks he was trying to get her back by showing her that he was able to be financially stable working as a pet psychic. Although I guess at some point he gave up on that too, because he went out and got himself a new girlfriend."

Matt nearly choked on his pie in surprise. "Really? His mom didn't mention that! Maybe we should go pay her a visit before we call it a day?"

"Sure, I've got her name and number. It's an interesting story. She's some lady that he used to write love letters to when they were kids. He did it under that name, Chesterfield Xavier. She never knew who he really was, googled that name one day and found him."

"Ah, the little girl down the lane!" Matt grinned his trademark lopsided grin. "Chester's mom mentioned her when I asked her about how he came up with that wild name of his. So they ended up together after all! The romantic in me likes that idea! Send me her number."

Earl picked up his phone and did as Matt requested. "You should have it now, the name is Kendra Varela."

"I see it. Let's see if she'll meet with us." Matt dialed the number, but it went to voicemail after a few rings. He left a brief message explaining that he was a detective who was looking for Chester and requesting a call back.

"No luck, huh?" Earl asked even though he knew the answer.

"Yeah, but I say we stop by her house and see if she shows up. There's things that a man will tell his girlfriend that he won't tell his own mother, and certainly not his ex-wife! She may have the best idea of what his recent mental state was like and what became of him. We don't have many leads yet, and she's the best we've got."

"Britney didn't think she knew much, but in my humble opinion, we might get more out of Kendra than she could." Earl agreed. He was already way ahead of Matt, as he'd been listening to him, he'd started doing a search on his phone under Kendra's name and number for her address. As a private eye, Earl had a subscription to a few websites that supplied such information-for a price.

"Bingo! I've got a current address for her. She's living out in an isolated corner of New Gretna. I'm sharing it with you now."

"Good work! What say we go and stake out the place together? We can leave your car here for a few hours and take mine down there."

"Sounds like a plan, my man!"

The two private investigators finished up their meals, asked for the check, and headed out the door. Little did they suspect that their phones had been hacked, and their entire conversation had just been monitored by a pair of men with less than honorable intentions....

Chapter 10: The Ne'er-Do-Wells

"Esmeralda Hazelton was one of the most influential witches of the Temple of the Old Gods during the 19th Century. Called 'The Great Reformer', she successfully advocated for a policy of less interference with the mundane world. She was behind the organization's mid-century name change and general softening of its positions regarding dealing with amateur psychics and occultists. A famous statue of her currently stands in the palace of the Pontifex Maximus at the center of Elysium to this day."

- From the Magna Historia Mundi by Dr. Naomi Waters-Spike

"They make me sound so terrible! So corrupt and greedy!" Balthazar Hazelton declared indignantly as he paced back and forth so rapidly on the carpet that his cousin, Gordon Hazelton, was scared he'd wear a hole in it.

Well, if the shoe fits... Gordon thought unkindly, but instead he said "Please! Your wounded pride is the least of our problems! Who on earth are these two detectives that your people hired? How can they possibly know so much about the Guilds and our family history? What are their names?"

Balthazar picked up a file on Gordon's desk and flipped through it. "Ah...let's see...oh, here it is! Yes! Their names are Matt Spike and Earl Rogers."

Gordon frowned. "Matt Spike...why does that name sound so familiar? His voice sounded familiar too." He typed the names into the computer in front of him. Within seconds it chimed. He scrutinized the screen and sighed loudly. "Earl Grey is a former ABC agent. So that explains that. And I just recalled who this Spike person is...he's not just a private eye, he's also the Guilds' Guardian of the Orb! I was briefly assigned to the ABC rapid response team that supports the Guardians at the start of my career, I even met him once! He's a personal friend of Bronson McDowell, the former Director of the ABC himself!"

The Orb is a powerful magical item that prevents magic users from casting any spells for miles around it. It effectively renders them completely vulnerable to conventional, non magical attacks. For millennia it was guarded by a secret brotherhood of assassins, who were sworn to use the Orb only if the Great or Lesser Houses of Magic abused their powers to go to war with each other or attempt to take over the world.

This arrangement had worked for ages, maintaining the balance of power within that ancient alliance of secret societies known as the Guilds. Until one day when a traitor within the ranks of the assassins allowed it to be stolen by a group of rogue magic users intent on global domination. This cabal was eventually defeated and the Orb replaced, but only after a great many people had been killed in the process. Ever since then, the Orb has been held by a secret Guardian so it wouldn't fall into the wrong hands again. Matt's friend Bronson McDowell had given this job to Matt and Naomi decades earlier.

"Oh, this is a fine mess you've gotten us into! If Spike learns the truth he might inform the Guilds! We can't make someone like him disappear, he's too important! He'll be missed and investigations will be launched which may inevitably lead back to us!" Gordon fought to get his breathing under control, he didn't want to lose his cool in front of his cousin. He had to maintain his air of control and superiority at all times.

"I swear, I had no idea that guy was the Guardian! All I knew was that Swan and Keith said he was very highly reviewed online," Balthazar protested.

"Well, in your defense the identity of the Guardian of the Orb *is* a tightly held secret. It has to be. I only know because I was once in that support squad," Gordon admitted.

"However, you shouldn't have entrusted a problem of this magnitude to those fools Swan and Keith. They've been nothing but trouble for our family ever since they came into our lives," Gordon scolded.

"They have their uses, they might not be able to cast spells anymore, yet they've still managed to use their knowledge to help me craft a few useful magic items for us."

"Not nearly useful enough!" Gordon hissed. "That cursed gun you made isn't nearly as potent as the one it replaced. Even if our former guest is still wearing the amulet which allows him to absorb the negative ambrosia from the weapon's victims, I fear that it won't supply him with enough nourishment to keep him alive for very long. Goodness knows that buffoon who stole him certainly won't be willing to do what it takes to keep him well fed. If he starves to death before we can find him, I doubt that we can replace him. Those creatures are impossible to capture without using ABC resources. It's a miracle I managed to do it once before without getting caught. I doubt I'll be so lucky a second time. I'm not willing to risk it. It's vital that we find him as soon as possible!"

"I know, I know," Balthazar said wearily.

"If only we'd eliminated this Chesterfield Xavier fellow when he discovered the truth like we did with his predecessor! Instead you sent him on vacation!"

"I only wanted to keep him around because it's so difficult to find anyone who can actually communicate with those beasts. You remember how long it took us to replace the first one?"

"I do, don't remind me." Gordon let out a groan of frustration. So much for keeping his cool demeanor. "I suppose there's no point in rehashing the poor decisions which brought us to this point, we need to concentrate on how to get ourselves out of this situation instead."

"I could ask Swan and Keith to take Spike off the case if you think it's too dangerous to keep him on it?" Balthazar offered.

Gordon rapped his long fingers on his mahogany desktop in concentration for a while before speaking.

"No, we'll allow him to do a bit more searching. He might very well find Xavier. He is quite a good detective and he seems very determined to do so. Even if he tries to deceive us, we'll know the truth since we can listen in on his conversations. Our missing guest might not be with Xavier when he locates him or he might keep him hidden from Spike. If he is with him when Spike finds him, then it might become necessary to deal with these detectives more forcefully. We can't kill them, but if we can capture them, there is a certain magical device I've liberated from the ABC vaults which can alter memories. We could use it on him and his partner if necessary."

Typically, when the ABC needed to change someone's memories they used an agent who was also a magic user to do it with a spell. Since Gordon was involved in various questionable activities that he didn't want to involve any of his agents in, he'd been forced to borrow this particular magic item to get that kind of a job done. In fact he'd even used it on other ABC agents in the past, such as the ones who'd helped him originally capture their former guest.

"I didn't know you had anything like that!" Balthazar sounded annoyed.

"Yes, I've had it for some time now. In fact, the night when we originally acquired our guest I ordered that witch, Agent Ember, to alter everyone's memories of the incident, then I used it to eradicate *her* memories of the affair," He bragged, savoring the sweet irony of it.

"If I'd known you had it, I could've used it on Chester to erase his memory of seeing that girl killed and avoiding this entire mess!"

"Well, you never asked. And as usual you foolishly chose to hide your problems from me until they grew to the point where they were beyond your limited ability to control."

Balthazar ignored this latest barb. "But what if Spike tries to call in that ABC rapid response team for backup when we try to capture him? We'll be in real trouble then!"

"That's easy enough to prevent. We can simply jam his Guild communicator. I know the correct frequency. Put all our security teams on high alert. I want them ready to roll out the moment he gets too close to discovering something we'd rather remain a secret. Remember: Matt Spike must *never* find out what we've been doing to feed our former guest. He's far too much of a goody two shoes and he'll report us for sure if he does. He also must not be allowed to find out that we're the power behind Humanaid. If either of those things should happen, send in our men to capture him and inform me right away. Do you think you can manage to handle that?"

"I won't let you down, cousin. You can count on me!" Balthazar swore.

Gordon massaged his temples. If only he could believe it, but the sad truth was that his cousin rarely did anything other than let him and the entire family down. Balthazar was the black sheep of the Hazelton clan, and had been completely disowned by the rest of them. Gordon only continued to associate with him because he suspected that he was not only his cousin, but also his younger half brother from a torrid affair his father had with his sister-in-law, Balthazar's mother and Gordon's maternal aunt.

He also felt a certain sympathy for him. It wasn't easy growing up in a family filled with so many famous and illustrious magic users and to have virtually no affinity for magic yourself. Gordon knew that pain all too well. It had led him into a career with the ABC, the Guilds' international police force, just as it had Balthazar. However, unlike his cousin, Gordon's career had proven to be far more successful. He now ran an entire branch office of the ABC, yet he still felt like most of the rest of his family looked down upon him and considered him to be almost as much of a failure as Balthazar.

That wasn't the only similarity between them. Like Balthazar, he'd also been raised in extraordinary wealth, only to be cut off from it when he became an adult. The wages of an ABC agent, even an important Branch Director like Gordon didn't even come close enough to covering the expenses of the kind of extravagant lifestyle he'd grown accustomed to. And so, he'd been forced to join his cousin in searching for lucrative new streams of income. They'd been fortunate enough to find a good one several years ago. Someday, Gordon's father would pass away and he'd get his fair share, but unfortunately the old man showed no signs of slowing down. Until that day, he had to protect his investments. Vigorously. Ruthlessly.

There wasn't anything he wouldn't do to ensure the money kept on rolling in.

Chapter Twelve: Enter Mothman

The two detectives headed down the Garden State Parkway towards the sleepy town of New Gretna, completely unaware that they were the subjects of so much consternation.

"Ya know, since Chester's ex apparently has a key to his place, we should ask her if she'll let us poke around in there and look for clues." Matt said from behind the wheel of his black Hyundai Elantra.

"That's a pretty good idea. I could text her and set it up." Earl offered.

"Yeah, see if she can meet us tomorrow at his place, at whatever time is most convenient for her."

"Okay, message sent, just waiting on a reply." Earl reported. But no reply was immediately forthcoming. That didn't matter much because there would soon be plenty to occupy them. Matt was already taking the New Gretna exit and within only a few more minutes his GPS had directed him to the long, heavily wooded side road where Kendra Varlea made her home. There were no other houses around as they made their way down the narrow path of sun bleached, cracked pavement. Finally they came to stop in front of a pleasant, two story Dutch colonial style house. No cars were parked in the driveway, and a large detached garage was visible behind the house and off to one side.

As the car came to a stop in front of the house, Earl looked at Matt. "Nobody's home. So what now? Should we just wait for her to show up, or do you want to dig around a little first?"

"We don't know for sure that nobody's home, there could be a car inside that garage, I wanna see if we can see anything through those windows." As Matt said it he was opening his car door.

"Okay, so I guess we're digging around a little first! I can dig it," Earl quipped, but Matt didn't hear his witticisms, he was already out of the car and moving towards the garage.

Earl hurried to catch up with the slightly younger man, who was looking through the grimy windows set into the door.

"There's something there, under a tarp," he announced as he heard Earl's feet grinding on the asphalt behind him. "See if that side door is unlocked, I'd like to take a closer look."

Earl was tempted to remind him of the illegality of entering the garage if it was, but he knew that Matt was already well aware of this fact and that it wouldn't dissuade him. He turned the knob and the door pushed open. Matt was already by his side and was soon shoving himself through the doorway. With a sigh, Earl reluctantly followed.

Earl found Matt peeking beneath the crumpled blue tarp. The outline of a vehicle was clearly visible beneath. Matt was at the back of it. He let out a whistle of appreciation. "Earl! Get over here, you won't believe this! The car under this tarp is exactly the same make, model and color as Chester's car! Do you remember his license plate number from the police report?" he whispered excitedly.

"Of course I do." Earl possessed a photographic memory when it came to numbers. He glanced at the plate under the section of tarp Matt was holding up. "That's the one! This must be his car."

Matt released the tarp and the two PIs looked at one another knowingly.

"This changes everything. If she's hiding his car, what else is she hiding? Him?" Matt asked.

"Or his dead body." Earl added grimly, although they didn't know of any motive Kendra might have for murdering him.

"Touché," Matt frowned. He hoped it hadn't come to that. "She might also just be pretending not to be home."

"What makes you say that?"

Matt pointed to a window on the opposite side of the garage. You could see into the backyard through it, and there was a car parked on the lawn behind the house.

"Oh. So what now?"

"Let's try knocking on the front door. If nobody answers, I'm going to pick the lock."

The ex-cop in Earl once more felt a wave of discomfort over his partner's frequent disregard for the law, but again he surrendered to the futility of arguing with him over it. Ultimately, Matt was going to do whatever Matt wanted to do. He was more of a hard headed detective than a hardboiled one.

"Don't sweat it pal," Matt said as if reading his mind. "I won't touch anything, she'll never even know we were inside. I just want to take a little peek."

Matt's words did nothing to calm Earl's worries. *And how do we explain ourselves if she is inside?* Earl wondered, *and what if she has a gun? She'd be perfectly justified in pumping us full of lead!*

Yet despite these fears, Earl found himself following Matt out of the garage, across the lawn and onto the front porch, resigned to whatever surprises fate had in store for them.

Matt rang the doorbell, the two detectives heard the chime sound on the other side of the door. They waited for a minute before Matt stabbed the button again. Earl thought he saw the curtains in one of the second story windows shift to the side, but he couldn't be sure. They waited again. Matt rang the bell once more.

More waiting.

"That tears it! I'm going in!" Matt snarled. He produced his lock picks from a pocket in his trench coat and went to work on it. They both heard what sounded like several pairs of feet running down the steps, then away from the front door.

The door sprang open under Matt's influence and the detectives rushed inside. As they entered the house, they heard more running feet from just ahead of them and a door being pulled open. Matt broke into a sprint, following the sound, Earl was right on his heels. A moment later they came skidding into the kitchen, but nothing could prepare them for what they found there.

"What the?" Earl asked the cosmos, but as usual, no answer was forthcoming. The cosmos can be an ass like that sometimes.

There was something stuck in the back door. It was a large, dark, man shaped *thing*. It had its back to them; a pair of enormous bat-like wings obscured most of their view of it. These same wings seemed to be what was stopping it from getting out the door, the creature kept getting them caught on the doorframe. Through a window, Earl saw a woman he assumed must be Kendra throwing open the door to the car that was parked out back and jumping inside. The engine roared to life.

"C'mon! Tuck your wings in more! You can do it!" Urged a man standing right behind the creature. That man was Ronald Hofnagel Junior, AKA Chesterfield Xavier.

"Wait!" Matt shouted, "we're not going to hurt you! We're here to help!"

"No! I don't trust you!" Chester shot back. As the creature in front of him continued to bang its wings up against the doorframe.

"Your mother trusts me, and I really don't want to let her down. The lady deserves answers!" Matt argued back.

"You know who really deserves answers, Chester?" Earl said, "Your daughter! Don't disappear again without letting her know that her father's okay!"

That seemed to strike a chord in Chester, he looked as if all the wind had been knocked out of him. "You've seen Vicki?"

Earl nodded, "That girl needs her father."

Chester placed a hand on the shoulder of the creature in the doorway. "Coathuan, it's okay. Calm down, we're not leaving. Not yet."

The creature ceased its fruitless efforts to exit and slowly turned to face them. Its face was nothing at all like a human face, the mouth was more akin to that of an insect, so were the eyes, which hung on the head like two massive red saucers. A pair of thick, twitching antennae rose from its head reminding Earl, absurdly, of bunny ears. It had a muscular build which was covered in a fine, dark gray fur which made Earl think of the soft down on a newly hatched bird. The hands were long, three fingered and terminated in sharp, nasty looking claws.

The eyes were the most terrifying thing of all, but Earl, as a former ABC agent, was able to push these feelings down and remain cool. It had been many years since he'd last encountered anything this strange, he'd thought he'd left all that behind when he joined Matt's detective agency. His overriding emotion in this moment was not one of terror, but annoyance that the weirdness had wormed itself back into the nice, normal civilian life he'd been carefully building for himself over the past decade.

"This is um, well his exact name is impossible to pronounce in English, but it sounds something like T'zzitch Coathuan. He won't hurt you, he's more scared of you than you seem to be of him, which is *odd*," Chester remarked. T'zzitch Coathuan waved cheerily and chittered something which indeed, did sound vaguely like his name.

Matt laughed. Heartily. Everyone looked at him like he was nuts. "I'm sorry, but I'm just having a real *Matrix* moment over here." He said, referencing the fringe theory that we're all living in a simulation, and that odd coincidences are evidence of it. "I know exactly what he is, he's the freak'in Mothman! A few old friends of mine I had dinner with just the other day were about to go out looking for him, and here I am, not even looking for him and I found him! What are the chances?"

"Why *aren't* you scared? Who *are* you two?" Chester asked suspiciously.

Matt smiled his lopsided smile. "Kid, nothing fazes me anymore. I've seen a few things in my day: frankencats, ape mercenaries and dragons. More wizards and witches than you can shake a stick at. A headless Frost Giant, Santa Claus, God, the Devil and Jesus H.Christ himself! Most of the ancient Greek and Viking Gods, a whole army of vampires and werewolves. Aliens from Venus, robots, a shape shifting alien too. I've traveled back in time and been to the Moon! This isn't anything all *that* new for me. It is pretty cool, though. My first cryptid! I wish I could tell Dennis."

Chester looked at him like he was a madman, yet his psychic senses told him that he was telling the truth, as improbable as that sounded. "And I repeat, who are you? You're not with Humanaid are you?"

"Relax, like I said, we're on your side. Why don't you call your girlfriend back into the house, we'll all sit down, have a nice cup of coffee and exchange our stories. I'm dying to hear yours, it must be a real doozy! You do have coffee, don't you?"

"Uh yeah," Chester said dully, "she's got some around here somewhere."

"Awesome! I think this is the beginning of a beautiful friendship, Chester," Matt grinned as he took a seat at the nearby table and winked at Earl.

Earl didn't wink back, all he could think of was the bizarre creature standing a few feet away from him, and those awful red eyes which seemed to be burning a hole into his very soul.

Act Two

ACT TWO

Chapter Twelve: On A Mission From The Other Side of The Scar

Dennis continued racing through the woods when finally, in a clearing up ahead he could see the large, terrible shape of the Mothman. Its back was to him, but he thought could see Athena standing in front of it. He couldn't see enough of her to tell if she was alright or not. His plan, desperate as it was, was to charge the creature, tackle it to the ground and pummel it with his fists. He took a deep breath and raced as fast as he could to gather up enough momentum so he could hopefully knock it to the earth. Then he heard something which stopped him in his tracks.

The sound of laughter.

But not just any old laughter, it was Athena's laughter. Rich and heartfelt, it was a sound he treasured. If she was laughing like that, then...that meant that she was okay? Or maybe just delusional? Perhaps she'd totally snapped and lost her mind?

In a fog of confusion he emerged into the clearing, all thoughts of trying to tackle the Mothman forgotten as he struggled to understand what was happening. Athena was sitting on a fallen tree in front of the creature and looked unharmed and content. She'd even wiped most of the blood from her nose off of her face. She glanced over at him as he arrived.

"Oh, hey hon! Meet my new friend!" she said cheerfully as if nothing had happened. The creature somehow turned its head despite having no obvious neck to fix its unsettling gaze upon him, then it bowed its head in greeting.

"Are you, are you alright?" he stammered.

"Oh yeah, that must've looked pretty scary when she carried me off, huh? I was really out of it for a minute there, too! She was feeding me so much information all at once, and it was a bit overwhelming! She thought it might be easier if we talked face to face with a little privacy to give me a chance to get used to how she communicates. She was right, so yeah I'm totally fine now."

"*A little scary?*" Dennis said hotly, "that's the understatement of the year! It was terrifying! I thought this thing was going to kill you! I was getting ready to beat the living shit out of it until I heard you laughing!"

"Whoa, don't go trying to beat the living shit out of her! She's totally friendly, freaky, but friendly. Anyway, I do appreciate the sentiment, good Sir Dennis, my ever gallant knight! Always ready to throw down with monsters on my behalf!"

Despite his current mix of anger and confusion, Dennis couldn't help but smile at her words. He took his first real good look at the creature. Now that he knew it wasn't munching on his wife, he could appreciate the fact that he'd found the object of years of his curiosity.

"So this is really the female of the species?" he asked rhetorically, it certainly wasn't obvious from looking at her.

She had none of the bodily features typically associated with human females, no pronounced hips or breasts. The shape of her body was humanoid in that she had two legs, two arms and a head, but that was where the similarities to human beings ended. Her wings were really more like that of a bat than a moth, although her eyes, mouth and antennae did give her an insectoid air. Her dull, dark brown color came from a short, fuzzy substance covering her body that he couldn't identify for sure being hair or small feathers. She had three elongated fingers on each hand, and a thumb which all terminated in claws. Her feet consisted of two thick toes, again ending in a claw. From afar they looked more like hooves. He noticed that she had a small, segmented tail which had a barbed end. Once you got over the disturbing effect of her eyes, she had a sort of wiry, majestic grace about her. She was almost regal in a way.

He couldn't believe that he was now standing mere inches away from one of the most mysterious cryptids of them all! Has anyone else ever gotten this close before? He reached for the video camera slung diagonally over his body by a long strap and started shooting. The Mothwoman didn't seem to mind. He wondered if she even had any idea what the camera was.

"You can really communicate with her, huh?"

"Yes. It was difficult at first. Her language is nothing at all like ours. A mouth shaped like that can't even approximate anything close to human speech, but it's not just that, the way that they think is also really, really different. It's closer to how animals think, although she's definitely way smarter than any animal. We have to communicate through pictures and feelings, kind of like how I do with Daniel and our pets. It took me a minute to get the hang of it."

"Wow!" was all Dennis could manage to say as he continued to film the Mothwoman, slowly encircling her.

The sounds of feet crashing through the underbrush drew their attention. Miranda and Lars were hurrying towards them.

"Athena! Omigod, are you okay?" Miranda called out to her as she approached.

"I'm right as rain, don't worry about me!"

Despite Athena's assurances, Miranda couldn't help but give her friend a warm hug as soon as she reached her.

"We really thought we'd lost you that time! Don't you ever do that to me again!" Her friend was almost in tears. Athena must've been greatly touched by her concern too, because her own eyes started moistening.

"Hey, don't make me cry in front of the Mothwoman!" she admonished jokingly.

Miranda released her grip on her and took a step back to appraise the creature in front of them. "Holy shit, that's the real thing, isn't it? So what? She's friendly now?"

"She was never truly unfriendly. She just wanted to get me alone for a minute to try and talk to me, because when our minds touched while I was meditating, she realized that I'm one of the few people in this world who can talk to her, and help her. She saw my life, and she knows that I'm a sorceress. In her world, I'd be considered a Holy Woman."

Lars craned his head quite close to the Mothwoman's body, his face was mere inches from her. She looked at him and made an odd chittering sound. He drew back reflexively. "Fascinating."

"Fascinating! That's all you've got to say?" Dennis reproached him, "Who are you, Mr. Spock? Mothman is real! We've got the proof right here on video! We did it! Maybe this time we'll be able to actually share this information with the world for a change?" Dennis was still a little annoyed that for various reasons, they couldn't reveal the existence of Daniel and his species to the world, although they were the creatures that had inspired the legend of the Jersey Devil.

"I wouldn't count on that, hon. She's asking for my help, and in order to help her, I'm afraid I might need to call on some help myself from some of our *secret* friends." They all knew that she meant her mentor, the wizard Clark Kismet when she mentioned secret friends. That meant they'd likely have to keep this entire encounter a secret.

"Dang! How many incredible discoveries can we possibly make without ever getting famous?" Dennis complained and lowered his camera. Athena knew that his irritation actually didn't run very deep. He did this for the thrill of discovery, a thrill that he was experiencing right now. It wasn't about money or fame for any of them, although a little bit of that sure wouldn't hurt!

"What kind of help is it asking for?" Lars inquired.

"Not 'it' Lars! *She*! She is T'zzitch Morgatchu, and she's here looking for her mate."

"Well tell her that I'm flattered. Even though I *am* available at the moment, I'm not interested." Lars joked dryly.

Athena laughed. It was a rare day when Lars blessed them with a joke. "No silly, she's already got herself a fine Mothman! He came here through the Scar some time ago. It's hard for me to understand exactly *how* long ago, because her people perceive time very differently from how we do. Our years feel like weeks to them. I think time passes differently in their world too. Anyhow, I only mention this because for her it doesn't seem like he's been gone all that long, but it could've been years over here. Her husband is like a sort of tribal chieftain. He promised his eldest son to the daughter of the chief of a rival clan to cement an alliance between them. But the crazy kid ran off with some girl from a totally different tribe the minute his old man left town."

"I can't really blame him, arranged marriages-ick!" Miranda said distastefully.

Athena shrugged. "Yeah, personally I'm not much of a fan of them either, but it's their way, so who am I to judge? Anyhow, the important thing about all of this is that breaking the marriage agreement like that could cause a big war between the tribes! Morgatchu is here on Earth looking for her husband because he's about the only one who can talk some sense into the kid and get him to honor the agreement."

"Why did he come here to begin with?" Dennis wanted to know.

"I was right about how they feed off of negative ambrosia. She shared some of the history of her race with me, and it's really interesting! Her people evolved psychic abilities to help them hunt a particular type of animal that was their main food source. This gave them such an edge that they eventually hunted it to extinction, but that was a long process. Before that animal went extinct, their psychic powers underwent a further mutation. As the numbers of that animal declined, her people evolved the power to also feed off of not only the physical meat of those animals, but the fear and terror they felt as they died. Supplementing their diet like that helped them remain strong as that animal became rarer and rarer. By the time that beast completely died out, this ability had become so developed that they could feed off of the suffering of any animals, and even sense future events that would cause massive suffering. They now feed entirely on negative psychic energy.

Her tribe lives in caves along the shore of a great sea. They fly out over the sea and feed off of the deaths of entire schools of fish that are swallowed up by the giant sea monsters on her planet. From time to time, when flying close to the Scar while it's open, they can sense future events in our world that will provide them with a good meal, so they cross over to have a feast. The Scar closes up and they get marooned here for a while until it reopens. They have to make do scavenging off of our nightmares until the Scar opens up again and they can fly back home. Her husband crossed over to gorge himself on something bad that was about to happen here, but he hasn't come back yet for some reason."

"Damn, that's downright *ghoulish!*" Lars replied.

"Is it really? We feed off of death too, all life does. Even vegetarians and vegans are living off of the bodies of living things. Sure, they're not animals, but they were still *alive*. Is it really any better than eating an animal, just because it's so different from us that we can more easily forget that it's also a kind of living being? Her people don't consume the bodies of *any* living things, they just eat the subtle energies given off by their feelings. They don't cause any suffering, they don't need to. The sad truth is that there's more than enough grief and misery in the world to keep them healthy."

"So how are we going to find Mr. Mothman for her?" Dennis asked.

"Honestly, I have no fucking clue." Athena admitted ruefully. "All the recent Mothman reports we've heard about can be traced back to her. That's why I wanted to ask Clark for help."

"Well, what are you waiting for?" Her husband urged.

"Yeah, I guess there's no time like the present. We don't want to cause a war on Mothman World with our dilly dallying."

She dug into the small purse she carried and produced a polished stone ball. She muttered a few strange words and it floated out of the palm of her hand and up into the air at the level of her eyes. This was a magical device which was rather unimaginatively called a 'sphere'. Magic users used it to call each other, like a magic cellphone. Morgatchu the Mothwoman chittered excitedly at this spectacle, obviously amazed by it. The others in the group were less impressed, they'd all seen her do it a thousand times by now.

Athena concentrated on her mentor, picturing him in her mind, but nothing happened. She tried again with the same lack of results. Recalling how the definition of insanity was doing the same thing repeatedly and expecting a different result, she tried instead to use the sphere to contact her brother Mark. He was probably with Clark and could put him in touch with her. She supposed Clark didn't have his sphere on him, although in her experience, a sphere was one of the few things that a magic user always carried on their person. It was as indispensable to their craft as the daggers, staves or wands that they sometimes used to cast certain types of spells. Athena was more of a wand girl herself, she didn't want to have to explain to people why she was always carrying a big knife around with her.

She imagined Mark. It was easy to summon a strong mental picture of him, he'd been on her mind a lot lately. She was really missing him. To tell the truth, she was scared of losing him to this weird world of wizards that they'd both blundered into. He didn't answer either.

"Okay, what the hell?" She swore, "Nobody's answering." She sighed quite loudly and searched through her purse once more. "Desperate times call for desperate measures." She was hunting in her purse for something Clark had given her years ago which could physically call him to her in an instant. It was an old business card with his name on it. She jokingly called it her 'get out of jail free' card since she knew that if she ever got herself in too far over her head, help from one of the greatest wizards of all time was always readily at hand. She found the card (and another stick of her favorite gum, which she popped into her mouth) and once more pictured Clark in her mind.

Nothing happened. Her card, somehow, had been declined. For once, help from one of the greatest wizards of all time was *not* readily available. She was completely on her own.

"Ah, to hell with them! Who needs them anyway? We can do this without them, right team? We found one Mothperson today, and we can find another!"

She said the words, and she wanted so badly to believe them—but she didn't. Just like she'd told Dennis earlier, she still had absolutely no fucking clue what she was supposed to do next.

Chapter Thirteen: Chester's Story

Matt Spike, Earl Rogers, Chesterfield Xavier and Kendra Varela all sat around a small kitchen table. T'zzitch Coathaun couldn't fit in any of the chairs, so he just leaned up against a counter casually, which was an odd sight.

Matt had already explained that he and Earl were a pair of private eyes hired to find him by a party which wished to remain anonymous. He was afraid that if he revealed that he was hired by Humanaid, Chester would try to run again. The fact that he'd been hired by Humanaid was irrelevant to Matt now, since he'd already resolved not to turn Chester over to them. He planned to call them on Monday morning and formally drop the case. He'd come up with some excuse for doing so, he had the whole rest of the weekend to think of one.

Their current host, Chester's girlfriend, Kendra was a petite and thin woman with short cropped black hair. Matt noted her resemblance to Chester's ex-wife, Britney. Aside from the fact that Britney was Asian and Kendra appeared to be a Latina, they were remarkably similar physically in many respects. Chester certainly had a definite 'type' that he preferred when it came to his choice of women.

"So we've told you who we are, now maybe you'd care to explain why you're on the run and how you came to make such an interesting friend?" Matt asked.

Chester found it much easier to psychically read animals than people, but his powers were developed enough to tell him that he could trust Matt and Earl, so he took a deep breath and started talking.

"Well, you know that the company I work for, Humanaid is involved in disaster relief right?" Matt and Earl both nodded. "They stockpile medical and other kinds of relief supplies in warehouses all around the country. These warehouses are always located conveniently *near* the disaster zones, but never *inside* them. The fact that they can quickly get these resources to the people who need them is the key to their success. But nobody ever thinks to ask how they always know exactly where to put these warehouses. If anyone bothered to look into it, they'd find out that these warehouses were first rented out and stocked only a few weeks before disaster struck. That's because Humanaid can predict the future, and profit off of it, all thanks to me and my friend Coathuan."

"So you're telling me that the Mothman here can actually predict the future?" Earl interjected.

"He does have a reputation as a harbinger of doom in the legends, so it makes sense when you think about it." Matt told his friend.

"Exactly!" Chester agreed, "Coathuan's people somehow eat the energy of negative emotions like fear, pain and suffering. They developed the ability to sense impending disaster as a way of locating their next meal."

Matt digested the information. The idea of using the Mothman's predictions to profit off of future disasters was as brilliant as it was insane. Matt bet that the people behind Humanaid were making money off of this foreknowledge in lots of other ways too aside from just disaster relief, like in real estate and insurance. There were lots of ways that someone with a bit of money to invest could make a fortune by knowing what communities would be hit by tragedy and when, if you stopped to think about it for a moment.

"So Humanaid used the Mothman to predict the future and get rich off of this knowledge, and you were what? Some kind of an interpreter for him?" Matt asked.

"Yes. Coathuan can read our minds easily enough, but he can only make himself understood by 'talking' to another psychic. His mind is so alien that even most other psychics have trouble making sense of his messages. That's why they needed someone used to dealing with the minds of completely different species."

Earl smiled broadly, all the pieces were starting to fit together now. "Like a pet psychic!"

Chester smiled too and did a little bow before continuing his tale. "When Humanaid hired me, they swore me to secrecy. They told me that Coathuan was an alien visitor to our world who wanted to help humanity by predicting upcoming tragedies. They said that while we couldn't prevent any of the bad things which would happen in the future, we *could* greatly mitigate the damage by quickly getting disaster relief to people who needed it desperately. It sounded wonderful to me. We were going to be helping people and they were going to be paying me a ridiculously generous salary to guarantee my silence. Plus I got to work with an alien being! That might scare most people, but to me it was an incredibly fascinating opportunity. How could I refuse? It sounded like it was the kind of thing I'd been waiting for my entire life! Unfortunately, I had no idea what kinds of terrible things they were doing to keep Coathuan alive." A dark cloud seemed to cast itself over Chester's demeanor as he said that last sentence.

"You can't keep on blaming yourself. You didn't know!" Kendra pleaded, and took his hand. He glared at her.

"Can't I? I'm a professional psychic! It's true that I can't read people as well as I can animals, but I still knew that my bosses were keeping things from me, that they weren't completely trustworthy, but I chose to ignore my instincts because I wanted their money so badly." He said bitterly.

"If you'd asked too many questions, they would've killed you just like they did with the guy before you!" Kendra reminded him.

"Whoa, let's back up a minute here," Matt interrupted, "what kinds of things were they doing to keep the Mothman alive?"

"Isn't it obvious?" Earl said darkly. "He's already explained that the Mothman feeds off of negative emotions. They were feeding him by torturing people, weren't they?"

Chester nodded grimly. "Yes. Coathuan can predict large-scale future suffering from thousands of miles away and even months into the future, but he has to be quite close to the event to be able to actually absorb it as food. He couldn't feed off any of these disasters without being physically present. They weren't about to risk shipping their cash cow around the country, so instead they started kidnapping people who they didn't think would be missed, held them prisoner and did unspeakable things to them. Coathuan wasn't allowed to tell me about it. He was told that if he did, they'd have me killed, and my blood would be on his hands. He knew they meant business because the first guy who did my job figured out what was going on. He knew that Coathuan wasn't a guest, that he was a prisoner, and that people were being hurt to feed him. When he confronted them about it, they killed him right in front of Coathuan. That's the one problem with their plan. It's difficult to lie to a real psychic. Fortunately for them, some of us are really good at lying to ourselves when large sums of money are involved."

"So how did you get wise to their scheme?" Matt inquired.

"They murdered someone in front of me too. A girl they'd captured escaped and ran into the room where I have my sessions with Coathuan looking for a way out. I recognized her from the news as a college student that had disappeared. I was going to help her, but they found her first and shot her! Then they gave me the week off hoping I'd just forget about the whole thing like nothing had ever happened." Both his voice and his body were trembling, he was obviously reliving the traumatic experience.

"So you decided to liberate your friend here so they couldn't do it anymore?" Earl asked.

"Yeah. I knew they could replace me, but I figured he'd be a lot harder to replace. Plus he really is my friend and it was obvious now that he wasn't there voluntarily. I wanted to give him his freedom."

"How the heck did you manage to free him?" Matt wondered.

"It was actually stupidly easy. I went back to my job late at night and told the security guard that I'd left something of mine up in the room where I talk with Coathuan. All the guards know me and trust me, so they didn't even bother to search me. Once we were up there together, I pulled a gun on him and forced him to release Coathuan. We knocked him out and made a run for it. We've been on the run since then. I hated to leave my dogs behind, but I knew Britney would find them and take care of them after I didn't show up to get Vicki. We came here because I'd already told Kendra everything the night that they murdered that poor girl. She was the one who encouraged me to take action, she gave me the strength to do the right thing."

Kendra took his hand and smiled. "They've been hiding out here ever since. It seemed like the perfect place. I don't have any nearby neighbors and not many people know that we're dating, or how serious we are about each other. He hasn't even told his own mother yet for some reason." There was a playful bit of accusation in her tone as she spoke that last part, and Chester blushed slightly.

"But where does Coathuan come from? How did he get here on Earth to begin with?" Earl wondered.

"I'm surprised you don't know already. The Men in Black are heavily associated with the early Mothman sightings." Matt said as he took a sip of his coffee. *How many cups has he had today?* Earl wondered, *and why isn't he running to the bathroom every five minutes?* Coffee tended to have that unfortunate kind of effect on Earl.

"From what I recall, the ABC did investigate those initial Mothman reports. In fact, many of the UFO sightings recorded at the time were really misidentified ABC reconnaissance craft. But the ABC never succeeded in capturing the Mothman and were never able to figure out exactly what it was or if it was even real," he informed them.

"Wait, are you telling me that you're one of the Men in Black?" Chester asked in an awestruck tone.

"Not anymore, but I used to be. And for the record, it's called the ABC, not the Men in Black. Nowadays I'm just a humble PI and I like it that way."

"No wonder nothing fazes you guys! What about you? Are you an ex-ABC guy too?" He asked Matt.

"My story is a little more complicated than that. Let's just say that I've got lots of friends in weird places, *very* weird places."

"You still didn't explain where the Mothman comes from," Earl reminded Chester.

"Oh yeah. Sorry. I guess it's another dimension. He sensed an upcoming catastrophe in our world when he was still back home and crossed over through some kind of a dimensional rift that links our world to his. We can't see it, but his people can and sometimes they come over here for a bite to eat. When he crossed over, it was at a place where someone, he doesn't know who, but I think it's the government, is somehow holding this dimensional gateway open all the time. The place looked like a military base and there were all these scientists there studying the gateway. I saw it in Caothuan's memories. They captured him and brought him to Humanaid."

Earl considered his words. "That dimensional rift sounds like what the ABC calls the Scar. It's a portal to other dimensions that's the source of lots of the weird stuff here in New Jersey, well, on the whole upper east coast really!"

"Oh, so that's where Snookie and the Situation are really from! It all makes sense now." Matt joked, referencing some of the stranger cast members from the notorious reality series *Jersey Shore.*

Kendra laughed. "God, I hate those clowns, they give us such a bad name and they're not even from Jersey, they're from Staten Island!"

"Or somewhere...*beyond!*" Matt couldn't drop the joke until the dead horse had been completely flogged.

"The place you described sounds like the ABC facility in Ong's Hat. I did some training there once. They've been studying the nature of the Scar at that place for years now," Earl told them.

"You know where it is?" Chester asked excitedly. "We've been trying to figure that out so we can get him back home! When Coathuan tells me about a disaster that's about to strike, we can usually figure out where it's at despite the language barrier by analyzing local landmarks, but the place where this portal is at was just someplace out in the middle of the woods, so exactly where it is has been puzzling us for days! We have to get him back home before Humanaid finds us! Also, he's not feeling very well, he hasn't had much to eat in days. He can feed off of the fear that local animals feel as they're hunted and killed, but we're afraid to let him out for very long, we don't want him to be seen and attract attention. He told me that the strange necklace he's wearing connects him to a gun that has a curse on it which makes people use it to kill. He can absorb the trauma from those deaths, but the gun isn't used often enough to keep him very well nourished. I'm afraid that he'll starve if he doesn't get home soon."

"It's been more than a few years since I've been there, but I'm pretty sure I could find it again. Unfortunately, the place will be crawling with security, it won't be easy to get in." Earl warned them.

"And we can't use any of our Guild connections to get them inside either," Matt added. "if the ABC turned him over to Humanaid once, they'd probably do it again. Besides, I don't trust the ABC anymore since my buddy Bronson McDowell retired from running it."

Earl was confused as to why the ABC had given him to Humanaid in the first place, or what those two ex-cons, Swan and Keith, had to do with all of this.

"I agree, but it still wouldn't hurt to have the help of some magic users that we know we can trust on this one. Maybe Randy or Keisha or Wendy or April could simply do a spell to teleport him past security and straight to the portal?" Earl suggested.

"Magic users?" Chester asked in surprise. "You guys know real life wizards too?"

"Witches mostly, but yeah, we do. I told you I had lots of friends in weird places, didn't I?" Matt replied, then turned to Earl, "That's some good thinking, pal! One of our magic-using buddies could send Mothman right to the portal and get us out before anyone even knew what had happened! I'm gonna give one of them a call right now!"

Matt produced a device from his coat pocket that looked something like a walkie talkie, only not as large and chunky. This was a Guild communicator, a kind of advanced satellite phone tuned into the special frequencies only used by the Guilds. First he tried Randy, his original partner in the detective agency and a powerful wizard. The communicator simply made a high pitched squealing noise when he tried to use it.

"This thing must be busted, it's not working right," he reported. Fortunately, all the people Earl had just mentioned also had cell phones and Matt had their numbers. He dialed Randy but there was no answer. Next he tried Keisha Bright, a young woman who had been Randy's apprentice. No luck there either. He tried to call Wendy Sommardahl, Randy's mentor and the former head of the Temple of the Old Gods. No answer. Lastly, he called Wendy's wife, the formidable witch April Sommardahl. Again, there was no answer.

Earl watched him end his last call. "No joy, huh?" As if on cue, Earl's own phone buzzed. He pulled it out and glanced at it. He chuckled. "Ironically, Britney finally texted me back about letting us into Chester's place to look for clues!"

"Somehow, I don't think that's going to be necessary anymore." Matt smirked, "Duh! I'll bet I know why they're not answering! There's some kind of a big wizard thing going on at Elysium this weekend. Some kid that Clark Kismet has been mentoring is graduating or whatever they call it. Randy told me all about it."

"Clark Kismet is still alive?" Earl asked incredulously. "That guy must be over 200 years old by now!"

"He looked younger than I did the last time I saw him!" Matt answered, "and that was about five years ago!"

"So what do we do now? How do we get Coathuan onto that base without the help of your magical friends?" Chester wondered.

"You know, the Scar does naturally open back up and close again somewhat regularly. And it isn't just located in Ong's Hat, it runs over the sky all along the entire northeastern seaboard. Mothman could just wait until it opens again and fly home through it then." Earl said.

"And when will that be?" Kendra asked.

"Impossible to say, but Chester said he could see it, so he should be able to recognize when it's open if he keeps an eye out for it," Earl replied.

"Unless it opens up in the next day or so, I don't know that Coathuan can stand to wait any longer. He's getting so weak and it's starting to affect his mind. You saw how confused he was just trying to get out the back door earlier!"

Matt let out a long breath, "I don't know yet, but somehow, we'll get him to that portal." Matt swore, despite the fact that he had absolutely no fucking clue as to how he was going to actually accomplish that.

Interlude:

Randy felt a sudden vibration in the pocket of his gray robes as he watched Mark mount the dias.

In his mind, he could feel who the call was from without even looking at the phone. He instinctively knew it was from Matt, and he was in deep trouble. He could feel his distress, even an ocean and a sea away.

Standing beside him, Clark Kismet leaned in closer towards him.

"Don't even think of answering that call!" He hissed with uncommon gravitas.

"But—"

"I'm sorry that your friend has gotten mixed up in this, but we must have faith that it will work out for the best," the older wizard said firmly.

Randy turned to Wendy who stood on his other side, "Mistress, he wouldn't call me at a time like this unless he was in over his head!"

Wendy shook her head. "Papa is right. We must have faith."

"Faith is a trap, you taught me that," Randy said somewhat petulantly.

"But not always. That is the Paradox of Life," April, who stood next to her wife Wendy, affirmed.

Clark nodded sagely. "Don't worry, m'boy. Things are unfurling in much the way I have foreseen. My visions are rare, but accurate—usually. How can our friends ever learn to stand on their own if we're always rushing off to their rescue? Now pipe down. This is Mark's moment and we mustn't ruin it with all these useless fears."

Clark's words and especially his comment about his visions only "usually" being accurate did little to calm Randy, but when he stopped listening to his anxieties and searched his intuition, he could see the truth behind them and he breathed a little easier, feeling not quite so guilty for letting the call go to voicemail.

Chapter Fourteen: Under Siege

Matt poured himself yet *another* cup of coffee as he racked his brains trying to figure out a way to get them into the ABC base without getting them all killed. A sudden bit of inspiration hit him and he set his cup down long enough to pick up his phone and call one more person, someone he was sure would answer.

Earl watched Matt talking animatedly to someone on his phone from across the kitchen, then his gaze fell upon the Mothman, or Coathuan, as Chester preferred to call him. Earl was surprised to find that he was already starting to take the presence of the strange creature for granted. He was even getting used to those piercing, spooky eyes of his. His ruminations were cut short by the sounds of squealing brakes and slamming car doors from somewhere outside.

Kendra's eyes grew wide as saucers. "Did you hear that?"

"Sounds like there's someone outside!" Chester stood up in alarm.

"More like several someones!" Earl added as he pulled his concealed pistol from its holster, and crossed over to the nearest window. He parted the curtains slightly and cautiously peered out of one side. What he saw there made his heart sink.

"Fuck! It looks bad! There's lots of cars outside, they've got the place surrounded, and they're all armed!" He reported.

"CHESTERFIELD XAVIER! WE KNOW YOU'RE IN THERE!" A voice thundered from outside. Earl thought it sounded like Mr. Swan. "WE HAVE YOU SURROUNDED! SURRENDER YOURSELF AND OUR GUEST AND WE WILL LET YOU AND YOUR FRIENDS LIVE!"

Coathuan chittered away in his weird alien language fearfully, and his antennae twitched spasmodically.

"Great! How did they find us?" Matt complained as he ended his call, putting his phone away and pulling out his own gun, a jet black 9mm.

As if in reply, a new voice blasted them. This time, it sounded as if it was Mr. Keith. "MATT SPIKE! THIS IS OFFICIAL ABC BUSINESS! DO NOT ATTEMPT TO INTERFERE, AND YOU AND YOUR PARTNER WILL REMAIN UNHARMED!"

"So, the ABC is in cahoots with Humanaid on this whole scam! I suspected as much!" Matt said angrily.

"I didn't want to believe that my old agency had become this corrupt, but obviously it has!" Earl said sadly. "At least this explains how they found us, the ABC can easily tap into any cell phone, they've probably been listening to us all along!"

"Damn, I'll bet you're right!" Matt swore.

"Everybody, listen up! Turn off your phones! Pull out the battery if it's an Android, if it's an iPhone, put it in the fridge." Earl ordered. The group quickly followed his unusual commands without question.

"Why hire us in the first place?" Matt wondered aloud now that they presumably had some privacy. "They've got an army of their own investigators, and all kinds of high tech spy doodads! They wouldn't need us for something like this!" Matt wondered.

Earl smiled, "I guess they just really think we're that good!"

"I'm flattered!" Matt replied sarcastically.

"Those guys out there can't possibly be ABC. They're not wearing nearly enough black, and I swear one of those cars is red!" Earl realized. "They're probably just working with the ABC."

"Humanaid security, then?" Matt speculated.

Earl shrugged "Makes sense, who else would it be?"

"Good, we stand a better chance against them. At least we don't have to worry about any ray guns."

"You're not actually going to try and fight them are you? If they surrounded my house we've gotta be hopelessly outnumbered, it's suicide!" Kendra shouted.

"It would be suicide to surrender to them!" Matt argued back. "They're obviously lying through their teeth! If they killed the last guy who found out their dirty little secret, they sure as hell won't spare us!"

Chester placed a hand on her shoulder. "He's right. We have to fight, it's the only chance we have."

"It's not much of a chance!" Kendra complained.

"That might be true, but I'd rather go down fighting, wouldn't you? Maybe take a few of those bastards down with us?" Earl asked her.

Before she could answer, Matt looked at Chester pointedly. "Hey, remember that gun you used when you freed Mothman? You wouldn't happen to still have it around would you?"

Chester grinned. "I do! It's upstairs! It's actually Kendra's gun, for self defense. I'll go get it!" With that, he ran from the room.

Matt smiled at Kendra. "See? Our odds are improving already!"

"Hardly!" She sighed. "You'd better let me do the shooting, Ron can't hit the blind side of a barn."

"It's your gun, isn't it?" Matt replied nonchalantly.

"So what's the plan?" Earl asked Matt.

"I'm thinking we can send our buddy Mothman here out the front door. While he's distracting them, making it look like he's surrendering, we all make a mad dash for Kendra's car that's parked right next to the door over there. They won't shoot Mothman, they need him alive, and he can just fly away and follow us in the car from the air. You're still strong enough to fly, right?" Matt asked the nervous cryptid.

Cauthuan nodded his head. Matt wasn't sure how he managed to do that since he didn't have a visible neck, but somehow, he did. Chester returned from upstairs, gasping for breath. Kendra held her hand out expectantly and he gave her the gun without argument, he knew he was a terrible shot. She checked that it was still loaded and took the safety off.

Kendra had to hand it to Matt, his plan sounded like it had a slight chance of actually working. "Where do we drive to?"

Matt frowned. "I'm not sure. My best thought was that we try to lose them on the road, then go to that portal in Ong's Hat. Hopefully, the last place they'd expect us to be going is their own headquarters! You'd better give your keys to Earl since he's the only one who knows the way."

"I don't like these odds." Kendra said sourly.

"Neither do I, but what other options do we have? If you've got a better idea I'd love to hear it, lady!"

Her silence spoke volumes. So did the fact that the next thing that she did was to pull the keys out of her pocket and toss them to Earl.

Outside the house, Mr. Kieth looked nervously at Mr. Swan, who, as always, was dressed in a snappy teal suit.

"How long should we give them?"

"However long it takes. We can't risk shooting up the place, we might accidentally hit the Mothman, which defeats the entire point of this exercise."

As it would turn out, they wouldn't have much longer to wait. One of the various security guards who was making up the gauntlet around the house had thought that he saw the glint of a gun barrel in one of the upstairs windows. In actuality, it was simply the reflection of the setting sun as it briefly emerged from the clouds. In his heightened state of anxiety, the jumpy guard decided he wasn't taking any chances.

"They're pointing a gun out the window!" He shouted in a trembling voice and immediately opened fire on that window. The other guards, who were all sheltering behind their car doors with their guns pointed at the place, followed suit, firing wildly into the building before them.

"Stop!" Mr.Teal shrieked. "Cease fire!" It was no good, nobody could hear him. Then he recalled that he'd given the megaphone to Mr. Keith, he tore the device from his diminutive companion in a rage. If only he could use his magic! He wouldn't need a stupid megaphone, he could amplify his voice with a simple spell. If he could use his magic, he wouldn't have needed to hire a detective, and he certainly wouldn't need all these gun toting morons to deal with this situation! But alas, as long as he had to wear the dampener, he was as weak and helpless as they were. He brought the megaphone to his mouth. "CEASE FIRE! I REPEAT - CEASE FIRE!"

But it was no good, even with the megaphone, he couldn't be heard over the sound of all the gunfire.

He had officially lost control of the entire scenario.

"Hit the deck!" Matt screamed as he did a belly flop onto the hard, stone kitchen floor. His body screamed in pain, but when he felt a bullet whiz by the spot where he'd just been standing he was grateful for his quick thinking.

The others got as low to the ground as they could, even Coathuan, although his large wings hung over him vulnerably. Matt crawled over to the nearest window and lifted up his hand to knock out the glass with the barrel of the gun. A few shards rained down on him, he brushed them off and crouched up high enough to see out the window and choose a target before opening fire. Earl bent down low and ran over to take up a position on the opposite side of the same window and began shooting too. On the other side of the room, Kendra scuttled towards the back door, knocked out a pane of glass with her gun and started shooting too.

Matt flattened himself against the wall as someone outside returned fire through the window, and took the opportunity to reload. He looked at Earl apologetically.

"This might really be the end, old buddy. I'm sorry I got us into this mess."

"Don't be sorry! These past few years working with you have been some of the best of my life. If it wasn't for you, I'd still be working for those assholes outside shooting at us! I think I'd rather die with my boots on anyway!" Earl told him earnestly. He meant every word of it. Earl didn't really want to die at all, but he knew that Matt, despite his many flaws, was a good man and he could think of much worse ways to go than fighting by his side.

A lump formed in Matt's throat. "Thanks, man." Matt wasn't so sure that he wanted to die with his boots on. This was never how he envisioned his death. Not that he spent much time envisioning his own death, in fact, he tried to avoid doing so as often as possible. He couldn't believe that he might never see Naomi again, or his kids, not in the flesh anyway. He knew from his previous adventures that death wasn't the end, but this fact still brought him little comfort. He liked his current life, and he wasn't ready to give it up just yet.

He gritted his teeth as he finished slapping another clip into his gun. He took aim outside the window again, screaming in rage at his assailants, at the awful unfairness of the entire situation. At first it looked like all his shots had missed, but he hadn't been aiming for the gunmen, he was targeting the gas tank on the nearest car. It exploded spectacularly, sending forth a fireball that engulfed the closest shooters. The flaming wreck flipped over and landed on the next nearest vehicle.

"Nice one!" Earl whistled appreciatively.

Their joy was to be short-lived.

From behind them, they heard Kendra cry out in pain, followed by a heart rending scream from Chester. When Matt turned his head to see what had happened, his eyes were assaulted by the awful vision of Kendra lying splayed out on her kitchen floor, her head had exploded from the back and her blood was spreading towards him like an unstoppable crimson tide of death. Chester was sobbing and rocking back and forth over the pitiful sight. The practical part of Matt wanted to shout at Chester to pick up her gun and shoot back, but he didn't have the heart to do it. *Let the man have his moment, we'll probably all be joining her soon enough and I don't want the last thing I ever did in my life to be yelling at someone for mourning their dead girlfriend!* He thought morosely.

Then Matt noticed something else. The Mothman looked unusually excited, and his antennae were moving back and forth in a peculiar, rhythmic way. His red eyes were glowing, illuminated from within by some nameless force. Matt realized that he was probably feeding off of all of the death and destruction exploding all around them. He couldn't help but feel a wave of revulsion wash over him.

He couldn't believe he was about to die because of that *thing*.

Chapter Fifteen: The Convergence

Back in the wooded expanse of the Edwin B.Forsythe National Wildlife Refuge, the Mothwoman T'zzitch Morgatchu was shrieking. It was an ear splitting noise which frightened the surrounding birds, making them explode out of the trees and up into the skies. The members of the JSPS covered their ears to protect themselves from the dreadful sound.

"What's gotten into her?" Dennis shouted to be heard over the deafening din.

"She's found her mate! He's scared! She can feel his fear—and use it to locate him! I know where he is too now, through my link with her! I can bring us all there!"

"What? You're talking about teleporting us there aren't you?" Dennis obviously wasn't too pleased, "We can't leave now! What about all my expensive trail cams? And Tim is supposed to come back and pick us up soon, remember?"

"We'll come back for that stuff later! We have to go *now* while the trail is hot! He needs our help! He's in some kind of danger!" She argued back. Dennis knew that she'd already made up her mind and there was no point in further argument.

"Everyone, link hands now!" Athena commanded. They all obeyed, even the Mothwoman, who had finally stopped making that terrible racket once she seemed to understand that Athena wanted to bring her straight to her missing mate. Dennis took one of Morgatchu's strange hands, being careful to avoid her sharp claws. Miranda took the other one.

Athena started reciting a chant that was already ancient when the first pyramid was erected in Egypt, and within an instant, they were gone from the woods, as if they'd never been there.

Athena and the others reappeared on the front lawn of a house under attack. It was surrounded by various cars of all shapes, sizes and colors. There were men taking cover behind the doors of these cars who were all shooting at the building. Near the back of the building there was a thick plume of black smoke billowing up from a pair of burning cars. Bodies were strewn around the wreckage here and there.

It was a total war zone!

And she had just stupidly teleported her best friends right into it. She knew that the Mothman was in some kind of trouble, but she never imagined it would be anything like this! Now she understood what that awful feeling of dread which had been plaguing her all week was about. She had been feeling this event rushing towards her, and the fear that even with all her newfound powers, she still couldn't protect the people most dear to her. For a moment she considered running away, teleporting them out of this chaos. She pushed those feelings aside. She had made a promise to help Morgatchu and she intended to keep it. She had a job to do now and no time for self-sabotaging doubts.

Thankfully, they had materialized far behind the gunmen, near the treeline across the street and nobody had noticed them yet.

"Take cover in those woods behind us—hurry!" she ordered. The others didn't need much encouragement. Within seconds they'd all found a tree to hide behind and were cautiously peering out from behind those same trees at the violent scene unfolding just a few hundred feet in front of them.

Miranda was the first to say something. "Where's Lars? I was holding his hand when we left and then he was just...gone."

"Oh shit! You lost him, didn't you? I told you teleporting was a bad idea!" Dennis accused.

Athena felt awful about Lars, she prayed that he wasn't lost forever in the *Place Between Places* that they passed through when teleporting. Then she recalled that the crystal amulets all the members of the JSPS wore to protect themselves from malevolent spirits also linked them together. She closed her eyes and touched her own crystal, reaching out with her mind for Lars. She could feel him on the other end of the connection, he was lost and confused, but still very much alive. Perhaps later she'd try to trace his location using the amulet, but that would have to wait for another time.

"Don't worry. He's okay. I'll pick him up later." This seemed to satisfy the others for the moment.

"What the hell is happening over there? Where's Mothwoman's husband at? Dennis asked.

"Morgatchu says she can feel him somewhere inside of the house that those guys are busy lighting up." Athena informed him.

"Great! He's probably gonna be full of holes by the time they're done with that place!"

"That's why I'm going to stop them."

"What? How?" Miranda asked fearfully. "I know that Clark has been teaching you some really amazing things, but you can't possibly take on an entire army by yourself!"

"Oh yeah? Just watch me! Besides, Morgatchu has my back! You guys hang back here, try to stay out of trouble, and enjoy the show."

And with that, she bolted out of the woods and towards the fight before the others, especially Dennis, could protest. Morgatchu silently lifted off the ground and flew along beside her. Athena was surprised to find herself smiling. She was equal parts terrified by what she was about to do, and exhilarated. She'd never cut loose with her powers before in the way she was planning on doing—it would be interesting to see what it was like....

Matt couldn't believe his eyes. He watched through the window as blue bolts of lightning struck some of the gunmen, sending them writhing to the ground. The lightning was coming from someone moving towards the house who was surrounded by a tall, transparent wall of emerald energy. He'd seen this kind of thing many times before. Magic users typically protected themselves with such impenetrable barriers when going into battle. But who was behind this particular shield? He couldn't really tell from this distance, it was definitely a woman. She almost looked like his friend Athena, but that was ridiculous wasn't it? Then a shrill sound pierced the air and Matt saw another Mothman flying towards the house, making that god awful sound. He supposed it was some sort of an alien battle cry. He watched as this new Mothman effortlessly picked up one of the gunmen, flew him high up into the air, then dropped him onto the windshield of a car. It swooped down again and impaled one of the attackers with some sort of a stinger, which Coathuan seemed to lack.

"Are you seeing what I'm seeing?" Earl asked in disbelief.

"I sure am!" Matt grinned. "The cavalry has arrived! We might just live through this one after all!"

"Then let's give 'em hell!" Earl cried as he fired a few more rounds out the window. Matt soon joined in.

All of this seemed to temporarily shake Chester out of his grief. As he saw their attackers starting to go down, he remembered a murder of crows that he'd befriended. He could sense this group of corvids nearby in his mind, curiously watching the conflict unfold from the safety of the nearby trees. In his mind, he asked them for help, and was soon rewarded by the sight of the dark flock swarming some of the shooters, mercilessly pecking at them. He fervently wished that whoever had shot Kendra was one of the men that his feathered friends were currently tearing apart.

"Damn! Are you doing that Chester? Are you secretly like Aquaman, except with birds or something?" Matt asked as he saw the unusual attack taking place out the window.

"Yes, but I can't just make any animal do what I want, I have to establish a rapport with them first before they'll consider helping me. For example, I've been feeding those birds for the past week."

Before Matt or Earl could comment further on this, Coathuan interrupted them by loudly repeating the strange call made by the other member of his species who'd been flying around outside. Coathuan was already looking far more robust, more energized by all the death and pain being unleashed around him. He stood up, stepped over Kendra's lifeless body and pulled the back door open so forcefully that he almost tore it off the hinges. This time he had no trouble getting out the door. He ducked down, tucked in his wings, stepped onto the back porch, spread his wings and took to the skies.

Athena really hoped she wasn't overdoing it. She wasn't actually *trying* to kill anyone, she just wanted to zap them with enough juice to knock them out, but it was hard to gauge how much to use. It wasn't like she'd actually had a chance to test out this kind of a spell on another person before. She winced as one of her lightning bolts burned a hole clean through one guy's guts.

Hmm, he's probably not going to live through that. She told herself that she shouldn't feel bad, after all, the men she was attacking were definitely firing at her with the intention of killing her, but she still couldn't help but feel a little guilty. It was actually pretty funny how frustrated and confused they looked as they fired over and over at the magical barrier surrounding her without any success. This was almost too easy for her, like shooting fish in a barrel. They couldn't hurt her, but she was free to do whatever she wanted to them. *'The Living Taser', that should be my superhero name. No, maybe 'the Electrifier'? Yeah I like that one better.* She decided.

A few feet in front of her, Morgatchu used her stinger to slice through another gunman, nearly tearing his head off with its razor sharp barbed end. His blood geysered out of his neck and splattered against Athena's magical barrier, dripping down the side of it.

Okay, now that's just gross! Her thoughts of disgust were jarringly interrupted by a feeling of pure joy which was suddenly emanating from Morgatchu. Athena looked up to see another Mothperson flying through the air. Morgatchu zoomed up towards him, and the two did a kind of elaborate dance around each other in the skies high above the conflict. She had finally been reunited with her mate!

Oh, isn't that sweet? Athena thought as she absentmindedly sent another bolt arcing towards a man to her left. A wet spot spread from his crotch as he lost control of his bladder under her electrical assault before crumpling to the ground, his body still twitching. Soon, Morgatchu and her mate were flying side by side, plucking gunmen from the ground only to release them from hundreds of feet up in the air.

When the mangled body of one of their victims landed in front of Athena she decided that "sweet" was probably not the right adjective to describe their reunion.

Athena heard a car engine from somewhere behind her. She whirled around to see an SUV racing down the road and pulling onto the grass. The vehicle looked absurdly like the one that Naomi Waters-Spike drove, even down to the bumper stickers, but that couldn't be could it? The driver's side door opened and a rather short person stepped out who was dressed from head to toe in a shiny blue suit of armor. It looked like something from out of the Middle Ages, only with sleeker, more futuristic lines. Their head was completely covered by a matching helmet. That wasn't the strangest thing about this new player though. No, the strangest thing was that there was a massive sword hovering in the air over their shoulder. The sword's blade looked like it was made out of a reddish glass or crystal.

Athena watched in fascination as this sword flew through the air and began smacking the nearest gunmen in the head with its handle, knocking them out cold. The armored newcomer remained next to the car they arrived in, but the sword was dancing all around the yard, taking out gunmen left and right. She found it peculiar that they weren't actually stabbing anyone with the sword. What they needed was a big club, not a sword.

Athena smiled. *Whoever they are, at least they seem to be on our side!*

Matt whooped in triumph. "There's my ace in the hole!"

"Is that really Naomi?" Earl asked in disbelief. He recognized her car of course, and the armor as being a suit bestowed upon Matt by a secret society called the Knights of Pendragon to help him in his duties as the Guardian of the Orb. He also recognized the flying sword he'd been given for the same reason, which was known as the *Vermilion Avenger*, but he'd never seen Naomi use any of these things before. He had no idea she could kick so much ass.

"It sure is!" Matt couldn't disguise the pride in his voice. Earl couldn't blame him, at this particular moment in time, he wanted to kiss Naomi too!

"So *that's* who you were calling!"

"Yeah, I was hoping she'd be able to help us break into that ABC base at Ong's Hat. She showed up right when we needed her! We're gonna have to get out of this house soon."

Earl didn't relish this idea. Although Naomi, the Mothpeople, and their unknown witch friend were making short work of their attackers, quite a few of them still remained. He had to hand it to them, these guys might not be ABC like they claimed to be, but they were still pretty tough. Most people would've fled in terror as soon as they came under attack from a magic user, not to mention a pair of cryptids.

"Why? What do you mean?"

Matt gestured out the window. Earl's eyes bulged in alarm at what he was indicating. The fire from the car he'd hit earlier had spread across the unkempt lawn and was getting closer and closer to the house with each passing second.

"Maybe blowing that gas tank wasn't such a hot idea after all?"

"Shit! This place is about to become an inferno! And it's still not safe for us out there yet!"

His point was neatly punctuated by a bullet which came whizzing past his face to bury itself in the wall across the room.

"Tell me about it," Matt smiled his lopsided smile, "caught between a rock and a hard place—that's the story of my life!"

Chapter Sixteen: Reunited And It Feels So Good

Mr. Swan didn't think anything could possibly get any worse once his men had refused to stop shooting at the house, and the people trapped inside, quite naturally, began shooting back.

He was wrong.

First, some witch appeared from out of nowhere and began using the classic lightning bolt spell (one of his personal favorites too) on his men. Then another Mothman started scooping them up into the air only to drop them back down to their deaths. As if that wasn't bad enough, *both* Mothmen started working together to kill his men in this way. The icing on the cake had been when someone showed up wielding the *Vermilion Avenger,* a legendary sword that Swan hadn't even believed was real up until now. He didn't know how he'd explain all of this to Balthazar. He'd be afraid of losing his job with Humanaid if it wasn't for the fact that they couldn't fire him or his companion on account of all the dirt they had on the Hazeltons. Blackmail, as it turns out, is an excellent way to maintain one's job security.

"Mr. Keith, I do believe that we can be of no further service in this situation." He said in a surprisingly calm manner considering the chaos exploding all around him. This wasn't because he had a knack for remaining cool in high pressure situations so much as it was that he was completely resigned to the fact that this assignment had devolved into an unsalvageable clusterfuck.

"Do I read you correctly? Are you suggesting a strategic withdrawal?" Mr. Keith asked eagerly.

"Yes, and with all due haste."

"Shall I announce it, or would you prefer to do the honors?" The smaller man indicated the megaphone Swan was still holding. Swan knew that the little fellow, who he'd often suspected of having a Napoleon complex, enjoyed having a large voice sometimes. Who was he to deny him such tiny pleasures?

"You can do it, for all the good it will do."

"Thank you," Mr. Keith smiled and took the megaphone from him. "It's important to always maintain the correct protocols, even when it seems futile. Anything less would be bad form."

"Yes, very bad form indeed!" Swan agreed as he took his car keys out of his pocket.

Mr. Keith put the megaphone up to his mouth. "ATTENTION! ALL HUMANAID FORCES! RETREAT IMMEDIATELY! RETURN TO HEADQUARTERS! I REPEAT—" but Mr.Keith would never have the opportunity to repeat his order. Before he could finish his sentence, one of the Mothmen, perhaps irritated by the sound of the megaphone, carried him off, high into the air and let go....

The unfortunate wizard landed a few inches in front of Mr. Swan, who uttered a cry of inarticulate fury upon seeing the dreadfully shattered state of his longtime friend and companion.

Swan needed no further urging. He turned and ran back to his car. He saw that several others were following his lead. Perhaps the diminished numbers of men shooting at the house now had made it easier to hear the latest megaphone announcement? Or maybe it was more likely that the men had recognized the encounter as being the hopeless bloodbath it had become and decided they'd had enough too? Whatever the case may be, the surviving men who hadn't already been shot, knocked unconscious, electrocuted, or dropped to their deaths were all now scrambling to get away. Some of them even had the presence of mind to grab their injured or unconscious comrades and haul them into their vehicles as they struggled to make their escape.

"They're all leaving! We've won!" Earl declared as he risked a glance out the window. He began coughing loudly as soon as he said it. The side of the house had already caught on fire and black smoke was beginning to fill the kitchen.

"Good! Let's get the fuck out of here before all this smoke does us in!" Matt said as he stood up and made for the back door. He was outside and gasping for air within seconds. Earl rose from where he'd been sheltering during the gunfight on the opposite side of the window to follow him. He moved past Chester, who was just sitting there despondently beside Kendra's body.

Earl paused in the doorway and turned back to face him. "C'mon Chester, we've gotta go!"

"I can't just leave her here to burn! Can you help me lift her?"

Earl frowned. Kendra was quite literally only useless dead weight now, but he couldn't blame Chester for wanting to preserve her body for a proper burial later on. He dutifully picked up one end of the corpse and helped the smaller man carry her out of the house, noting angrily how much blood he was getting all over his favorite dress shirt in the process, then hating himself for being so petty in the face of tragedy. Shirts could be replaced, but Chester had just lost the love of his life. Soon, they were joining Matt out on the back lawn near Kendra's car. He was grinning as he watched the last of their attackers' vehicles roaring down the road and away from the house. They set her body gently down on its hood.

"I can't believe we all made it out of that house alive. I really thought that was gonna be the end for us." Matt said as he watched the house continue to burn, the smoke still stinging his eyes and making them water. The pair of Mothpeople, Coathuan and Morgatchu landed next to the group.

"Where did this other Mothman come from?" Earl asked Chester, as much to satisfy his own curiosity as to distract the man from his palpable grief.

"It's his mate. She's been looking for him too." Chester said robotically, without looking at Earl. He couldn't take his eyes off of Kendra's lifeless form. *So much for distracting him from his mourning,* Earl thought sadly.

Matt raised an eyebrow at the idea that one of the Mothpeople was a woman, since he couldn't tell from looking at her. Aside from her stinger, having a slightly more diminutive build and a duller, lighter color she seemed identical to Coathuan.

Matt spied a woman behind a glowing green barrier slowly walking across the big lawn towards them.

"Time to find out who our secret savior is." He said and began striding towards the mystery woman. From behind her, he noticed Naomi running towards them too, the *Vermilion Avenger* now hovering over her shoulder.

I must be seeing things. That one guy over there looks just like Matt Spike, right down to that pretentious hat! Athena thought. The sound of feet from behind her drew her attention and she turned her head to see the armored person with the ridiculously big flying sword sprinting towards her. She could now see that this person was a woman, and a tiny one at that. As she drew nearer, the woman flipped up the visor on her helmet and Athena was greeted by a familiar face which made her stop dead in her tracks.

"*Naomi*? What the fuck? What are you doing here?"

"What the fuck indeed! I knew you were a little psychic, but I never dreamed that you were a witch too!"

"I'm not 'a little psychic' I'm a whole lot psychic, and I prefer to be called a sorceress!" Athena replied a little testily. She made her energy shield disappear with a gesture and a muttered word. She didn't need it anymore.

"Oh, sorry. Well if you know about the Guilds then I guess that the easiest way to explain all of this is that Matt and I are secretly the Guardians of the Orb. We've been given special weapons and armor like this to help us do that job. Matt ran into a little trouble on his latest case and called me in for some back up."

"The Guardians of the Orb?" Athena thought for a moment. "I think Clark mentioned that once. You guys hold onto the Orb of Thoth right?" Athena knew that this was a powerful magic item which prevented spells from being cast for miles around. Obviously Naomi didn't have it with her or she wouldn't have been able to use her magic when she'd arrived. That made her wonder who was guarding it at the moment.

For her part, Naomi was tempted to correct her and tell her that the Orb she guarded was actually the Orb of Sinister, which had replaced the original Orb of Thoth, but decided that such minor details didn't matter, especially at a time like this. Something Athena had just said had piqued her curiosity though.

"Yeah, that's us. You don't mean Clark Kismet do you?"

"Yeah, I'm his apprentice. You know him?"

"I do. He practically raised my friend Wendy. He loves to tell me all the things I got wrong in my *Magna Historia Mundi* volumes. He gives me copies back with sticky notes full of corrections on the pages. It's pretty annoying actually."

"I've met Wendy too, she's cool! So you really wrote all those books, huh?" Athena's head was spinning. She'd seen those *Magna Historia Mundi* books lying around Clark's home, but had never paid any attention to who the author was.

"I did. Did you say you're his apprentice? I thought his new apprentice was some young guy?"

"That's my brother Mark! They're initiating him this weekend. I'm kind of like Clark's secret, under the table apprentice."

Before Naomi could react to this latest revelation, Matt had caught up with them.

"Holy shit! Athena! That really was you! Thanks, you really saved our bacon by showing up when you did. So you're really a witch, huh?"

"Sorceress!" Athena and Naomi said in unison, then both chuckled.

"Sorceress, witch, whatever! I never understood the difference." Matt confessed irritably.

"There really isn't much of one. Sorceress just sounds cooler," Athena admitted."

"Guess what?" Naomi said "Athena knows Wendy! She's another one of Clark Kismet's apprentices."

"Damn, it's a small world, after all isn't it?" He gave Naomi a peck on the cheek. "Thanks for coming so quickly. You must've driven like a maniac."

"I don't know any other way to drive! Are you and Earl okay?"

"Yeah, but the lady who owns this place wasn't so lucky." Matt said grimly and looked meaningfully over at the car.

Athena followed his gaze. "Is that her? Take me to her, maybe I can do something for her with my magic."

Matt sighed, "Okay, but I'm afraid it's probably a little too late for that."

Earl watched as Matt and Naomi neared him, accompanied by the mysterious witch.

"Hey everyone, this is my friend Athena. She's the sorceress who just rescued us." Matt announced when they were within earshot. Earl muttered a greeting.

"A sorceress?" Chester repeated hopefully, "can you use your powers to help her out?" He pointed at Kendra.

"That's what I'm here to see about." Athena walked over to where Kendra's body was laid out and looked down at her appraisingly. Her heart sank at what she saw. Now she understood what Matt had meant. The poor woman was missing part of the back of her head and had already been dead for some time. Mercifully, her death had probably been instantaneous. Athena could use her magic to heal, but there were definite limits on this ability. It was certainly well beyond her powers to resurrect the dead. She didn't even sense Kendra's spirit lingering around the place, which was a good thing.

"I'm afraid it's too late for her. She's gone, there's nothing I can do for her." She said quietly.

Chester turned away from her, a pained expression on his face.

"Thanks for the assist." Earl said to Athena. "How did you know that we were in trouble?"

"I didn't. It's just a crazy coincidence that it turned out to be you guys. I was out in the woods looking for the Mothman and ended up befriending his wife. She sensed that he needed help, so I brought her here."

"You were *looking* for the Mothman?" Earl asked incredulously. "We just kind of blundered into ours."

"She's a paranormal investigator." Matt explained.

Athena proudly pointed to her JSPS tee shirt. Then she made a face! "Oh shit! That reminds me—Dennis and Miranda! They're still hiding out in the woods across the street! I'd better go check on them! I'll be right back!" She turned away and started running across the long yard towards the road.

Earl stepped closer to Matt as they watched Athena's hasty departure. "We need to talk about what our next move is gonna be. We can't hang around here all day next to a burning house! Sooner or later someone will notice all this smoke and call the authorities. I'm not in any mood to try to explain any of this to the police, are you?"

Naomi waved her hand over the yard turned battleground. "And we'd better figure it out soon! When those guys left, they took most of their own with them, but they missed a few of them. Pretty soon they'll start waking up and I don't expect they'll be any friendlier when they do!"

"Where can we go that's safe if the ABC really is in on this? It's virtually impossible to hide from them-I should know, I used to be one of them!" Earl complained.

"I don't know about that," Matt said as he rubbed his stubbly chin. "Chester managed to evade them for an entire week. Humanaid must not have the full resources of the ABC behind them, or they wouldn't have needed to hire us, or these goons. I think we're just dealing with some rogue elements within the ABC, not the entire organization. The problem is we don't know who's in on it and who isn't, so we can't go to *any* of them for help. I don't think we could call them for help even if we wanted to anyhow. I'm pretty sure they were jamming my Guild communicator earlier." Not that he had his communicator on him anymore anyway. He'd put it into the refrigerator of the house that was currently burning down along with his phone at Earl's urging. Naomi carried one too, but he assumed it would be jammed as well.

Coathuan began making lots of excited sounds in his bizarre alien tongue. Morgatchu joined in.

"What are they saying?" Earl asked Chester.

"They're telling me that it's important for Coathuan to get back home ASAP. He's needed urgently to defuse a situation which could lead to war on his world."

"Well, that decides it!" Matt said. "We'll return to our original plan of getting the Mothpeople to that portal at Ong's Hat. I still think that the last thing our enemies will be expecting is for us to come to them."

Naomi nodded. "If Athena is still willing to help us out, we've got a pretty good chance of success."

"That was so cool!" Dennis gushed as Athena got within earshot. "I captured the whole thing on video! My wife-the total ass kicker! Too bad I can't share the footage with the world, but we can still enjoy it!"

"Yeah! You were amazing! Remind me to never get on your bad side!" Miranda laughed. "I had no idea you could do any of that!"

Athena flushed a bright red color in response to their adulation—and also at the fact that since she'd inadvertently killed at least one of the men she'd zapped, her husband had just made an accidental snuff film. Not that she was about to tell him that. It would destroy the whole vibe of the moment.

"Yeah, well I didn't want to risk scaring any of you off by showing you how powerful I've become. I guess the cat's out of the bag now. Don't worry, underneath it all I'm still the same old Athena I've always been. I promise not to smite anyone with lightning unless they really piss me off!" She was trying to turn it into a joke, but both Dennis and Miranda knew her well enough to tell that a part of her was truly frightened of how she'd be perceived by them now. Athena had a deep need to be seen as just a normal woman, although she'd always been far more than that. Her exceptional nature was something which everyone around her appreciated except for herself.

Dennis gave her a long hug. "You could never scare me away. You should know that by now," he whispered seriously as he looked into her eyes. "For better or for worse, remember? I'm in it for the long haul."

"That goes for me too," Miranda added. Dennis waved her over.

"Group hug!" He declared playfully. Soon the three were all locked in a somewhat awkward embrace. Athena broke the group up and lifted up her glasses to wipe a tear from her eye.

"You guys are the best! I definitely would've turned to the dark side by now without you two."

"So what is this all about? Who were those guys you were fighting? Who's that character with the big flying sword and the cool armor?" Dennis asked breathlessly.

"You'll never believe this, but that's Naomi, Matt's wife! He's here too. They're part of the Guilds, just like Clark is. They even know him too!"

To her surprise, Dennis took this shocking news in rather calmly. "It makes sense. I had the feeling they were holding things back from us during dinner. So that's what all that 'we can't tell you or we'd have to kill you' stuff was all about!"

"You noticed that too, huh?"

"It's one of the reasons why I was so bothered afterwards. The idea that they had secrets they couldn't trust us with made me realize just how far we'd drifted apart as friends."

"Well stop being so butthurt about it and come on over and say hello." She started to lead them over to the others, who were still gathered a little too close to the burning house for Miranda's comfort. As a realtor, she also hated to see such a sterling example of a Dutch Colonial going up in flames. They sure don't make 'em like that anymore.

The trio of paranormal investigators picked their way across the tall grass of the wide lawn, having to occasionally step over the odd mangled corpse or unconscious gunman. Athena spotted one of them groggily starting to come to and groping around in the grass for his fallen weapon. She quickly gave him another jolt of electricity, almost as an afterthought.

"You still haven't explained who these men are and what this is all about." Miranda reminded her.

"That's because I honestly don't know." Athena confessed in embarrassment. "In all the excitement I forgot to ask! Let's see what Matt has to say about it when we get back over there."

In short order, the two groups were reunited. Introductions were made and explanations were hastily given. Naomi stripped off her armor and gave it to Matt, and it miraculously adjusted itself to fit him. Matt then filled them in on his plan to get the two Mothpeople to Ong's Hat, and Athena agreed to help get them there. She offered to teleport them if Earl would open his mind to her to show her where the ABC base was, since she had to have a clear idea of this for her teleportation spell to work.

Dennis delicately reminded her that she'd just lost Lars and that teleportation spells did not appear to be her forte. Everyone then agreed that perhaps it would be much safer to simply drive there. They split themselves up into two groups for the ride, divided along gender lines. The four men would drive in Matt's car, with Earl behind the wheel to guide the convoy. The three ladies would ride with Naomi in her SUV. The Mothpeople would fly high overhead and try to remain out of sight as best they could, which would be a little easier now that the sun was finally starting to sink below the horizon.

It was difficult for Chester to leave Kendra behind. He was especially afraid that the fire would consume her body before any firefighters inevitably arrived. Athena, who was a fan of cremation, but not of wanton environmental destruction, was more concerned about the blaze spreading to the nearby woods. She impressed them all by casting a spell which created a torrential rain centered squarely over the house, extinguishing the inferno with uncanny speed.

Matt fetched the tarp that had been concealing Chester's car from the garage and delicately placed it over Kendra's body.

"I barely knew the woman, but from what little I saw, she was brave and she deserved way better than this." The detective said in a subdued voice.

They allowed Chester a few moments to say his final goodbyes before he joined Matt, Earl, and Dennis in the lead car.

"Let's get the hell out of here." The pet psychic growled.

And so it came to pass that the unusual group left behind the smoldering remains of a once handsome Dutch Colonial and a lawn strewn with the bodies of their enemies for an uncertain future as the sun finally gave up and surrendered to the onyx darkness of the night.

Unbeknownst to them, that future was made all the more uncertain for them by the fact that they'd forgotten to tell the newcomers that their foes could tap into their phones.

The Hazeltons were still listening in, and thus were well aware of their plans. They were already busying themselves preparing various countermeasures.

The night of the Mothman had only just begun...

Act Three

Chapter Seventeen: An Eldritch Horror From Beyond The Edge of Human Memory

Mr. Swan and the two remaining cars of men who hadn't already turned in their notice after today's fiasco swerved to a stop in the middle of the deserted country road. They quickly arranged their vehicles so they were completely blocking the road and Swan reached into his back seat. His long, manicured fingers found the handle of a stainless steel briefcase and with a grunt he hauled it onto the front passenger seat and snapped it open.

Inside the foam padded interior were very two different kinds of magical devices. One was a golden headband which could be used to rearrange someone's memories. Balthazar had given it to him to use on the pair of detectives when they surrendered, but of course, that opportunity had yet to arise. It was still the plan to alter the memories of the Guardians if they surrendered or could be captured. The other item was a clear, crystalline egg about the size of a pineapple. This was something he'd been given to use strictly as a last resort, only if things truly went bad. It was the magical equivalent of the nuclear option. However, when things had gone to shit earlier, he'd been in such a state of mental distress that he'd completely forgotten he had it. When Gordon Hazleton (who almost never deigned to deal with him directly) had called him with new orders as he sped away from the disastrous siege on the Dutch Colonial, he'd explicitly instructed him to now use this egg as a bargaining tool.

Swan could see a tiny, green blob of a creature squirming around inside the egg. He muttered a quick prayer to the Gods that he wouldn't have to actually use the thing contained inside. He grabbed the egg and stepped out of the car. According to his sources, his quarry was currently speeding along Route 72 and would be turning onto this road, Magnolia soon enough. The four men who'd been desperate or stupid enough to remain in this fight took up their positions behind their cars and pointed their guns out into the night. Swan looked fearful towards the skies. He felt vulnerable and exposed outside of his car like this. He hoped he wouldn't end up like poor Mr. Keith. If the Mothpeople decided to suddenly swoop down and grab him, he doubted that his men would be able to react in time to save him. There was nothing but an impenetrable, oppressive darkness overhead. No moonlight to give him any warning. He didn't know what he was more scared of, these moth creatures, or the monstrosity writhing within the crystal egg. Swan gulped nervously as he thought he saw two pairs of headlights approaching. The egg felt cold in his clammy grasp, despite the loathsome creature burning with nothing but pure hatred trapped within it.

"Jesus Christ! These guys really don't know when to quit!" Earl exclaimed as his headlights reflected off of the loud teal of Mr. Swan's suit. Swan was standing before a trio of cars parked lengthwise across the road. He was flanked by a pair of men on either side aiming pistols at them. Matt caught sight of the spectacle and groaned.

"How did they know where we were headed?" Chester shouted in a panicked voice.

"Should I try to run it?" Earl asked.

"No, this isn't the movies. There's no way we can smash our way through those cars without totaling this one, and there isn't enough room on the shoulders to try and get around them. Hey Chester! How close are our flying friends to us right now?"

The pet psychic closed his eyes and brought his fingers to his temple. "They fell a little behind, we've been driving so fast that they've had a hard time keeping up but they're not that far off."

"Good. Slow down and come to a stop. It looks like they want to negotiate. Let's try and buy ourselves a little time until Mothman and his honey are close enough to give us a little death from above."

"I'll make sure they understand the plan." Chester said, and closed his eyes again.

Swan looked on as the lead car rumbled to a stop a few hundred feet away from him.

"Matt Spike!" He shouted, suddenly missing having his megaphone. "Surrender now, or I shall unleash something so dire, so dreadful, that the mere sight of it will shatter your feeble mind into a thousand pieces!" He held the egg out before him. "Behold! For within this crystal is an eldritch horror from beyond the edge of human memory! An abomination which imprinted itself onto the very nightmares of our ancestors!" Swan was actually starting to enjoy himself a little. He always did have a flair for the dramatic. He hoped that he wasn't laying it on too thick. Hamming it up, as it was.

Inside the car, its occupants were not impressed.

"Sheesh! This clown has read way too much Lovecraft!" Matt critiqued.

"Wait, I'm confused. If it's supposed to be an eldritch horror from beyond the edge of human memory, then how could it have imprinted itself on the nightmares of our ancestors? I mean, beyond the edge of memory means that nobody remembers it right? If you can't remember it, how can you have nightmares about it?" Dennis commented.

"That's what I would think too." Chester agreed from the back seat.

"This asshole never knows what the fuck he's talking about." Earl griped.

An unearthly screech pierced the night; it was soon joined by a pair of screams from somewhere behind Mr. Swan. He turned his head quickly enough to see two of his men from each of his sides lifted up into the air, their feet flailing, only to disappear into the night. The remaining two men fired wildly into the sky. A moment later, the first pair of men crashed back down, one of them dented the top of one of their cars. The other one smashed a windshield then bounced onto the road. His lifeless eyes stared back up at Swan accusingly, looking eerie in the shadows cast by the headlights. Swan's remaining men continued to fire blindly into the darkness above.

"Light 'em up!" Matt Spike shouted as he and his partner leaned out of their car windows and began shooting at the roadblock.

"Fools!" Swan shrieked. "You leave me no choice! You brought this upon yourselves!" He smashed the egg to the pavement and threw himself into his car. In the rear view mirror he spied his last two men being carried up into the air.

The egg shattered on the asphalt, releasing a small green blob. Within a matter of seconds, it began growing to an immense size until it filled the entire road, completely blocking the view of the cars forming the roadblock. In less than a minute, it was taller than the tallest tree along the side of the road. The beast had one massive red eye in the center of a bulbous, elongated, cone shaped head. Large veins pulsed malevolently on the sides of the head. Countless thick tentacles which terminated in claws like those of a lobster snaked out from it. A ring of beak-like mouths was arranged around the base of the creature. It lifted up into the air, until it was hovering about eight feet above the road, held aloft by some unseen force.

"It's a Despoiler!" Naomi and Athena exclaimed from the front seat of her SUV, which was currently stopped behind Matt's car. They each looked at one another with a renewed appreciation for the other.

"What do you know about Despoilers?" Naomi asked.

"Only that they're one of the many magical creatures created as a living weapon during the Great Magic War. It's supposed to be illegal to make any of them nowadays, but that doesn't stop some people from trying. Most of them just do it for the challenge of it. Clark loves to tell me the story about how the Queen of Wyrms tried to use one on him once," she sighed. "If I had a nickel for every time he told that story I'd have two fifty. And I don't mean two dollars and fifty cents, I mean two hundred and fifty dollars!"

"How can you two be so calm? It's a fucking giant monster!" Miranda shouted from the back seat.

"Because we know that Despoilers are impossibly dumb, almost mindless. They're only a real threat when someone is controlling them. All we have to do is kill the guy who smashed the egg. The Despoiler automatically follows the mental commands of the person who released it. Once he's gone, it'll be easy to destroy." Naomi explained as if lecturing one of her students.

"That thing really isn't all *that* terrifying," Matt said appraisingly. "Weird yes, but terrifying, not so much. I'm just saying, I've seen worse."

"You know what it reminds me of? The beholder from our old D&D games!" Dennis exclaimed. The recent revelation that his wife was far more powerful than he'd ever imagined, coupled with the knowledge that he had a pair of Mothpeople on his side had combined to give Dennis a dangerously smug air of invincibility and fearlessness.

"Yeah, that's right!" Matt agreed. "It's like a really big beholder, just with lots of beaks for some reason. Why does it have beaks? Not just one, but like seven. And crab claws on the ends of the tentacles! Who dreamed up this thing? What kinda drugs were they on?"

"I dunno, but whoever they are, they're going to get sued for copyright infringement." Dennis joked.

"That guy was definitely overselling it." Chester chimed in.

"It *is* pretty damned silly looking," Earl said dryly.

The Despoiler howled angrily with all seven of its beaks, as if sensing how the men were mocking its menace. It brought one mighty, meaty tentacle crashing down onto the hood of Matt's car, instantly destroying the engine. The women watched as the men all ran out of the car and scattered. Matt and Earl shot at the monster, the bullets failing to penetrate its thick hide.

"Aww, Matt loved that car," Naomi observed. Matt screamed obscenities at the monster to that effect as he continued to shoot at it.

"Do you suppose that the boys know that part about killing the guy who broke the egg?"

"Matt would if he ever bothered to read my *Magna Historia Mundi*, but he always says he doesn't have the time to," Naomi noted sourly.

"I suppose we'd better tell them then. And I guess I can do some cool sorceress stuff to it," Athena said as she opened her door.

"And I can do some cool floating sword stuff to it," Naomi said, opening hers. The *Vermilion Avenger* lifted itself out of the back cargo area of the SUV, hovered past Miranda and out the door. Naomi slipped a necklace she'd been wearing out from around her neck and placed a ring that had been dangling from it onto her finger. A glowing bubble of emerald energy similar to the one which had surrounded Athena earlier now shielded her. Miranda suddenly understood why Naomi had given her suit of armor to Matt. Apparently she had her own ways of protecting herself in a fight.

Athena glanced back at her friend, who was cowering in the back seat. "Mira, stay in the car. Unless the monster attacks it, in which case, definitely get out of the car as fast as you can! But otherwise, just stay inside—are we clear?"

Miranda nodded, but as soon as Athena slammed the door shut she snarled "Yeah, as clear as mud!"

The Despoiler wasn't nearly as filled with pure hatred and rage as Mr. Swan had been led to believe by all the legends of his youth. In fact, it wasn't filled with much of anything. He was oddly disappointed by this. He was expecting to be pitted in an epic struggle for his own sanity with a mind of pure evil in order to control the actions of the beast. Instead, he'd discovered that controlling it was much easier than driving a car in most of the video games he played.

The moth creature with the stinger barreled towards the Despoiler's eye and tried to poke it out. Swan laughed maniacally at the futility of this gesture. Even the Despoiler's eye was too tough to pierce! He brought up another tentacle and used it to swat the monster aside. He watched through the Despoiler's eye with satisfaction as it smashed into the pavement. The other moth creature swooped down and punched at the Despoiler with impotent fury. Swan simply wrapped a tentacle around it. It was easy to recapture the monster with the might of the Despoiler at his command! He'd already fulfilled half of his mission! Now all he had to do was capture the Guardians of the Orb, wipe their memories, and kill all the other witnesses. But not necessarily in that order. He decided it would be more fun to kill the most expendable ones first. He swung a tentacle at the SUV...

Miranda saw the massive tentacle rushing towards her and bailed out the side door with seconds to spare as the SUV was swatted high into the air only to crash back down onto one of the pine trees lining the side of the road.

"My insurance doesn't cover acts of Despoilers!" Naomi roared and sent the *Vermilion Avenger* into the eye of the monster.

Unlike when Morgatchu had attacked it, this time a thick yellow substance erupted from the huge red eye as the sword sank itself deep into it. The blade of the *Vermilion Avenger* was made of a substance that could cut through anything. It then pulled itself out of the eye and began hacking off tentacles left and right, including the one holding Coathuan. The monster flailed its remaining tentacles blindly, one of them nearly came down on top of Naomi, but she was saved by her glowing green energy shield. Athena blasted the beast with thousands of volts of electricity. There wasn't any need for her to hold back this time! The monster bellowed in pain.

Inside his car, Mr. Swan screamed. He couldn't see anything through the Despoiler's eye anymore! And worst of all, he could feel its agony as it was swiftly dismembered and electrocuted. Then he heard his car door creak open. He looked up to see Matt Spike's partner, Earl standing over him pointing a gun his way.

"Surprise, motherfucker!" He said, fully channeling his inner Samuel L. Jackson.

These would be the last words Mr. Swan would ever hear.

With the inside of Swan's head now decorating the interior of his car, the monster completely stopped fighting back. It just hung there, floating above the road spewing a gooey yellow liquid from the dozens of stumps where its tentacles used to be, and screaming from its seven beaks.

Coathuan struggled out of the grip of the lifeless tentacle that had been holding him and ran over to help his stunned mate to her feet.

Miranda joined the group, who were now all staring up at the thing.

"So how do we get rid of this thing? More lightning?" She asked Athena.

"Nah. I mean, I *could* do that, but then all that nasty yellow pus inside will probably splash all over us when this thing explodes. It'll be worse than when the Stay Puft Marshmallow Man blew up at the end of *Ghostbusters*!"

"We could just leave it here, like some kind of an avant-garde surrealist art installation." Matt suggested.

Chester shook his head. "No, it's a living thing and it's in lots of pain. It's wrong to leave it like this, we should just put it out of its misery."

"Oh! I've got an idea!" Athena smiled.

Soon she was chanting an incantation which created a pocket of impossibly cold air around the monster. It froze solid, died, and came crashing down to the road. As it did so, it shattered into dozens of pieces, much like the crystalline egg which had birthed it. Dust to dust, ashes to ashes.

Unfortunately for them, these individual pieces were huge. As they fell, they completely crushed the cars making up the roadblock-the only cars which had still been intact enough to drive.

"Oops." Athena winced as the boulders of solid ice which had once been a monster smothered their chances of driving the rest of the way to Ong's Hat.

"Great! Just great!" Matt whined. "I guess we'll have to hoof it the rest of the way!"

"Chill out Matt, it's not so bad," Earl assured him. "I'd say we're only about half a mile from the trail that leads up to the secret base. Also, it'll be easier to sneak up on the place on foot. We would've had to abandon the cars and walk soon anyway."

"Easy for you to say pal, you still have a car!" Matt grumbled.

"We have another little problem." Chester announced haltingly. "Morgatchu's wing and her hip was hurt when that monster hit her. She can't fly. She can still walk, but she needs a little help." The others now noticed how Morgatchu was standing with one arm wrapped around Coathuan for support.

"Let me take a look at it." Athena said as she walked over to the Mothwoman. She felt along her leathery wings and then on her hip. She closed her eyes and concentrated, then frowned. "It's no good. Her anatomy is too alien, I'm afraid I might end up doing more damage if I try to heal her. She's gonna need to see a doctor in her own world."

"Do you think she's still up for this little hike?" Matt asked Chester.

Morgatchu chittered a response.

"Yes, she doesn't have much of a choice does she? But it's going to slow us down." Chester translated.

Matt threw his hands up into the air. "Wonderful!" he said sarcastically.

Earl ignored his partner's complaining. "C'mon! We need to get off this road before they send someone or *something* else after us. We can walk parallel to the road through the woods to avoid detection until we reach the trail." He dashed off towards the woods without waiting for a reply. Naomi shrugged, unable to find fault in his logic and sprinted after him, the *Vermilion Avenger* trailing behind her. Soon the others joined them until they were all crunching through the underbrush in the dark towards the hidden base, and the inter dimensional portal that would bring Coathuan and Morgatchu home.

Chapter Eighteen: The Road To Ong's Hat

"Hey Matt, I've been meaning to ask you," Dennis said as they walked through the woods, "how did you ever get mixed up in all this Guild business to begin with?"

"It was on another missing persons case, way back in '95. These damned missing persons cases are always nothing but trouble! I should stop taking 'em."

"I don't know about that," Earl chimed in, "you met on one of those 'damned missing persons cases' and that worked out pretty good, didn't it?"

Matt smiled, "Yeah, it did. What about you guys? How long have you secretly been a sorceress, Athena?"

"Not very long. I guess the easiest way to explain it all is that Clark Kismet is an old friend of the family, a *very* old one. He's been bugging me for years to let him train me in how to develop my psychic abilities, but I kept on turning him down. I wanted to hold onto my nice, cozy, relatively normal life. Then a few years back we got into a really dangerous situation on one of our paranormal investigations and one of my teammates died. After that, I vowed that I'd never let that happen again, so I finally told Clark he could train me."

Naomi laughed. "You know, most people in the Guilds would kill to have a wizard as famous as Clark Kismet as their teacher. Only someone like you would dare to string him along for years!"

Athena wasn't sure if that comment was intended that way, but she decided to take it as a compliment, then she remembered something she'd been meaning to ask Matt and Naomi about.

"You guys are supposed to be the Guardians of the Orb, right? But if you're both here, then who's guarding it?"

"Our son Joe. He moved back home recently and I asked him to keep an eye on it while I was gone. He's not too thrilled about it either. The kids hate all this Guild stuff, it scares them," Naomi explained.

"Which is a perfectly sensible reaction since we nearly get killed every time it comes into our lives like this." Matt reminded her.

"So your kids know all about this stuff?" Dennis asked.

"Truly spoken like someone who doesn't have any!" Matt laughed. "We tried to keep it a secret from them at first, but it's kind of impossible. Kids find out *everything* sooner or later."

"No secrets are safe!" Naomi agreed with a chuckle.

The group walked along in silence for a while longer, until Earl decided to break it. He'd been wrestling with whether or not to bring up this particular subject or not for some time, and realized that he may not get another opportunity.

"Chester, I know that you're still really hurting from losing Kendra, and unfortunately I'm sure you will be for a long time, but, well it probably isn't my place to say any of this, but I think you should know that Britney is still carrying a torch for you," he said in a hushed tone.

"What?" Chester replied incredulously. "How would you possibly know something like that?"

"She told me. In my experience sometimes people tell strangers things that they won't even tell their best friends."

"You're right, it isn't any of your damned business!" Chester said tartly, then stormed off to the back of the line to walk beside Coathuan and the limping Morgatchu instead. Earl had just inadvertently reminded him of why he typically preferred the company of nonhumans.

Earl shook his head as we watched him go. Matt placed a reassuring hand on his shoulder.

"Hey man, you tried. You know what they say? You can lead a horse to water, but you can't make it drink! It's just way too soon for him to be worrying about his love life."

"I know. I should've kept my stupid mouth shut. I'm a detective not a match maker!" Earl lamented. "What was I thinking?"

"You were thinking that you'd like to see a broken family back together again. It's not the worst thing a person can wish for, give yourself a break," Matt reassured him.

"Thanks."

"So what can we expect when we reach this base?" Matt inquired more loudly so everyone could hear.

Earl took the hint and increased his own volume too. "Most of the base is underground. In fact, we're probably walking right over it right now! But the place where they're studying the Scar is outside, above the ground. The Scar is normally in the sky. They've used some sort of foreign technology to pull a small section of it down closer to the ground and hold it open. The place looks like an amphitheater. The portal is surrounded by all manner of scientific instruments that are constantly measuring and monitoring the energies of the Scar. In a little while we'll reach the trail that leads to the entrance to the base. The perimeter of the base is surrounded by a high concrete wall. If we follow the wall, we'll eventually reach the section where they're studying the Scar. I figure Naomi can use the *Vermilion Avenger* to cut a hole in the wall, then our moth friends just have to make a run for it to get to the portal."

"How will we know when we're on the other side of the place where they're holding the Scar open?" Naomi asked him.

"It's not hard to tell. I can even see it from here! See that lighter part of the sky over there?" He pointed through the trees. There was indeed a small section of the sky nearby that wasn't quite as dark as the rest of it. "That's from the flood lights in that amphitheater area. Also, the energy field that's holding it open is always making a really loud, crackling sound."

"Also, I can sense when I'm close to a part of it that's open." Athena added. "Won't somebody see Naomi cutting a hole in the wall and attack us? Wouldn't it be safer if I just teleported the cryptids to the portal?"

"No, it won't be!" Dennis answered hotly. "No more teleporting! Remember Lars!"

"I haven't forgotten him, I feel awful about losing him! But if these guys are armed with laser guns and other sci-fi stuff, this plan doesn't sound all that much safer. I'd hate to bring them all this way just to watch them get zapped before they can reach the portal."

"It's a risk we'll have to take," Matt said. "I'm sorry Athena, but we've been over this before and I'm still with Dennis on this one. When a teleportation spell goes bad it's usually *really, really* bad. You're lucky that Lars is still in one piece. He could've ended up anywhere in the universe! He could've rematerialized somewhere in outer space, or under the ocean, or inside of a wall! We simply can't take the chance that won't happen to any of us."

"It's not a very long distance from the wall to the portal. If they run into any trouble along the way, we can cover them until they reach it," Earl explained.

"And then what? Assuming they get to the portal and make it home, what happens to us afterwards?" Miranda asked in a trembling voice. She wasn't very happy about this increasingly frightening mess that she'd landed herself in.

"Honestly, I'm not sure. I haven't thought past that point in any great detail, " Matt confessed. "If we do manage to escape from here, then we'll be fugitives, possibly for the rest of our lives. If we can't escape, there's a very good chance that they'll execute us on the spot in order to keep their secrets. If we're lucky, they'll take us prisoner instead. If they do, I can only pray that some of our more powerful friends within the Guilds find out about it somehow and come to bail us out."

"You really think they can beat us?" Dennis asked doubtfully. "I watched Athena take out a whole army of them like it was nothing, and we just killed a giant monster too! We're total badasses!"

"We may not be badass enough, and we're certainly not invincible. We've just been really lucky so far. Those guys back at the house weren't ABC agents," Earl elaborated. "ABC agents are much better armed and trained, and some of them are very skilled magic users too. They're definitely capable of defeating us, especially since this is their base. They've got the numerical advantage, we're going to be hopelessly outnumbered once they're onto us. Considering the fact that Mr. Swan was expecting us on the road, they may have a similar surprise waiting for us when we reach the portal."

"In other words, we're walking straight into a trap," Miranda said sourly.

"Probably," Matt agreed. "But that doesn't matter so long as we can get Coathuan and Morgatchu close enough to use that portal. If they get captured again, these dirtbags will just keep on kidnapping and torturing innocent people to keep them alive. Not to mention the fact that Coathuan has a war to stop in his home world."

Naomi nodded, "Focus on the big picture, Miranda."

Miranda shuddered. She'd like to be a hero, but all she could think of was her husband and her son and if she'd ever get to see them again. What if she got killed out here? Her family would likely never know what happened to her. They'd never know that she lost her life trying to prevent a war in some distant dimension.

Was it worth it? She wanted to believe that it was, but Coathuan and Morgatchu were so utterly alien and unsettling to be around that it was hard for her to think of them as being people, or to care very much about a war amongst creatures so completely different from anything she was used to. Call her crazy, but it was hard to have much compassion for creatures who literally fed on human sorrow. She wondered if they were feeding on her sadness right now!

She definitely didn't like the idea of random people being kidnapped and tortured, and she *did* want to help put an end to that. However, since she hadn't witnessed any of that first hand it felt like such an abstract concept that it was difficult for her to place it above her own wellbeing.

When she got out of bed this morning, she had no idea that she might end up getting killed today, or becoming a fugitive or a prisoner. She felt like her entire life had just been ruined. How did it happen? How had things spiraled out of her control so quickly? It was so unfair! What was she even doing here? What could she really contribute? She didn't have any super powers or weapons, she was just a realtor who liked to go ghost hunting on the weekends! She hadn't signed up for any of this—and yet here she was!

Earl must've sensed Miranda's growing despair, because he next tried to offer her a glimmer of hope.

"Of course," he began, "as far as I can tell they haven't sent any actual ABC agents after us. Which is *curious* to say the least! To me that suggests that not everyone in the ABC is in on this. True, the fact that they turned Coathuan over to Humanaid originally does indicate some sort of a relationship between the two groups, but if they're truly working together then I think they would've used the full power of the ABC against us by now. Especially since they seem so desperate to recapture Coathuan. The fact that we've managed to get this far tells me that the ABC hasn't been completely compromised. So we do have a *chance*. A chance that there won't be a massive ambush waiting for us on the other side of that wall. And a chance that if we're captured, someone will listen to our story and realize that we're not the real bad guys in this scenario."

Miranda frowned. So if they didn't get themselves killed breaking into a top secret base, then the best they could hope for was that somebody someday would eventually figure out that they'd been justified in doing so? As pep talks went this one was an absolute stinker, but she did appreciate the effort, lousy as it was.

"Always look on the bright side of life!" Dennis suddenly sang out.

Matt whistled the next few bars of this song from the classic Monty Python movie, *The Life of Brian* (which had been one of his and Dennis' favorites as teenagers) before singing the next line: "Always look on the bright side of death!"

Dennis picked up the next bit, whistling once more.

Miranda rolled her eyes. Maybe death wasn't so bad after all? It might actually be preferable to being stuck in the woods with these two geeks for much longer!

Chapter Nineteen: The Chapter of Infinite Penultimatenitude

The impromptu sing-a-long came to an abrupt end as soon as the group reached the gates of the facility with its numerous grim warning signs assuring them that any trespassers would be shot on sight. They skirted the edge of the twenty foot wall at a distance they hoped would keep them hidden from any hidden cameras. In time they reached a spot where the sky was at its brightest. Just as Earl had explained, there was a disturbing cracking sound coming from the other side.

Surely, this was the location of the portal!

Matt turned to Chester, "Maybe you could ask Coathuan if he wouldn't mind flying up long enough to give us a clue about the security on the other end?"

"Good idea," He closed his eyes and held his hand to his temple in that peculiar way that he did when communicating with the Mothpeople.

Coathuan took his arm out from around Morgatchu, who leaned herself up against a tree for support. They all watched as the Mothman silently rose up into the air without beating his wings. Not for the first time, Matt wondered if there was some type of telekinesis involved in his flight, with the wings just being used for gliding, steering and when sudden bursts of speed were needed. But if that was the case, then why did Morgatchu's injured wing prevent her from flying at all? He realized that he still had so many questions about the mysterious alien creatures, questions which he'd likely never have answered.

The Mothman flew straight up, careful to stay on the periphery of the area lit up by the floodlights below. He came back down quickly, making excited sounds and gesturing with his hands. Chester nodded dejectedly.

"It doesn't look good. There are dozens of people armed with weird silver guns standing around waiting for us. Coathuan says that he might be able to fly up and make a quick nosedive straight into the portal without getting hit, but he can't do that kind of fancy flying while carrying Morgatchu, and he's not willing to leave her behind. He thinks they'll make a less conspicuous target if they try to run for it on foot."

"Shit!" Matt swore. "They're definitely gonna need us to cover them while they try to reach the portal, and we can't do that without making a hole in the wall. Once we do, they'll know right where to concentrate all their fire."

"I have an idea," Naomi said. "It won't take very long to cut a hole with the *Vermilion Avenger*, even in a wall this thick. What if I made two holes? That way they won't know which one to concentrate on? We could even split up and attack through both of them. Maybe get some of them in a crossfire?"

"A two pronged attack? I like the sound of that!" Matt smiled, then he looked at Dennis, Miranda and Chester with a suddenly grave expression on his face. "You three had better start heading back to the road. Now that we know they're waiting for us, our chances of living through this aren't great. There's no point in all of us getting killed or captured. If by some miracle we make it out of this one, we'll come looking for you."

"No way, I want to fight! I picked this up before I left the house," said Chester, producing Kendra's gun from where it had been stuffed into the waistband of his pants, gangsta style.

Matt eyed the weapon skeptically. "Does that thing still have any ammo left in it?"

"It's got almost half a clip left," Chester revealed.

"You had that thing when we fought the Despoiler and you never used it?" Earl asked in a surprised voice.

"Yeah, well I saw how useless shooting it was and didn't feel like wasting my bullets."

"Give me the gun, Chester. Kendra told us you were a lousy shot and you've got a kid. You're sitting this one out," ordered Matt.

Chester turned red in the face. "So what? You've got kids too and you're not going home! I want payback for what they did to Kendra!"

"My kids are adults! They don't need me anymore the way your daughter still needs you!" It hurt Matt to say those words out loud, but it was the truth. "And doing this won't bring Kendra back! Now for the last time, give me the fucking gun." Matt said forcefully, yet somehow still quietly.

Chester scowled, but placed the weapon in Matt's outstretched hand nonetheless.

"Let me use the gun, Matt! I'm a really great shot!" Dennis said enthusiastically.

"Since when?" Athena scoffed. "You hate guns!"

"C'mon! You've seen how good I am at Call of Duty!"

Naomi chuckled. "That's just a video game, trust me, those skills don't translate into real life."

"Nobody else is getting the damned gun, okay? I'm using the gun as a backup because I'm almost out of bullets for my own piece!" Matt declared testily. Both he and Earl had in fact both ran out of ammunition during the gunfight at Kendra's house. They'd reloaded on the ride over using spare ammunition Matt kept in his car, then wasted a great deal of it fruitlessly shooting at the Despoiler.

"Give me your gun too, Earl. I'm sending you away with the others. Your boys aren't much older than Chester's girl."

Earl shook his head. "No way, pal. You're gonna need me."

"I don't need you dead! This is insubordination!" Matt argued.

"So what're ya gonna do about it? Fire me?" Earl said sarcastically.

"Okay, okay fine! You can stay, but it's your funeral. Now the rest of you guys get a move on! We won't start the attack until we've given you a chance to get far enough away."

"It's funny, a few minutes ago I was so scared I wanted to run away, but now that you're actually ordering me to leave, I don't want to go. I feel like I'm abandoning you to your death!" Miranda told Athena tearfully.

"It's okay, Mira. It's better this way. What could you really do anyway? Throw rocks at them? Hang around and watch me die? Go home to your family. If we don't come back, tell Clark and Mark what happened to us, maybe they can get us some kind of justice." She hugged her friend and whispered "Thank you for everything."

"I don't want to leave you either!" Dennis cried, his voice catching in his throat. "It's my job to protect you!"

She stroked his cheek. "My dearest, you've been protecting me ever since we were kids, but you can't protect me any longer. Nobody can. Don't look so sad. I don't have any intention of dying today, but even if I do, we both know that death isn't the end is it? I promise that I'll come back to you, in one way or another. Now go home, somebody has to feed the pets!"

Dennis leaned in and whispered in her ear. "If things get too crazy, you have my permission to teleport the fuck out of there and take as many of our friends with you as you can!" She nodded and they kissed, one long final kiss before she pushed him away. "Go! Before I change my mind!" she bawled.

Dennis went to shake Matt's hand, but the detective pulled him in for a hug instead. "It's been wild getting to know each other again, hasn't it?" said Matt. Dennis simply nodded his head, too shook up to respond with words. He gave Naomi a salute and she saluted him back.

Chester put one hand on Coathuan's shoulder and another on Morgatchu's. "It's been an honor being your friend. I'll never forget you. Good luck to you both," he said it out loud, although there was really no need to, they already knew what was in his heart.

He started to walk away, but then a sudden thought froze him in his tracks. He turned around and looked Coathuan in the eye. "Go easy on your son when you get back home. My own parents ran away from home to be together too when they were still just barely kids, and their parents never forgave them for it. I know how much that hurt them, how much it hurt us *all*, and I'd hate to see the same thing happen to your own family." The Mothman nodded his understanding, Chester smiled and hurried back to where Dennis and Miranda waited for him.

The three waved one final time and walked away, Dennis and Miranda still sobbing and pausing to look back every so often. In time, their retreating forms were lost, swallowed up by the darkness of the forest.

"Do you think we'll ever see them again?" Naomi asked.

"I'm going to make damn sure that we do!" Athena said with a renewed determination.

Agent Ember was incredibly bored. All the personnel at the base had been standing around in the IRA (Interdimensional Research Area) for over an hour with their weapons drawn and so far nothing had happened. She was beginning to think that her boss, Sub Director Gordon Hazleton, had lost his marbles. He'd told her that he was expecting an imminent attack upon the IRA from enemies intent on using the portal and he needed her to assemble everyone for an ambush. But so far, the enemy has failed to show.

When she'd pressed him for more details, he told her a very odd story. Something about a pair of demonic creatures who had been summoned to our world by an unregistered witch. They had then taken over the minds of the Guardians of the Orb and were planning on using them to break into the IRA. If these demons reached the portal, they would be able to expand it so that an army of similar monsters would pour in to overrun the Earth. Her orders were to stop the demons from reaching the portal at all costs. Her people were to only shoot to stun the Guardians, but they were allowed to use maximum force on anyone else who may be assisting them.

Ember was one of the few people who knew the identities of the Guardians. For years she had been assigned to a squad of ABC agents they could call upon for backup if they were ever about to lose control of the Orb. That's how she first met Gordon Hazelton. He'd served on that same team for a brief time before his ever ascendant career took him elsewhere, and eventually to command of this entire base. She owed a lot to him. He'd been the one who'd convinced her to transfer to this branch office and given her a promotion as one of his top lieutenants. She trusted him implicitly, yet something about his story didn't ring true for her, but she couldn't put her finger on quite what it was. If she didn't know better she'd suspect that he'd been lying to her. She was a powerful witch in her own right, but she always found her superior to be impossible to read because as a security protocol he wore a magical bracelet which prevented psychics from getting into his mind, and all the classified information locked away inside.

Ember had known better than to suggest that they simply close the portal to stop the demons from reaching it. She knew all too well that once it was closed, they might not be able to open it again, at least not without risking creating a power surge that could render the entire eastern part of the country without electricity for days. Even after decades of studying the Scar, they seemed to still know so little about it.

And so here they were, standing around like a bunch of idiots. She wished her friend Agent Method hadn't transferred to a branch in the UK a few months earlier. She would've kept her entertained while they waited. Instead, she was stuck with Agent Fresh for company. He was a well meaning young man, but he had all the personality of a walnut and was often dull as bricks to talk to. None of the other nearby agents were any better as conversationalists. It had been a very long night indeed.

Agent Fresh indulged in his nervous habit of spraying his mouth with an aerosolized breath freshener before speaking. "Where are these attackers already? Maybe the boss's intelligence was wrong?"

"I'm beginning to wonder the same thing," she confessed.

"If they've taken control of the Guardians' minds, does that mean they've captured the Orb too? Do you think they'll have it with them?" he asked in a shaky voice. This was a frightening thought, since it would mean that none of the assembled ABC agents who were magic users would be able to cast any spells.

"I don't think so, supposedly they've got a rogue witch with them. She'd be making herself helpless too if that was the case." Still, the idea of this made Ember tighten her grip on her pistol. If her assumption was wrong, the weapon would be her only line of defense.

Agent Fresh continued to prattle on. "I wonder how those demons knew who the Guardians were? It's such a big secret! Of course, now all of us know what they look like since they had to show us so we won't kill them. They're definitely not what I was expecting. I thought they'd be...younger somehow."

Mercifully, this conversation was cut short as they saw a large circle of sparks appear on one end of the wall, then moments later an identical one was traced out on the opposite end.

It looked like the attack was finally beginning....

As soon as the pair of holes were cut, Athena used her magic to push the six foot cylinders of concrete they'd formed outwards. She did so as forcefully as she could, so they'd be launched out like projectiles into the amphitheater. The nearest ABC agents scrambled to avoid these deadly missiles, a few of them weren't fast enough. One or two were simply struck with a glancing blow and knocked to the ground as the lethal objects sailed past them, but several others took the full brunt of the impact and it wasn't pretty to say the least. The missiles pulverized every bone in their bodies, turning the agents into a pulp.

Ember cursed. She held up both of her hands and sent lightning bolts arcing over to each of these flying columns, they shattered instantly, showering a choking mist of thick dust onto her people. Through this smokescreen she struggled to see their attackers as they burst into the IRA. Through one of the holes she saw the witch, hiding behind her energy shield. Two odd, winged creatures with big red eyes were with the witch, sheltering behind the shield.

She assumed these were the demons. They reminded her more of the Mothman, a creature that the ABC knew surprisingly little about. Many years earlier, one had come through the portal at this very facility. They'd captured it, but it had died in captivity before they could learn much about it. If she remembered correctly, it had starved to death because they didn't know how to feed it. She found it strange that the winged creatures were walking instead of flying. Even odder still, one of them appeared to be injured and had to walk with the support of the other one.

On the other end of the IRA, she saw the Guardians. There was Dr. Naomi Waters-Spike, surrounded by a bubble of protective energy, directing the movements of *The Vermilion Avenger* as it danced through the air, knocking agents out by striking them with its handle or the flat side of the blade. That was strange too, Ember knew that Naomi preferred to use non lethal attacks, but if her mind was truly being controlled by demons, surely she wouldn't still be holding back and would use the sword to cut up more than a concrete wall? Her husband Matt was soon flying through the hole, dressed in his full suit of armor, which allowed him to fly for very short bursts. He was carrying two pistols and even he seemed to be holding back, shooting her agents in the legs instead of the chest or head. There seemed to be someone hiding on the other side of the wall who was firing on them. Whoever this was, they also showed a similarly unusual level of restraint, shooting to disable rather than kill. Or maybe she was reading too much into it? Perhaps they were both just incredibly shitty shots?

Ember quickly realized how useless her subordinates' attacks on the Guardians were. With their weapons set to stun they couldn't possibly weaken the bubble around Naomi, or come close to penetrating Matt's armor. She felt bad doing it, especially since the Guardians were handling her own people with such kid gloves, but she ordered her people to take their weapons off of the stun setting.

She noticed that even the witch wasn't using lethal force, she was zapping her agents with just enough electricity to knock them out. As she looked on, the witch took out a large number of agents in front of her by casting a spell that collapsed the ground beneath them so that they all tumbled into the deep fissure she'd created. Effective, but not deadly. So far, the only deaths their assailants had caused were from those concrete columns they'd sent out, and only because they hadn't been able to control their flight path.

Something definitely didn't feel right about this whole thing.

Nonetheless, her orders were to stop these so-called demons from reaching the portal she now stood in front of and she intended to carry out her mandate. She ordered most of her remaining agents to concentrate their fire on the witch and the demons. The witch's mystical shield protects her from energy based weapons like the ones used by the ABC, but if they struck it enough times, they would eventually weaken and then shatter it. If they struck her before she cast a spell to create a new shield they'd be able to eliminate her threat—permanently.

Athena was enjoying herself. So far, this wasn't nearly as bad as she'd expected it to be. They were still kicking plenty of ass! Maybe they'd live through this after all? These people's weapons might be different, but they still couldn't get through her shield. She also hadn't been attacked by any other magic users yet, which was her biggest fear. In fact, the only other magic she'd seen used so far was when that one tall lady in the long black dress standing near the portal had used lightning to destroy her concrete projectiles. She'd have to keep an eye out for her.

Just as Athena was thinking that they could actually win this fight, everything seemed to go wrong all at once. She looked on in horror as a male magic user levitated the energy bubble protecting Naomi into the air and violently threw it up against the wall surrounding the amphitheater. He repeated this move over and over again, so forcefully that cracks began to appear in the wall. Naomi screamed as she bounced around helplessly inside. Since she was distracted by this onslaught, she lost control of the *Vermilion Avenger* and the mighty sword clattered uselessly to the ground.

Athena sent a lightning bolt sizzling towards Naomi's assailant, but he managed to erect his own magical shield seconds before it could reach him. Athena tried a new tactic, casting a spell which caused a pair of gigantic arms to form out of the very earth beneath this wizard's feet. These earthen limbs seized him by the legs and battered him against his own shield until he passed out. As he lapsed into unconsciousness, his shield disappeared, and Naomi's bubble dropped to collide with the ground in front of the wall. Naomi seemed to have been knocked out by his attack, she just laid there motionless inside the bubble. Dozens of ABC agents converged on her, all firing their ray guns at the bubble in unison. Was it Athena's imagination, or was she beginning to see cracks appear in the surface of the bubble?

Matt swiftly came to his wife's rescue. He flew down, landing in front of Naomi, brandishing the *Vermilion Avenger*. Normally the sword was too heavy to lift, but Matt's armor greatly enhanced his strength, making it possible. He swung it like an oversized baseball bat, so that the flat of the blade struck the nearest agents, knocking them over like bowling pins. As Athena watched, the agents now concentrated their fire on Matt. He continued swinging at them and swatting them down, until a lucky shot seemed to penetrate a gap in the armored plates protecting one of his legs. Matt dropped the sword and went down on one leg as more agents surrounded him, blocking him from Athena's sight.

They were starting to lose!

Athena was alarmed to see cracks beginning to appear in her own shield as line after line of agents swarmed around her, all firing upon her. Coathuan chittered nervously from behind her.

No! They were so close! She could see the portal hovering over the ground only a few hundred feet away, but it might as well be a mile away.

If only she could make these people understand that they weren't the real enemy! She could sense their collective confusion over this entire situation. This feeling was especially strong coming from the woman in the black dress, the witch who seemed to be directing the battle. Athena knew that this woman suspected something was fishy about this fight, that she was filled with so many doubts. She had to find a way to exploit those doubts, she had to get through to her!

A desperate plan formed in Athena's mind. There was a way to rapidly share one's experiences with someone else, a special technique Clark had taught her, but it required making physical contact. She locked eyes with the witch in the black dress, and the witch immediately threw a magical shield over herself, covering the front of her body. Then the woman raised her arms and began chanting a spell. Athena had no intention of waiting around to see what kind of spell she was about to hit her with. She took a deep breath and decided she had to chance doing the one kind of spell that everyone had been trying to prevent her from casting all day-a teleportation spell. She knew she could pull it off! And besides, Dennis had told her it was okay to do it if things got too crazy, and her current predicament was the textbook definition of "too crazy" as far as she was concerned! Dennis had expected her to use this move to escape, to save herself and the others rather than allow themselves to be captured or killed, but that's not how she planned to use it.

Instead, she teleported mere inches behind the witch trying to cast the spell on her, leaving Coathuan and Morgatchu behind her ever weakening energy shield. The confused witch looked around, saw Athena standing behind her and scowled. Before she could do anything else, Athena stretched out her finger and touched the woman's forehead.

Contact!

A torrent of images, words and sounds flooded into Agent Ember's head. They were all of Athena's memories from the past twenty four hours. As she experienced these moments in time and her understanding increased, a cold fury built up inside of her. Gordon Hazleton had lied to her! He'd callously risked her life and the lives of all the agents under his command to further this shameful money making scheme that he was surely a part of.

Gordon had been in charge when the ABC had captured that first, unfortunate Mothman, the one who had starved to death. Apparently, he'd discovered more about the nature of these creatures during that time than he'd revealed to anyone else and that knowledge had inspired this entire enterprise. She also recalled a wizard she'd busted a few years back for creating Despoilers, and all the eggs they'd taken into custody. It was suddenly obvious where the one Athena and her friends had fought against came from. It would be child's play for someone with Gordon Hazleton's clearance to make such a thing 'disappear' from the inventory of the ABC Vaults. There could be no doubt about it, this man whom she'd so long admired and trusted was guilty as hell. Her sense of betrayal was epic in proportion, surpassed only by her anger over it.

"Do you understand now?" Athena asked.

"I do," Ember answered. She quickly cast a spell which greatly amplified her voice and spoke: "CEASE FIRE! ALL AGENTS STAND DOWN IMMEDIATELY! DO NOT ATTACK THE INTRUDERS!"

All around them, ABC agents lowered their weapons, confused looks adorning many of their faces.

An angry voice buzzed from within the earbud Ember wore, it belonged to Gordon Hazleton. He'd been watching the entire battle from the safety of the IDR control room overlooking the amphitheater. "What are you doing? Don't trust her, she's lying! She's possessed by those demons! Resume your attack immediately!"

Ember wanted to believe him, she really did. It would be so much nicer to believe that he hadn't betrayed her, and everything that the ABC was supposed to stand for. But her gut told her otherwise, and had been trying to tell her this entire time. Now all of the odd things she'd noticed during the battle suddenly made sense. There could be no doubt that the visions she'd just experienced were the truth and not the result of some demonic deception.

She responded to him by instead addressing everyone in the IDR, her voice remained thunderous. "I HAVE JUST LEARNED THAT SUB DIRECTOR GORDON HAZELTON IS A SUSPECT IN A SERIES OF HEINOUS CRIMES AND MUST BE ARRESTED IMMEDIATELY PENDING A FULL INQUIRY. HE HAS ORDERED THIS ATTACK UNDER FALSE PRETENSES IN AN ATTEMPT TO CONCEAL HIS CRIMES, PLACING ALL OF US IN UNNECESSARY DANGER! AS THE NEXT MOST SENIOR RANKING OFFICER ON

DUTY, I AM TEMPORARILY TAKING COMMAND OF THIS FACILITY EFFECTIVE IMMEDIATELY!"

Athena looked around the amphitheater and she saw a group of agents step back to reveal Matt, he was clutching his injured leg, but otherwise appeared to be unharmed. Behind him, she saw Naomi stirring within her energy bubble. Further down along the wall, she spied Earl cautiously poking his head through the hole. Morgatchu and Coathuan were still okay, safely encircled by her own energy shield only a few dozen feet away.

She allowed herself a small smile of satisfaction. Everyone was still alive and they'd won! Against all odds, somehow they'd won!

Chapter Twenty: Karma Police

Inside the IRA control room, Gordon Hazelton screamed and slammed his fist into one of the control panels before him. Why did they oppose him? Why couldn't they understand that he was just taking what he deserved? Why should he be persecuted merely for having the courage and initiative to seize what the world clearly owed him for having to suffer under the constant expectations of having to fulfill a legacy that no one could ever possibly live up to?

The two technicians in the room with him looked at one another questioningly, then one of them stood up and drew a silver pistol from beneath his lab coat.

"Sir, I'm sorry, but I'm going to have to place you under arrest." The words were barely out of his mouth before Gordon's fist was flying towards his face. The man staggered backwards, and Gordon was upon him immediately, savagely bashing his head into a control panel. As the man's gun clattered to the floor, Gordon scooped it up.

The moment it was in his hands, he shot the man he'd been brawling with, burning a hole clear through his chest. He whirled on the other man just as he was pulling out his own pistol, but Gordon was quicker on the draw. The man fell to the ground, his body smoking. Gordon took a deep breath, stepped over the body and made sure the door was locked.

I can still salvage this situation, he told himself, *I am still in control!*

He sank down into a vacant seat, pulled out his cellphone, and dialed up Balthazar.

"Initiate the contingency plan immediately!" he ordered, ending the call as soon as Balthazar acknowledged.

Gordon looked down upon the group below and smiled. *They think they've won, but this isn't over! I'm not so easily beaten! I always have a back up plan! They're about to find out what you get when you mess with me!*

The deafening sounds of approaching helicopters interrupted Athena's triumphant thoughts.

"What's that?" she asked in alarm.

"That's impossible! The area around this base is supposed to be a restricted airspace!" Ember exclaimed.

Several large, black choppers appeared over the amphitheater, each emblazoned with a stylized "B.S." in a font which reminded Athena of the logo for the punk band the Dead Kennedys. Before the helicopters even landed, scores of men leapt out. They were all armed with assault rifles, dressed in black body armor, helmets and balaclavas. In a matter of seconds, they'd surrounded the entire amphitheater with a chilling military precision. They all had their weapons trained on the ABC agents.

Agent Ember immediately recognized this as being the Blackstone Group, a particularly ruthlessly mercenary organization suspected of various human rights violations on numerous continents. Somebody had very deep pockets if they could afford to hire this many of them. A pair of heavily armed helicopter gunships buzzed back and forth menacingly over the amphitheater, their weapons trained on them all. Judging from the uncanny speed with which they'd arrived, they must've already been deployed in the air nearby, likely circling around the no fly zone over the base, just waiting for the signal to attack.

A man in a well tailored business suit stepped out of one of the choppers wearing a smug smile. Ember immediately recognized him as Balthazar Hazelton, Gordon's notorious cousin. Suddenly, Gordon's dishonorable actions made a lot more sense, if he'd fallen under the influence of his hopelessly corrupt relative.

Balthazar raised his voice so he could be heard over the din of the chopper's still whirling blades.

"Stand down now or be killed! We have you surrounded, outnumbered and outgunned! It's suicide to resist us!" He barked as he approached her.

Ember estimated that the mercenaries outnumbered the still conscious ABC forces by at least three to one. Even with their superior weapons, the ABC was badly outnumbered. She did have three magic users on her side, but Athena had knocked one of them out earlier. This left herself and Athena as the only ones capable of fighting back with magic. Matt Spike was injured and Naomi was barely conscious, so the Guardians would be of little help. They might be able to win, but the outcome was far from certain. Either way, more of her people would definitely die, people whose lives were her responsibility. She didn't want their blood on her hands.

"Order your people to throw down their weapons," Balthazar said. He was now only a few inches in front of Ember and Athena, who were themselves only a couple of feet away from the glowing, crackling sliver of brilliant light that was the portal.

Ember lowered her eyes in resignation. She couldn't believe she was about to do this. "ALL AGENTS, DROP YOUR WEAPONS AND SURRENDER."

Balthazar chuckled. "Gordon always said you were quite reasonable, he thinks very highly of you, Agent Ember isn't it? Lower your magical shield, and the ones over those two creatures. I also want the Guardians to get rid of their armor and shields." With a wave of her hand, the shield over Ember shimmered then dissipated. She looked over at Athena expectantly. Athena grimaced in anger, but had to give in to the reality of the situation she made an identical gesture in the direction of her own shield and it disappeared. Mercenaries near Coathuan and Morgatchu moved forward and roughly seized them by the wrists, handcuffing them. Morgatchu nearly fell over as they separated them, and Coathuan hissed at them furiously, earning himself a rifle but to the head.

"MATT SPIKE AND DR. WATERS-SPIKE, REMOVE YOUR ARMOR AND TAKE DOWN YOUR SHIELD!" She commanded. Even from across the amphitheater Athena could see Matt's scowl as he took off his helmet and struggled to remove the rest of his armor. Inside her bubble, Naomi shook her head as she pulled the ring from her finger and the bubble disappeared.

Balthazar looked at Athena "Don't even think that you can get away with casting any more spells." He snapped his fingers and a mercenary rushed forward with a briefcase in his hands which he now snapped open. Inside was an odd looking kind of bracelet. Balthazar removed it from the briefcase and turned it over in his hands contemplatively. "Do you know what this is, my dear? It's called an Inhibitor. It's kind of like a very weak version of the Orb of Thoth. It prevents the wearer from casting any spells. Don't worry, you won't be wearing it for very long. Once Agent Ember here uses her particular talent for altering minds to ensure your loyalty to us, you will become quite a valuable new asset to Humanaid. We've needed a skilled magic user for quite some time. We couldn't risk removing the Inhibitors from those fools Swan and Keith without alerting their parole officers, but you my dear, are a different story! An unregistered magic user! Nobody will miss you! You belong to us now. Don't worry, you'll enjoy working for us. I can have her rewrite your memories so that you won't even remember anything of your old life, you'll never even know what you're missing. Now hold out your wrist."

Athena reluctantly held out her wrist. She felt a sharp pain as the teeth on the ends of the bracelet sank into her flesh. For a moment it felt as if all the color had drained out of the world. "You're wrong about nobody missing me. My mentor is Clark Kismet, and he'll be coming for you!"

For a second, Balthazar looked worried, but then he smiled his usual smug smile, the one that made his face so eminently punchable. "That old fossil? If he does, we'll deal with him too. Perhaps we'll even use you to destroy him!" He leered at her, then turned to regard Agent Ember.

"Agent Ember! So named because you can reduce someone's memories to naught but smoldering embers! My, how poetic! Before you burn a hole through this witch's mind, I will first need you to rearrange the memories of all your agents assembled here. They will remember this incident as being a training exercise. A drill to simulate an attack on the Interdimensional Research Area. Unfortunately, a few agents forgot to put their weapons on stun and there were a few casualties as a result."

Ember looked at him defiantly. "I have never used my powers to alter the memories of my own agents! I would rather die!"

Balthazar laughed again. "Oh really? My, what a noble stance! There's that lovely ABC hypocrisy on full display! You alter the memories of civilians all the time and think nothing of it, yet draw the line at doing it to your own people as if that's somehow any better? How sanctimonious! You see my dear, it simply isn't true. You *have* altered their memories before. My cousin told me all about it. You were part of the team that captured this Mothman creature the night it first came through this very portal!" He pointed at the portal which was mere inches away dramatically.

The portal! This gave Athena a sudden idea. He told her that the Inhibitor prevented her from casting spells, but she wondered if it interfered with her natural psychic abilities too? They were two different things. One didn't have to be psychic to be able to cast spells (although it certainly helped) and vice versa. If she could still use her psychic powers, then they had a chance. She tried to send a telepathic message to Ember.

Hey Ember! Are you reading me?

Yes, the witch replied. Athena felt a burst of joy.

Keep this idiot talking, I have a plan to get us out of this, but I might need a few more moments.

Okay, it shouldn't be very hard, I have lots of questions for him, and he sure likes to gloat!

Ember knit her brows in confusion. "I don't remember any of that! You're making it up!"

"Yes, it's all true! You and your team captured the Mothman and took it to a building owned by my cousin. Then he had you erase their memories of the entire episode. I believe he had to threaten the lives of your family to get you to comply, and this threat still stands. We know where you live and we will not hesitate to kill them all."

"What? But if that's true, how is it that I have no memory of it? I can't use my powers on myself!"

"We have a certain magic item which can also alter memories. He used it on you afterwards."

"If you have something like that, then why force me to do it at all? Just do it yourselves!"

"Oh, come now! Where's the fun in that? There's nothing quite as satisfying as forcing someone to violate their own self righteous principles! Besides, you're the master of this kind of thing, nobody else has quite your panache for it, and you're far more efficient, you can alter dozens of people's memories all at once." There was also the added complication that the magic item in question was currently trapped under tons of frozen Despoiler carcass, but she didn't need to know that.

"Now do it, or your family dies!" he promised darkly.

While this conversation was happening, Athena was stretching out her senses to look beyond the open portal. On the other side she saw a series of tears in the fabric of time/space, tunnels that led to various worlds. Her awareness moved past them in rapid succession until she found one that looked particularly familiar. She sent an urgent call out, down into that tunnel and hoped that it would be heard in time....

A pair of red, clawed legs emerged from the portal and latched onto Balthazar Hazelton by the shoulders. A second later the rest of the beast flew through the column of light and carried the screaming Balthazar into the air directly above Athena.

The sorceress looked up at her friend and grinned mischievously. "Hiya, Daniel! Show 'em what you can do!"

Her loyal familiar blew out a long trail of flames fifteen feet into the air.

Athena quickly uttered the spell that amplifies one's voice and gave an ultimatum. "I AM IN CONTROL OF THIS WYVERN! I WILL COMMAND HIM TO ROAST THE MAN HE IS CARRYING UNLESS ALL OF HIS PEOPLE DISARM AND SURRENDER! AND I WANT THOSE TWO CHOPPERS CIRCLING OVERHEAD TO COMPLETELY LEAVE THE AREA - RIGHT NOW!"

"Listen to her!" the terrified Balthazar blubbered. In his earbud, he could hear his cousin Gordon screaming "NO!NO!NO!" He ignored his cries. "Do it!!" Balthazar reiterated.

As one, the Blackstone Group dropped their rifles. The two gunships buzzed off away from the amphitheater. The ABC agents wasted no time in picking up their own weapons and training them on the mercenaries. Athena looked at Coathuan and Morgatchu, still in shackles.

"UNCHAIN THE MOTHPEOPLE!" she commanded. Two of the men who had put the shackles on them hesitantly moved forward and removed them. Coathuan and Morgatchu started moving towards Athena. Matt, Earl and Naomi were hot on their heels, slowed down by Matt's injured leg. Naomi was helping him walk, in an odd inversion of how Coathuan had to assist Morgatchu. Once it was obvious that the ABC had all the mercenaries firmly under their control, Athena commanded him to drop Balthazar a safe height, and the wyvern came in for a landing. She rubbed him under his chin affectionately, and he nuzzled her back.

"Such a good boy," she told him, using her "inside voice" again. Agent Fresh stepped forward and pointed his gun at Balthazar, who raised his hands fearfully.

"It's the wyvern from your dream!" Agent Ember said, remembering him from when she'd seen the last twenty four hours of Athena's life. "Nicely done!" Athena mimed a courtesy. "Let me take care of that nasty thing for you!" Ember said, pointing at the Inhibitor. She chanted a few words and the bracelet fell to the ground. Athena rubbed her wrist and thanked her.

Matt and the others had finally caught up with her. "Wow! Dennis said something about you having a pet dragon on the ride over here, but I thought he was kidding!" Matt remarked.

"It's a wyvern!" Naomi and Athena corrected him, then giggled.

"Wyvern, dragon, what's the difference? I can never tell!"

"Wyverns have smaller front legs, and are typically smaller in general," Athena informed him.

"Great job, Athena! I thought we were done for!" Earl told her.

"Yeah!" Naomi agreed.

"Thanks, I'm glad you're all okay. Well, relatively speaking! You'd better let me take a look at that leg Matt!"

"It can wait, it looks like our moth friends are eager to get back home, we'd better say our goodbyes!" Matt pointed to where Coathuan and his bride waited beside the portal.

"Oh yeah, literally the entire reason why we're here!" Athena laughed and she bowed to the two creatures. They inclined their heads to her and to all the others, then they both sent a series of images and feelings to Athena. The sorceress nodded her head in understanding.

Athena addressed her friends on behalf of the mothpeople. "They are both very grateful for all that we've done for them and would like to request that this guy," she pointed to Balthazar, "be allowed to accompany them back to their home world to face justice for his crimes against them."

"What? No! Don't let them take me!" Balthazar pleaded, looking squarely at Agent Ember.

Ember smiled back at him. It wasn't a friendly smile. "I have no trouble transferring custody of the suspect to these two. He's caused nothing but trouble in this world for long enough!"

"You can't do this!" Balthazar screamed at her.

"I just did," she said cooly, then leaned closer and whispered "You shouldn't have ever threatened my family, motherfucker!"

Coathuan grabbed Balthazar by the arm, bent down until he was level with the whimpering man and hissed in his face, spraying him with bits of his alien spittle. Then he dragged the screaming, crying man through the portal and they disappeared together.

"I still had so many questions for him." Matt said wistfully as he watched him go.

Naomi placed a hand on his shoulder. "It's okay, hon. Sometimes it's better to let the mystery be."

Matt could appreciate what she meant and smiled his little half smile.

Morgatchu was still lingering behind. She bowed to the group one last time, then spread her wings, which already seemed to have done some healing, turned and walked into the glowing aperture.

"She seems to have made a speedy recovery!" Earl noted.

"That guy's fear provided her more than enough juice to supercharge her healing." Athena explained. "Who was that asshole anyway?"

"Just a big nobody," Ember answered. "Nobody at all."

In the control room, Gordon Hazelton contemplated the barrel of his gun. He couldn't believe it, all his carefully laid plans had come to naught! Defeated by an amateur witch and her pet! The humiliation was too great to bear. There was nothing left for him now. In a matter of minutes they'd find him up here, break through the door and he'd be finished.

All his life, he'd portrayed himself as the respectable one. True, he lacked any talent for magic and this had earned him plenty of disdain from the family, but he'd still managed to make something of a success out of his life despite this "disability" as his family saw it. Especially compared to that perennial fuck up, Balthazar.

But all of that was gone now; he'd be seen on the same level as Balthazar, perhaps even being held in greater contempt if such a thing was possible. The shame he had brought upon the family was unimaginable. From now on, the Hazeltons would be seen as a hopelessly corrupt bunch. He'd destroyed the legacy of that insufferable paragon of goodness, Esmeralda Hazelton for all time. That monumental ancestor who had loomed over his entire life, casting a shadow it was impossible to escape out from under, constantly daring him to be what he could never be. Fuck you Esmerelda! Shattering her monument was *his* monument!

In a flash of sudden insight, such as people often have in moments of crisis, he realized that this was all he'd truly wanted out of life-revenge on the family who had brought him into this cruel world, and then refused to soften the blow by giving him the love he deserved. He smiled at that idea. Perhaps, in a way he had won after all? Was ruining the reputation of the family which had done nothing but bring him pain and sorrow not the most fitting revenge for everything they'd done to him ever since he was a child?

He'd just had to lose in order to win. How ironic!

He almost wished he'd be around to see it, the look of shame on his father's face. Perhaps that's the final jolt that would be necessary to give the old fool the heart attack he's been skirting around? Wouldn't that be something!

But he wouldn't be around to see it. He didn't have the strength to endure the circus they'd make out of him, and he knew it. He wouldn't give them the satisfaction of seeing him break.

He closed his eyes and squeezed the trigger, a bright blue beam of energy disintegrated his head and his corpse slid from his seat to lay beside the bodies of his other victims. All of them now companions in death.

Epilogue One: Dinner With Friends

A week later, Athena and Dennis Arden were guests at Matt and Naomi's house. The Guardians had thought it was only fair that they should have them over for a meal this time around to repay them for everything.

Matt and Dennis walked together as Matt proudly showed him around his spacious study, decked out with Matt's own array of nerdy collectibles. Matt walked now with a slight limp, he had waited too long before allowing Athena to try and heal his wound. Even with Agent Ember's help, the two of them had only been able to repair the severe burns to his leg, but not all the deep muscle and nerve damage from the ray gun shot that had eaten away at his flesh.

"I have to admit that I was a little disappointed with you when we had our last dinner together," Dennis admitted suddenly.

"Oh?"

"Yeah. At first I thought it was because I could tell that there was so much that you wanted to share with me, but were afraid to. I didn't like knowing that you felt like you couldn't trust me with your secrets anymore. But now I know there was more to it than just that. You've *changed* Matt, you're not the same kid I played D&D with back in the day! I was mourning the loss of my old friend, and at the same time, trying to figure out if I liked this new guy who you've become well enough to bother trying to get to know him."

Matt laughed, "Honestly I felt very much the same way, only I didn't quite know how to say it!"

"Well, I just wanted you to know that I do like the new Matt, a lot! You've grown into a good man, and a fine leader." Dennis imitated Matt's gruff voice for a moment, "Chester! You suck at shooting and you've got a kid! Go home!"

They both laughed, in that special way that only good friends can.

"God! Do I really sound that harsh?" Matt asked.

"Sometimes, but it's cool. You really knew how to take charge out there, making plans and everything, I admire that."

"I dunno about that! My brilliant ideas almost got us all killed, your wife is the one who really saved our asses. She's the hero. You got lucky there, she's a real catch."

"I know. Naomi's pretty amazing too."

"I like to think so! We both did pretty well for a couple of geeks from the sticks of south Jersey, didn't we?"

"You know it! Let's see what those two special ladies are getting up to, shall we?"

"Sure, but first, let me tell you what I appreciate the most about you, Dennis. I've gotten really used to all the weird shit that I've seen since joining the Guilds, I find most of it to be interesting, I enjoy some of it, but I've never really *loved* it. In fact, although I try to put a brave face on it, it low key terrifies me, like in an existential way! It's everything I always thought I ever wanted to experience as a kid. You know-adventure, excitement, and all that jazz. But the truth is, I've never been completely comfortable with it. You, on the other hand, have never lost that spark, that sense of childish wonder over it all. You adore it! You are absolutely in love with it! With the great mystery of life! That's why you continually chase after it! Even after you've seen how dangerous it can be, you still actively seek it out! You don't even have any weapons or armor! That, my friend, true bravery. I wish I could figure out how to be more like that. I think my life would be a whole lot simpler if I could ever crack that particular secret."

Dennis was beside himself for a moment. "Jesus! Thanks, man. That means a lot coming from you. Yeah, you've got it right. I'm definitely in love with the strange and unusual-just look at who I'm married to!"

"Yeah, you're totally like Darrin from *Bewitched* now, only much, much cooler!"

Dennis laughed "Why does everyone keep on telling me that lately? C'mon, let's go see what my Samantha is up to."

Dennis' Samantha was currently hanging out with Naomi in the kitchen as she was checking on her lasagna for the umpteenth time.

"That seems like an awful lot of food for just the four of us," commented Athena.

"That's because it's not for just the four of us, there's a mystery guest or two who will be joining us shortly," Naomi revealed slyly.

"Hmmm. I'm tempted to try and read your mind, but I like a good surprise every now and then."

"No! Not the mind probe!" Naomi practically shouted, mimicking a notoriously cheesy line from an old episode of *Doctor Who*. Naomi liked to pretend that she wasn't as nerdy as Matt was, but in her own way she was just as bad. Athena, who was definitely as nerdy as all of them combined and felt not the slightest hint of shame over that, immediately got the reference and chuckled.

"You know, I always used to think you were a little snooty back in high school, but of course now I fully grok the awesomeness that is Naomi," Athena admitted.

"Snooty huh?" Naomi considered the comment. She had always seen herself as a very practical and down to earth kind of girl, and always assumed everyone else did too. Then she recalled how much she secretly loved it whenever someone called her by one of her many titles like "Professor", or "Doctor" or best of all "Supreme Archivist of the Guilds". She also remembered that she'd given her multi-volume history of the world an incredibly pretentious Latin title. "Okay, yeah I guess I can come off as a little snooty sometimes, I'll own it. I'll admit that until recently, I wasn't always your greatest fan either. I was probably jealous about how free you were when it came to flying your freak flag. Plus I've always had a bit of a grudge against you for stealing my boyfriend back in high school."

"I stole *your* boyfriend? You stole *my* boyfriend!"

Matt and Dennis walked into the kitchen at that time. "You're not talking about George Jablonski are you?" Matt asked.

"He was dating both of you at the same time, he used to brag about it in the locker room. What an ass," said Dennis.

"So you see, neither one of you stole him from the other one," Matt continued. "How did you not know that? Half the school knew it!"

"I never pay attention to gossip," Athena replied.

"Neither do I," Naomi agreed. "Besides, he's not worth carrying a grudge over. He was a bit of a shit anyways. Isn't he in jail now or something?"

"I read about that too! It had something to do with arson didn't it?" Athena commented. "But I'm with you, he was no prize. And I'd say we won the real prizes in the end." She waved her hand in the direction of their husbands.

"You're right, even if they are a couple of nerds, they're *our* nerds! Now why don't all of you get out of here and go to the table? This food looks about ready."

As he took his seat in the dining room, Dennis was puzzled by the number of places set. "Are we expecting more people?"

"You could say that." Matt grinned his lopsided grin.

"Is it your mom or your son? Didn't you say they both live here too? I haven't seen them around." Dennis tried to guess.

Matt imitated the buzzer sound in a quiz show with his mouth. "Try again! My mom lives in a little house on the other end of our backyard. She pretty much keeps to herself. My son is out with his girl tonight."

"Your daughter?" Dennis couldn't give up the game.

"Nope. She lives over in the Hub City with her roommate Celine."

There was a sudden flash of intense light a few feet away from the table. When all the spots had cleared from everyone's eyes, the answer to the minor mystery was apparent.

Clark Kismet and Athena's brother Mark had teleported into the room. They weren't the only ones, with them was also Wendy Sommardahl, who was basically Clark's unofficial adopted daughter, her wife April, and her former apprentice and Matt and Naomi's old friend, Randy Grumman.

"Greetings! I do hope we're not too late?" Clark asked.

Naomi poked her head out of the kitchen. "You're right on time! I'll have dinner on the table in a sec!" She announced, then disappeared back inside.

"Mark! Clark!" Athena exclaimed and ran over to embrace them. She hadn't seen them since they'd left for Elysium over two weeks earlier, and hadn't been able to speak with any of them since before the night of the Mothman.

"Congratulations on your initiation!" She told her brother.

"And congratulations on surviving yours!" He replied. The peculiar wording of his response made her raise an eyebrow, but she was so excited to see them again that she decided to brush it aside as something to possibly ask him about later.

"Hey Wendy, hey April, hey other guy!" Athena said.

Randy laughed. "I'm Randy, a former student of Wendy's and a friend of Matt and Naomi. It's nice to finally meet you, Athena. I've heard so much about you."

She shook his hand. "Only believe the good parts! Wait? There were some good parts, right?"

"One or two," Mark replied playfully. Athena punched him in the arm, then noticed that her brother was carrying a large oval shaped gift wrapped object tucked beneath that arm.

"What's that?"

Mark glanced over at Clark questioningly for a moment. The senior wizard told her "Something for later on."

Naomi emerged from the kitchen, her hands swathed in oven mitts carrying a huge, steaming ceramic cooking pan before her.

"Sit down! Sit down! The food is ready!" she commanded. All of them knew better than to defy Naomi, especially when she used that particular tone of voice and promptly found a seat. She set down the lasagna in the center of the table with a spatula.

"Help yourselves!" She called as she vanished back into the kitchen.

"It's great to see all of you guys. This was a really nice surprise, but I'm a little confused about something. How did you teleport here if the Orb prevents any spells from working?" Athena asked.

"That's easy, it's not here right now. My son took it with him when he stepped out," Matt explained.

Clark started speaking jovially. "I hear all you had quite an adventure in our absence. You even fought a Despoiler! Did I ever mention the time that the Queen of Wyrms tried to use one to—"

"Oh no you don't! I'm not gonna listen to that story again!" Athena interrupted him.

Wendy looked at Athena and mouthed a silent "thank you" to her. She'd no doubt heard this tale even more often than Athena had over the years.

"But it's a great story! One of my most epic battles! It was practically made to be told around the dinner table!" Clark argued.

"Today is supposed to be about Athena, Clark," Mark reminded him gently.

"Ah yes, quite so, quite so."

Naomi reappeared with a large salad bowl and a pair of tongs that she set on the table only to speed back into the kitchen once more. She came back out a final time with a pitcher of tea in one hand and an uncorked wine bottle in the other. She placed these down and threw herself into her seat.

"Okay, that's it for now, everyone dig in!" She announced.

"Everything looks great," said Matt.

"Smells great too." Randy complimented as he prepared his plate.

"Indeed it does! And I have something for you as a special thank you for this excellent meal, Naomi!" Clark said and pulled a large, leather bound volume from the breast pocket of his purple suit jacket, despite the fact that it was impossible for it to fit into such a small pocket. He handed it to Naomi, reaching across the table.

She immediately recognized it as being an edition of her *Magna Historia Mundi*. Countless yellow sticky notes protruded from the pages.

"I've finally finished all my corrections to volume four!" Clark declared joyously, as if he'd just discovered a new continent.

"Gee, thanks, Clark," Naomi replied acidly from between gritted teeth.

"Think nothing of it, my dear! It's always a pleasure! I know how important historical accuracy is to you!"

As happy as Athena was to see the other guests, something was still bothering her, and bothering her quite a lot. "How exactly *did* you hear about our little adventure?" Athena asked Clark in an injured voice. "I haven't heard anything from any of you for days!"

"Obviously, we've been in communication with Naomi and Matt since then, otherwise we couldn't have set up this surprise," her mentor replied breezily.

"You're missing my point, I tried calling you for help and you ignored me when I really needed you. Then you show up days later and wanna pretend like none of that happened?"

"But you didn't really need me! You proved that magnificently! And that's precisely why I did what I did, and instructed the others to all do the same."

"Stop talking in riddles! It sounds as if you're trying to say that you knew all of this was going to happen, but you've always told me how hard it is for humans to predict the future in any great detail or with complete accuracy. The act of observing the future inevitably changes the outcome. So if you did have some sort of a premonition, you couldn't have possibly known for certain that we'd all survive."

Wendy leapt to the defense of her adoptive father. "Papa doesn't have visions of the future very often, but when he does, they do tend to be far more accurate and reliable than anyone else's."

"No, she has a right to be upset," Clark asserted in a softer voice. "And it's true, even with my particular gift, I didn't know one hundred percent for sure that they'd all make it through that ordeal perfectly safe and sound. However I did what I did because I have absolute *faith* in Athena. Faith that she'd be able to successfully navigate the crisis without help from any of us. And she did not disappoint!"

He met Athena's eyes. "Don't you see, my child? It was a test! Your trial by fire! When I had my vision of the future, I decided to treat it as your final exam. One that you passed with flying colors! Mark is done with his training and so are you, for the most part. It sounds as if we may have to review teleportation spells a bit more." He tutted and said under his breath "Poor old Lars! I'll have to help you track him down and bring him home later on." Then he smiled toothily. "Anyhow, I hereby officially declare you to be a full fledged and proper sorceress and this gathering to be your graduation party!"

Athena, for once, was left completely speechless. She wasn't sure how to feel about this. While she was touched that her teacher had such faith in her, and thrilled that her apprenticeship was over, she was also still miffed that he'd known she'd be in tremendous danger and abandoned her to it.

"It wasn't easy for him to ignore your call for help," April told her, sensing her mood.

"It wasn't easy for *any* of us to avoid helping you guys," Randy said looking at Matt and Naomi in particular.

"I've already told you I forgive you, pal." The detective reassured him, but it was obvious that the younger man was having difficulty forgiving himself.

"So what is that thing supposed to be? My diploma from the Clark W. Kismet School of Wizardry?" Athena asked, pointing to the gift wrapped oval that was now leaning up against a nearby wall.

"No, something much better!" Clark grinned and levitated the object so that it was hovering over the center of the table. With a wave of his hand, the gift wrap melted away into nothingness. Athena could now see that the oval was a heavy looking polished wooden plaque. Carved into it and expertly painted was the image of a stylized red wyvern, and a woman in a white gown who looked very much like Athena. Arcane glyphs in the ancient language of M'bogish were carved around the perimeter of the oval. The plaque rotated slowly as it hung in the air so that everyone could see it.

"Umm. That's really pretty but I still don't know what the heck it is," the baffled sorcerers confessed.

"Well, I can't have you running around as an unregistered magic user, especially now that an entire ABC branch knows that you exist, it's quite illegal. And you've reminded me on countless occasions how you'll never join the Temple of the Old Gods, so I came up with an alternative solution. What you're looking at is an official seal which certifies your very own Lesser House of Magic, the House of the Mistress of the Wyverns, as being a part of the Guilds."

"My what?"

"You are now your own Lesser House of Magic, the House of the Mistress of the Wyverns."

"You can do that? You can have a secret society with just one person in it?"

"It's not just you, technically I'm also in it because there has to be at least two members in such an organization, but you're the one in charge of it. Such a thing is highly irregular, but the Guilds owe me a few favors, so they allowed it."

"I'm not sure what to say! Thanks, it sure is an *interesting* solution. The House of the Mistress of the Wyverns, huh?

Sounds like I'm having a torrid affair with them or something! Maybe you should've workshopped the name first?"

Clark laughed.

Athena punched her brother in the arm again playfully. "Did you hear that, Mark? I've got my own super secret club now and you're not in it! However, if you're really, really nice to me and should ever have any kids, I'll *consider* letting them in."

"Don't hold your breath on that one!" Mark answered as he rubbed his arm.

"I dunno about that, it looked like things were starting to get serious between you and that nice young wizard you met on Elysium," Randy teased.

"I *am* interested to see where that relationship might go, but I was actually referring to the possibility of me kissing Athena's ass, not my interest in ever having children someday!"

"Oooh! Mark has a new boyfriend ? Tell me all about it!" Athena leaned in towards her brother, ready for him to spill the tea.

Clark cleared his throat and made her seal fly back over to where it had been sitting up against the wall earlier. "Perhaps we can discuss your brother's love life a little later on? There's more that I must tell you about your status as a new Lesser House of Magic, and it's rather important."

"Ya know, I'm not too wild about that 'Lesser House' part either, are they trying to give me an inferiority complex?" joked Athena.

Clark ignored her lack of seriousness. "In order to get the Guilds to grant you such a unique status, I also had to agree to giving you certain responsibilities. Namely, you'll be taking over as the new Guardian of the Scar. It's a position which is normally held by a member of the Temple of the Old Gods, but the current Guardian will be retiring soon, so the duty will be transferred to you. It's most fitting since it's a position once held by your ancestor, Marlena Anderson."

Athena wondered if this had been Clark's plan all along, to have one of Marlena's descendants replace the Guardian? She knew that her mentor had a great fear that his old foe, the Queen of Wyrms, might return someday through the Scar. Clark probably felt more secure having a descendant of Marlena as the Guardian should that ever happen. The man liked to pretend that he was the stereotypical bumbling mage, but she knew that beneath his clownish facade he always had multiple plans within plans going on. For better or for worse, she had become his pawn in whatever long chess game he was playing with the universe the moment she agreed to become his pupil.

"Yeah I remember. The Guardian of the Scar is supposed to deal with any bad stuff that comes out of it. Shouldn't I know how to open and close the Scar if I'm supposed to be the Guardian?"

"Quite so. I'll teach you how. You could've avoided much turmoil if you'd already had this knowledge during your recent ordeal." Clark sighed, "Marlena and Esmeralda Hazelton were close friends, almost like sisters. I knew them both very well. It's a tragedy what's become of Esmeralda's family. It would've broken her heart to know that they'd end up as bitter enemies of her best friend's descendant."

"What ever happened with all of that Humanaid stuff anyway?" Dennis asked. "Did they shut that place down?"

"Oh yeah, they sure did!" Matt told him. "The ABC raided their headquarters and found a bunch of cells in the basement where they'd been holding people prisoner under appalling conditions. All those people have been freed and given some of the company's money as compensation, although they can never truly be compensated for the hell they went through. The Hazeltons were really exploiting their knowledge of future disasters to the fullest. Humanaid was just the tip of the iceberg, they had other companies involved in real estate and insurance schemes too. Those two clowns, Swan and Keith had all the dirt on the Hazeltons, they each had implanted heart monitors. In the event that both of them died, a bunch of files would automatically be uploaded to the ABC world headquarters detailing all the Hazelton's dirty dealings within the next 24 hours. It was their insurance policy, none of these guys trusted each other. The Hazeltons only knew that if they openly moved against Swan and Keith, their secrets would get out somehow. They didn't understand that the minute Earl shot Swan their fates were already sealed."

"Has anybody heard anything about Chester? How's he doing?" Athena wondered.

"Yeah, I have," Matt answered. "As you already know, after we told Dennis, Miranda and Chester to vamoose, Miranda called her husband to come pick them all up. Chester asked to be dropped off at his ex-wife Britney's place so he could see his daughter and the two of them got to talking. It sounds like they're trying to work things out and might end up getting back together. And that's not all! There's actually renewed interest in his idea for a pet psychic TV show. The ABC has lots of contacts in the entertainment industry. Gordon Hazelton was the one who used his influence to squash the network's interest in Chester in the first place so he'd have to come work for Humanaid instead."

"Well, it sounds like a happy ending all around." Naomi said, pouring herself a glass of wine. "We should toast to the future."

"An excellent suggestion, my dear!" Clark agreed. Within minutes, everyone was pouring themselves a glass. They all held them aloft.

"To the future-whatever it may hold!" Matt declared.

"To the future!" they all echoed and toasted.

Epilogue Two: Tahitian Treat

Most of the time, when a person is lost in the great interstitial expanse known as *the Place Between Places*, their body will drift in a kind of mystical suspended animation for years, decades, centuries, or even millennia while their mind is still perfectly awake and aware. It's a living nightmare, the kind of hellish existence that can break even the strongest of minds.

Fortunately, none of this is what happened to Lars Ericson. Somehow, he defied the odds a million to one and only spent a few minutes lost in this infinite limbo dimension. When he returned from it, he defied the odds even more greatly than before by emerging not only in the same universe, in the same galaxy, in the same solar system, but on the same planet in the same year and month as when he'd left. He could've arrived in the cold wastes of Antarctica, or a thousand fathoms beneath the Atlantic Ocean, but instead this hopelessly lucky man ended up suspended a few dozen feet in the air over the tropical paradise of Tahiti.

When he came crashing back down to the earth, he happened to land on top of a man wielding a gun, instantly knocking him out. The confused reporter looked up to see another man nearby now aiming a pistol at him. Without missing a beat, he charged the man, tackled him, wrested the gun away from him, and swiftly pistol whipped him into dreamland.

The hyperventilating Lars looked around to make sure there weren't any more of them, only to instead see a frightened looking, but rather beautiful woman attired in an elegant dress standing only a few feet away.

"Thank you, whoever you are! Those men were trying to kidnap me! You saved me!"

Lars stood up and gave her his most winning smile. "All in a day's work for Lars Ericson." He replied in his suave announcer's voice. The woman's heart melted at the sound of his dulcet tones. Lars' heart beat faster at the sight of the woman, a red head like himself, and ravishing one at that.

It was love at first sight, for both of them.

The woman turned out to be a fabulously wealthy heiress vacationing on the island at her summer estate. The men threatening her were part of an international gang who had targeted her, hoping to win themselves a handsome ransom. Lars and the woman turned the two men over to the local authorities. The would-be abductors promptly squealed on their compatriots to get themselves a lighter sentence, and the gang was soon broken up.

All in a day's work for Lars Ericson.

So it was that when Clark Kismet and Athena Arden materialized one day on a Tahitian beach in front of the two strolling lovers, Lars told them that there was no need for him to come back with them right away. He could fly back to New Jersey on his fiancé's private jet whenever he wanted to. He did, however, invite them and the rest of the Jersey Shore Paranormal Society to their wedding next month.

Athena was overjoyed to find out that her old friend was not only not the least bit mad at her for her bungled spell, but doing impossibly well for himself as a result of it.

Clark however, left the beach darkly muttering something about "the convergence of so many waves of quantum uncertainty converging in one nexus over Lars creating a massive cosmic imbalance". Or something like that. It was hard to hear him over the sounds of the pounding surf and Clark likes to mumble.

"Chill out, why don't you? Sometimes you have to accept things for what they are, no matter how weird or improbable it might seem and just be happy."

Even Clark couldn't argue with that. The student was becoming the teacher and finally starting to live up to her divine namesake's reputation for wisdom.

And that realization filled him with a joy which was as boundless as the cosmos itself.

Epilogue Three: Three Epilogues? Isn't That Gratuitous?

I mean really! We've already been given two perfectly serviceable endings already, haven't we? It's as if the author doesn't know how to let go! Surely all the loose ends have been tied up by now?

Oh.

Yes, that's right, there is one matter which perhaps could use a bit of clarification.

(Ahem)

So it was that one night, not too long after the Night of the Mothman, Athena Arden was watching her eldest fur baby, the dog amusingly known as Mr. President, take a shit in the backyard. As the geriatric canine's ancient bowels struggled to move, he made that peculiar face that dogs make when shitting. Athena tried to look the other way. Even after all these years, she always felt uncomfortable violating the privacy of creatures who had no sense of privacy in this matter. She chose to look up at the moonlit suburban sky instead. She noted that the Scar was open tonight, pregnant with all the unknown dangers and delights that such a state of affairs offered.

Suddenly, the animal paused in mid-shit and began barking with a gusto Athena hadn't heard from him in the better part of a decade. Athena glanced around to find the source of the disturbance.

She was greeted by the sight of a large, dark shape perched on her fence. Two red eyes burned in the darkness at her.

She smiled. "Hey, Morgatchu. How's it going?"

She soon learned that her unusual new friend had arrived to fill her in on recent developments in her own world. Communicating in that peculiar mix of mental pictures and emotions that she employed, Morgatchu told her the tale of her and Coathuan's return home.

Coathuan had been successful in averting war between the great tribes of their people. In fact, he'd managed to do more than simply stop a war, he had united the various factions in a new alliance. He'd done this by allowing his wayward son to marry the girl who had stolen his heart, and also the one he'd already been promised to.

Athena couldn't conceal her shock over the idea of a double wedding. She wasn't sure she approved of such a thing when it came to humans. Morgatchu told her that it was unusual in her world too, but not completely unknown. However, Coathuan was not a particularly conventional Mothman, and he had somehow convinced all the parties involved that it was a good idea, and united all three tribes under one alliance in the process. The Mothwoman thanked Athena again for all her help and took wing back to her own world before the Scar could close up, or the neighbors could file a complaint about the still barking dog.

Athena watched her dark, strangely beautiful form disappear into the night and experienced a wonderful sense of harmony and gratitude over the fact that she lived in a universe where such wild and wonderful things as mothpeople really existed.

This lovely sense of peace was quickly shattered by the sounds of Dennis calling to her from within the house.

"Athena! Get in here! Check this out! You're never gonna believe it!" And other such hyperbole issued in a seemingly endless torrent from within her abode.

Athena followed the stream of excited exclamations to Dennis' home office, where the Great Seal of the House of the Mistress of Wyverns now proudly hung beside a poster which purportedly showed a remarkably clear photo of a UFO, with the words 'I want to believe' written below it, along with other collectibles and knickknacks from their many investigations over the years. Dennis had been busy within, reviewing the footage from the trail cams he'd recovered from the nature preserve. He pointed at his computer screen as she entered the room.

"Here! Look at this!" He clicked the mouse and a portion of the video played which showed a four legged, dog-like creature briefly move through the frame. Dennis rewound it and paused it as the animal was about to exit the picture.

Athena wasn't sure what all the commotion was about. "So? It's a dog."

"No, it's not just any dog, it's El Chupacabra! Look at those spines along its back! Have you ever seen a dog that looks like that?"

El Chupacabra, which roughly translates to "the goat sucker" is a cryptid originally spotted in Puerto Rico, but since reported throughout the Spanish speaking world. It was notorious for attacking livestock and vampirically draining them of their blood. A few years earlier someone had supposedly shot one in Texas and preserved the body in a freezer. When experts examined the corpse, they found it to be nothing more than a hybrid of a dog and a coyote with a bad case of the mange.

Unsurprisingly, Athena did not believe in El Chupacabra. She squinted at the screen to get a better look at it. She really needed to get an updated prescription for her glasses, she was long overdue.

"Yeah, sorry hon, but that's just a dog with a wet back. Those 'spines' are the hairs standing up on its back in clumps. Besides, who ever heard of El Chupacabra being in New Jersey?"

Dennis laughed. It never failed to amuse him how stubbornly Athena clung to her skepticism even after all they've been through. "Yeah, well you said the same thing about the mothman!" He reminded her.

Athena was sticking to her guns. "I'm putting my foot down this time. I'm not about to go back out into that nasty swamp again, getting eaten alive by mosquitoes to chase after another so-called cryptid. No more kooky adventures with cryptids! From now on, we're sticking to our specialty-ghosts! They're not nearly as dangerous."

Dennis opened his mouth to protest, then closed it. He knew more than anyone the futility of arguing with Athena once she'd made up her mind.

The End
(Yes, we really mean it this time!)

Athena and the Jersey Shore Paranormal Society will return in "Ghost Town"

The author would like to apologize to the good people of West Virginia for stealing their wild and wonderful state cryptid and putting him in a story set entirely in New Jersey.

Other Books by R.E. Sohl

A Dead End World:

Book 1: The Shadow of Death

Book 1.5: Tales From a Dead End World

Book 2: Beyond the Veil of Death

Book 2.5: Tales From A Dead End World Volume Two

Book 3: Matt Spike and the Vampire's Curse

Mistress Of The Wyverns:

Book 1: Jersey Devils

Book 1.5: Romance Of The Gun

Coming in 2024:

Book 3.5: Tales From A Dead End World Volume Three

Book 4: Matt Spike Against The Amazon Saucer Women From Venus

About The Author

R.E. Sohl (if that even is his real name) is the alleged author of entirely too many stories in which members of an ancient, global conspiracy are actually the good guys and the space aliens are just here to harmlessly observe us. This is obviously all part of a massive disinformation/propaganda campaign to make you feel all warm and fuzzy when our Illuminati/Lizard-people masters inevitably emerge from the unholy depths of the Hollow Earth to rule us more openly. All of the proceeds from any of his books which you may purchase are funneled into a Swiss bank account used to help fund various nefarious Black Ops.

He recently moved to Fairfax, VA so he can be within convenient boot licking distance of his beloved CIA overlords.

Printed in the USA
CPSIA information can be obtained
at www.ICGtesting.com
LVHW031748051124
795791LV00011B/291

9 781959 860495